Carl Weber's Kingpins:

Cleveland

Carl Weber's Kingpins:

Cleveland

Brandi Johnson

URBAN BOOKS

www.urbanbooks.net

Urban Books, LLC
97 N18th Street
Wyandanch, NY 11798

Carl Weber's Kingpins: Cleveland

ISBN 13: 978-1-62286-486-7
ISBN 10: 1-62286-486-7

First Mass Market Printing May 2017
First Trade Paperback Printing March 2016
Printed in the United States of America

10 9 8 7 6 5 4 3 2 1

Distributed by Kensington Publishing Corp.
Submit Orders to:
Customer Service
400 Hahn Road
Westminster, MD 21157-4627
Phone: 1-800-733-3000
Fax: 1-800-659-2436

Carl Weber's Kingpins:

Cleveland

Brandi Johnson

Acknowledgments

Six books later and all I can say is . . . BUT GOD!

First and foremost, I gotta give a shout out to the woman I get my strength from, my mommy, Maggie Johnson. I love you, lady!

And as always, Nikki Ajian, we did it again!!!! I don't know where you find the time to do what you do. All I know is that you show up and get the job done with NO hesitation and NO complaints. Thank you for NOT telling me what I wanted to hear, but what I needed to hear with each novel, attitude or not. That's what "REAL" friends do. Thank you for always being here for me.

To my three sons—Montias, Brei'yonte, and Amir'aki—everything I do is for you. I don't know how y'all put up wit' ya momma when I'm facing a deadline, but y'all do. Y'all have to be three of the strongest young men that I've ever met. All I can do is pray that y'all will continue to grow stronger by the day.

To my future, Harvey Barnes, thank you for being so patient with me. I know I can be difficult at times, but you continue to hang in there with me. You make sure that I know I am special and that I feel like the queen you always tell me I am. You go above and beyond to keep a smile on my face, and for that and many other reasons, I LOVE YOU to life! Thank you for loving me so completely and unconditionally.

To my agent, Joylynn Jossel-Ross, thank you for always thinking of me. After every book, I always say this will be my last one, and you are the ONLY one that can talk me into giving it one more try. Thanks for everything.

Shout out to my big brother, Capone. You wear so many names and play so many roles in my life. People don't know how big your heart really is! Thank you for ALWAYS havin' your baby sister's back without questions and with no limitations. I love you, big bruh!

To my homie, Tarkington Johnson, thank you for always being there to give me that extra push. I appreciate all that you do.

Candra Carter, my homie for life (thirty plus years to be exact) you already know that I love you and thank you for being the gentle soul that you are, the voice of reason (Sometimes lol).

To Carl Weber, thank you for continuously taking a chance on me. I appreciate ya!

Shout out to everyone else that I didn't mention by name. You know what it is. Just know I love and appreciate y'all too.

Last but not least, I gotta give my fans a BIG UP. My goodness, y'all been hangin' in there with me and supportin' me to the fullest. I know y'all been patiently waitin' on my next joint to drop, and I never wanna disappoint ya. Without y'all there would be no Author Brandi Johnson! Thanks so much!

Chapter One

"You guys are goin' to miss the bus," Ke'yoko's mother hollered from the bottom of the stairs.

"Here we come," Ka'yah and Ke'yoko hollered simultaneously. Ke'yoko and Ka'yah rushed down the stairs, giggling the whole way down.

"How come you're not wearin' the outfit that I put out for you?" Ke'yoko's mother looked over at her and asked.

"Mom, I'm almost eighteen years old. Don't you think I'm too old to still be dressin' like my twin sister?" Ke'yoko asked.

"Go back upstairs and put on the clothes that your mother laid out for you," Ke'yoko's father said sternly as he walked out of the kitchen smoking on a pipe.

"It's okay, Emi; they are a little too old to still be dressing alike," Ke'yoko's mother said letting out a nervous chuckle, and hoping things weren't about to get ugly inside of the Cho household as usual.

"Do what I said," her father repeated.

"I don't wanna dress like Ka'yah," Ke'yoko stated.

Ke'yoko's father walked toward her with a frown and raised his hand. Ke'yoko didn't flinch. She stared into her father's cold, dark eyes and waited for his hand to connect with the side of her face.

"The bus is here," Ka'yah yelled, relieved, before her father's hand could connect with her sister's face. Both girls ran to the front door.

"You girls have a good day at school," their mother called out as the girls were running out the front door, leaving it wide open.

Neither Ka'yah nor Ke'yoko responded. They were already out the door and off the porch. Their mother had to walk over and close the door.

"Man, that was close," Ka'yah said, out of breath from running.

"It is what it is. I ain't thinkin' about that nigga," Ke'yoko said as they boarded the school bus.

"Where did you learn that language from?" Ka'yah inquired as she and her sister took their seats. "You've been talking a lot differently here lately."

"I got it off an episode of *Money & Violence*," Ke'yoko said and laughed.

"*Money & Violence?*" Ka'yah asked, confused.

"Yeah, *Money & Violence,*" Ke'yoko said and laughed again. "It's a show that comes on YouTube."

"And just where are you watching television at? Because we sure don't own one," Ka'yah asked, looking at her sister and waiting for her to answer.

"I be watchin' it on my cell phone," Ke'yoko replied as she opened up her book bag and pulled out her Mark Cross Grace purse and dug through it, pulling out a new iPhone 6.

"Where did you get that purse and phone from? They look expensive!" Ka'yah asked, taking the phone from her sister's hand and examining the device.

"They are expensive. Ja'Rel said I deserve all the finer things in life," Ke'yoko said, smiling at the thought of her newfound friend.

"Who is Ja'Rel?" Ka'yah pried while handing her sister's phone back.

"You know, the guy I be sneakin' off to see when we supposed to be at the library," she replied as she put her phone and purse back into her book bag.

"The tall one with the green eyes?" Ka'yah asked.

"Nope," Ke'yoko replied.

"The short, fat one with the chipped front tooth?" Ka'yah guessed again.

"Nope."

"Well, which one is he? Dang!" Ka'yah laughed.

"The one who drives the silver Lincoln MKC," Ke'yoko stated.

"Oooooh, okay, he's cute," Ka'yah said and smiled.

"He sho'll is," Ke'yoko said.

"Sho'll?" Ka'yah asked.

"Oh, sorry. He sure is," Ke'yoko said jokingly.

"All I can say is you better be careful, Ke, 'cause if Father finds out that you're sneaking off with some boy, he's going to kill you!" Ka'yah said, worried about her twin sister.

"So? I don't care if he does find out! That nigga ain't none of my real daddy, so he can't tell me what to do!"

"Why do you always say that?" Ka'yah inquired.

"My poor naïve sister," Ke'yoko replied while shaking her head.

"I guess," Ka'yah responded, not really wanting to hear why all of a sudden Ke'yoko had been running her mouth, saying their father was not really their biological one.

All Ka'yah could do was shake her head. She didn't know what had gotten into her sister the past couple of weeks. She'd been sneaking off school property with her best friend, Nadia, to meet up with these dudes, and lying to their parents about being at the library and sneaking out of their bedroom window when she thought everyone was asleep. Ka'yah didn't know what her father was going to do once he found out Ke'yoko's grades were going downhill, too; all she knew was it wasn't going to be pretty. All Ka'yah could do was hope and pray Ke'yoko would get it together before it was too late. Ke'yoko didn't seem to care about all the drama she caused with her actions and the backlash Ka'yah took because of it.

"I'm nervous about the test we gotta take in English class," Ka'yah said, shaking her head as the bus pulled up in front of Laurel, the all-girls school that she and her sister were forced to attend.

"You'll do okay," Ke'yoko said while grabbing her things and standing up.

"I sure hope so," Ka'yah replied as she followed her sister off the bus. "You don't seem too worried. How do you think you gon' do? Did you even study for it?"

"Nope," Ke'yoko said, stepping off the bus and onto the pavement, and waving over to Nadia, who stood across the street.

"Girl, you better get it together," Ka'yah warned as she started up the walkway.

"Whatever! I'll see you after school, though," Ke'yoko said, turning to walk in a different direction.

"Wait, where you going?" Ka'yah asked, confused.

"I got somethin' to do. I'll be back in time to catch the bus home," Ke'yoko turned back around and replied.

"So, what am I supposed to tell Miss Dennis?"

"Shit, tell her anything you want," Ke'yoko said uncaringly.

Ka'yah watched as her sister crossed the street to join her friend, and a few seconds later, the silver Lincoln MKC pulled up.

Ke'yoko smiled, waved at her sister, and got in the front seat of the car while Nadia joined some light-skinned cat in the back seat.

Ka'yah shook her head in disbelief all the way into the school building.

"What do you mean you don't know where your sister is?" Ka'yah's father yelled at the top of his lungs, intimidating her. "You left this house together this morning!"

"I don't know where she at," Ka'yah cried, trying her best to convince her father.

"Was she at school today?" her father yelled.

"Yes, she was there," Ka'yah lied.

"Don't think I'm not going to call the school in the morning to find out if she was really there! And if they just happen to tell me she wasn't, you're going to get exactly what she's going to get when she gets home! Now get out of my face and go to your room!"

Ka'yah looked over at her timid mother and little brother, Kailo, before heading up the stairs with her brother following close behind. She knew when her father found out the truth about Ke'yoko not being at school, he was going to kill her too! Once again she was caught up in Ke'yoko's mess.

Twenty minutes had passed when Ka'yah finally heard the front door open, and within seconds it sounded like World War III was taking place down in their living room.

"Where the hell have you been?" their father snapped.

Neither Ka'yah nor Ke'yoko had ever heard their father use that word before.

"I missed the bus so I had to walk home," Ke'yoko said nonchalantly.

"So do you really expect me to believe that?" her father asked angrily.

"Believe what you wanna believe," Ke'yoko said smartly and started walking toward the stairs.

Her father snatched her by her book bag, making it fall to the floor. Ke'yoko watched as all the contents spilled out.

"Where did you get this purse from?" her father asked, bending down and quickly picking it up.

Ke'yoko didn't open her mouth. She didn't really know what to say.

"Oh, you don't hear me talking to you?" her father asked as he unzipped her purse and began going through it.

"Gimme my stuff," Ke'yoko screamed, attempting to snatch her purse out of her father's hand.

"Where did you get all this money and this cell phone from?" her father asked. "I'm sure you didn't buy it, did you, Anda?" he asked, looking over at his wife. When she didn't answer he continued fussing. "Now, I'm not going to ask you again, young lady; where did you get this stuff from?"

Ke'yoko still refused to answer. She stood and stared at her father as if he'd said nothing to her.

"Oh, so you going to stand here and play deaf with me? Okay. You won't be talking on this," he said before slamming the cell phone down on the hardwood floor.

Ke'yoko watched as her phone shattered. "What you do that for?" she snapped.

"I do what I want to do around here. This is my house," her father said smartly while emptying the rest of the contents onto the floor.

"May I be excused?" Ke'yoko asked with an attitude. Before her father could answer she turned to walk away, only to be grabbed by the back of her long, silky hair, and thrown to the floor.

"So you're not going to tell me where you got the money and cell phone from?" her father yelled as he climbed on top of her and pinned her down.

"Emi, stop it!" their mother yelled. "Get off of her."

Ke'yoko's father slapped her across the face, busting her lip in the process.

Ka'yah flew down the stairs with Kailo in tow to see what was going on. Ka'yah watched in disbelief as her four foot five inch mother tried her best to get her husband off of her sister.

"Get the fuck offa me!" Ke'yoko screamed as she struggled to get up.

Ka'yah and Kailo couldn't believe what was transpiring. Ka'yah wanted to run over to her sister's aid, but she knew their father would do the same to her if she tried to help Ke'yoko.

"Oh, so now you hood?" he asked before slapping her again. "What are you going to do if I don't get up?"

"Get the fuck up offa me," Ke'yoko yelled again.

"You come up in my house two hours after school let out, smelling like weed and alcohol and think it's supposed to be okay?"

"I'm grown," Ke'yoko yelled as she struggled to get her father off of her.

"Grown?" Her father grimaced before smacking her again.

"Emi, please stop!" their mother cried frantically.

"Fuck that! She thinks she grown, well, grown people pay their own bills, have their own car, buy their own clothes and, better yet, have their own house!"

"I don't need you to do shit else for me!" Ke'yoko screamed.

"Oh, you don't? Anda, pick that shit up off the floor," their father yelled.

Ka'yah watched in disgust as her mother did as she was told.

"Well, since you're grown, I'm going to treat you as such. When I let you up off the floor, get your shit and get out my damn house!" her father said as he slowly rose up off her.

Ke'yoko got up off the floor and wiped her tears away. "Give me my shit," she yelled at her mother.

"No. You won't get any of that back," her father said, taking the stuff from his wife's hand.

"I don't give a fuck! Ja'Rel will replace everything you took and then some," Ke'yoko snapped.

"Who's Ja'Rel, the nigger you've been sneaking around with?"

"Don't worry about who he is! Just know he takes good care of me," Ke'yoko said, rolling her eyes.

"Well, stop wasting time and go pack your shit and move in with Ja'Rel!"

"Emi, we can't let her go! She's too young," Anda said, frightened for her daughter.

"Oh, so now you wanna speak up for me?" Ke'yoko looked over at her mother and asked as tears steadily flowed. "Where were you at all these years when I needed you to protect me from this muthafucka?"

"Ke'yoko," her mother called out and tried to reach for her daughter's shoulder.

"Don't 'Ke'yoko' me," she said and quickly turned her shoulder so her mother couldn't touch it.

"This is your father you're talking about in that language!" her mother said, hurt.

"This corny-talkin' nigga ain't none of my father! Hell, he not even black. How the hell did you think you were going to keep passing that lie off? You let his punk ass adopt us after you were raped by our real father. You didn't think I knew that, did you? Yeah, I knew. Na Na made sure she told me before she died because she knew you never would. I always knew that me and Ka'yah wasn't fully Japanese; I just never knew what we were mixed wit'. That explains why we're so much darker than Kailo," Ke'yoko said, wiping her tears away.

Ka'yah eyes grew big like saucers, wanting her mother to tell Ke'yoko to stop with all the lies, but she never did.

"Ke'yoko, I'm sorry," her mother said as she tried to catch her breath. The drastic pain she felt, remembering the night she'd been raped by a black man while walking home, hit Anda like a ton of bricks. Having her daughters know the truth, a truth that she had sworn she would take to her grave, hit her even harder.

Ka'yah and Kailo both stood on the stairs in shock from the news that they'd just heard.

"Where you gon' go?" Ka'yah finally found enough nerve to ask her sister, breaking the silence, as tears filled the rims of her eyes.

"Ja'Rel said I can come live wit' him," Ke'yoko replied.

"Good, you can be somebody else's burden. But I'll tell you what, when his black-ass gets to disrespecting you, putting his hands on you, or when he goes to the penitentiary because I'm sure he's going, they all do, don't come crawling back this way, because once you leave here you are never to return, do you hear me?"

"I don't give a fuck!" Ke'yoko frowned.

"Please, don't leave," Kailo said, sadly.

"I got to, Kailo, and if y'all had any sense, y'all would come wit' me," Ke'yoko said.

"They're not going anywhere with you! You won't corrupt these two. They will turn out nothing like you! They have a future. You bring shame to the Cho name!" her father spat.

"I won't be a Cho for long, you just watch and see!"

"This Ja'Rel will never marry you. He'll just keep you barefoot and pregnant while we hard-working taxpayers take care of all of you!"

"I don't give a fuck what he does to me. It can't be no worse than livin' in this hellhole!" Ke'yoko said.

"Are you done?" her father asked. He stared at the daughter he had raised as his own for all these years. Ke'yoko was spoiled and ungrateful. He was sick and tired of all the heartbreak and disrespect she brought to them. He had tried and failed. All the lies, not coming home for days at a time and now running around with a thug, he was done!

Ke'yoko didn't respond. She just looked at her mother with pure disgust on her face, then over at her father and wanted to spit on them both, but decided not to. She then looked over at Ka'yah and Kailo, and shook her head. The looks on her siblings' faces tore her up on the inside. Knowing there was nothing she could do for them right now, she turned and walked out of the front door.

Chapter Two

Seven Years Later

Ke'yoko was awakened by a tender kiss on the side of her cheek. She slowly opened her eyes and looked up at her husband with a smile.

"Mornin', baby." He smiled back.

"Mornin'," she replied through a yawn as she sat up and stretched out her arms while looking out the patio doors at the beautiful light blue Turks and Caicos water. "Man, I wish I could wake up to this view every mornin'."

"It is breathtaking, ain't it?" Ja'Rel replied, taking in the beautiful view as well. Ja'Rel was a thin, clean-cut dude. He was average height, not quite six foot, with a dark complexion and brown eyes, and he sported a fade with a nicely lined-up goatee. There was nothing spectacular about Ja'Rel's looks; it was his swag and personality that had attracted and kept Ke'yoko as well as all the other women he messed around with. Ja'Rel stayed dressed from head to toe and smelling good at all times. He had beautiful white teeth, kept a smile on his face, and got a compliment on his thick, sexy lips from all the ladies he came in contact with. Ja'Rel was the type of man who could keep you laughing and make you feel protected: two traits women love in a man.

"Just think, if business keeps boomin' the way it is, we will be wakin' up to this view every mornin' in no time."

"Do we have to leave today?" Ke'yoko whined.

"Yes, baby, we have to leave today. I got a empire to run." Ja'Rel smiled at his wife as she pouted.

"You left Ka'yah in charge of the business, so I'm sure everything is runnin' smoothly," Ke'yoko said, hoping to get at least one more day on this beautiful island.

Ja'Rel walked over, grabbed his suitcase, and tossed it on the bed. "Look, baby, don't take this the wrong way: I know Ka'yah is ya twin sister and all, but she ain't too bright when it comes to certain things and runnin' a business is one. The only reason I left her in charge is because you begged me to, remember?" Ja'Rel said, opening up the drawers and grabbing some of his clothes.

"That's not nice, Relly. How hard can it be to answer the phone, take orders, and send the men out to do the jobs? I do it every day." Ke'yoko laughed, knowing that her sister did act like a straight blonde at times.

"It might not be, but remember the truth ain't always nice. And here I thought all Japanese people were smart," Ja'Rel said jokingly as he continued packing.

"That was such a stereotypical and racist comment." Ke'yoko smiled as she tossed the blankets back. "But don't forget, our biological father was a black man, so maybe she got her brains from him."

"Oh, and that comment wasn't racist and stereotypical?" Ja'Rel asked as he zipped up his suitcase.

"Maybe a little." Ke'yoko smirked as she climbed outta bed.

"Damn!" Ja'Rel snapped as he looked over at his wife, who was wearing only a teal lace panty and bra set. "Come here, girl," Ja'Rel said while grabbing Ke'yoko by the arm.

"I thought we were about to leave," Ke'yoko said as she enjoyed the kisses her husband planted on her neck.

"We are, but not before you give me some of this wet-wet." Ja'Rel wrapped his arms around his wife's waist, grabbing a handful of her ass.

"Okay, but don't forget Ka'yah is runnin' the company," Ke'yoko reminded him.

"Oh, yeah, let's get the fuck up outta here before we won't have no business to go home to," Ja'Rel said, quickly composing himself.

"You somethin' else." Ke'yoko smiled as she headed to the bathroom to shower.

After the long flight home, all Ke'yoko wanted to do was shower and get some rest, but instead Ja'Rel drove straight to his office to check and make sure everything was running how it should have been.

"Look what the cat dragged in." Ka'yah smiled as Ke'yoko and Ja'Rel walked into Barne's Pest Control.

"Everything seems to still be intact," Ja'Rel teased, looking around the office.

"Oh, shut up, nigga." Ka'yah laughed.

"Fo' real," Ke'yoko agreed with her sister.

"Look at'chu, girl, you done got yourself a tan lyin' out there in all that sun," Ka'yah said, walking over to her sister and giving her a tight hug. "How was your vacation?" Ka'yah asked, standing back and gazing at her twin sister.

Ke'yoko and Ka'yah were both truly stunning women. Born identical twins, no one could tell them apart when they were little. You could only tell them apart as they grew older and their figures developed. Their mother was full-blooded Japanese, and their unknown father had been African American. The mixture of the two races had blessed both young ladies with beautiful features. Both sisters had beautiful long, silky jet-black hair, clear and flawless complexions, and beautiful light-colored eyes.

Ke'yoko was slightly taller than Ka'yah and used to have a perfect hourglass figure, until she got married. You couldn't pinch an inch if you had wanted to; she was still stacked and tight in all the right places, with just a little more to hold on to now. Ka'yah had always been thick. She had a shapely waist, followed by a plump tail and thick legs.

"Girrrrl, let me tell you. We stayed at the Seven Stars Resort on Grace Bay. You talkin' about heaven."

"Well, I'm quite sure that's the closest Ja'Rel gon' ever get to heaven," Ka'yah joked.

"Ha ha ha, very funny," Ja'Rel said with a smirk.

"For the record, I made his body feel like he was in heaven several times a day. So, anyways, like I was saying, our room was the bomb.

We had a panoramic view of the water, heated marble floors . . . Oh, and let's not talk about the sandy white beach. It was so sexy," Ke'yoko replied.

"I bet," Ka'yah replied, slightly enviously.

"Excuse me. I gotta take this call," Ja'Rel announced before walking into his office.

"Okay," Ke'yoko replied and continued bragging to her sister about the resort.

"Well, I'm glad you enjoyed yourself. You needed it." Ka'yah smiled.

"Who you tellin', girl. It was nice to get away. I needed to get the miscarriage off my mind," Ke'yoko said, sullenly.

"Don't worry, sis, it'll happen one day. You just have to remember everything happens for a reason," Ka'yah said, hoping to lift her sister's spirits up.

"Yeah, I know. Until then I guess I can just keep spoilin' my nephew." Ke'yoko smiled. "Speakin' of Aiko, where is he?"

"He's wit' his stupid-ass daddy," Ka'yah said, rolling her eyes.

"He still trippin'?"

"Yes! Now he talkin' 'bout his momma said Aiko ain't none of his son and he needs to get a DNA test done on him because all his other kids look just like him, and all kind of crazy shit!"

Ke'yoko and Ka'yah shook their heads simultaneously.

"As long as I was wit' him, he claimed Aiko, but soon as I decided to leave his punk ass, now all of a sudden Aiko ain't his child."

"Typical nigga." Ke'yoko frowned. "Aiko looks just like that bum."

"Just like him," Ka'yah replied. "But it's all good. He gon' be well taken care of wit' or wit'out Daron in his life."

"Without a doubt! Me and Relly wouldn't have it no other way," Ke'yoko stressed.

"Thanks, sis," Ka'yah said.

"You ready, baby?" Ja'Rel stepped out of his office and asked.

"Yes, I'm tired," Ke'yoko responded.

"A'iiiight, Ka'yah. I'll get up wit' you in the mornin' to go over all the work orders and whatnot," Ja'Rel said, yawning.

"Okay. Y'all have a good night," Ka'yah said, waving to her sister and brother-in-law.

Ka'yah finished up the little work she had left over, locked up, and dropped the money off at the night deposit box before heading home to get herself a much-needed drink.

Chapter Three

Ke'yoko was in the shower when Ja'Rel walked in.

"I'm out, baby. I'll see you at the office in a coupl'a hours," Ja'Rel said.

"You leavin' already? It ain't even eight o'clock yet," Ke'yoko said as she rinsed the soap off her body.

"I know. I need to get down to the office and make sure everything is in order," Ja'Rel replied as he looked at his reflection in the slightly steamed mirror.

"Well, aren't you gon' at least eat some breakfast?" Ke'yoko asked as she stepped out of the shower.

"Ain't shit here to eat. I thought you was goin' to Walmart when you left last night. I'll just grab somethin' from ya ancestors at Koko's bakery." Ja'Rel smirked while grabbing Ke'yoko's towel off the sink and handing it to her.

"I did go to Walmart, but I forgot my wallet at home so I had to put everything back; and, nigga, that's an Asian bakery." Ke'yoko laughed, snatching the towel from Ja'Rel's hand.

"Asians, Japanese, Koreans, y'all all the same to me." Ja'Rel smiled.

"You ignorant," Ke'yoko said jokingly as she wrapped the towel around her body.

"But you love me though," Ja'Rel said, leaning in and giving his wife a kiss on the lips.

"Yes, I do."

"All right, baby, I'm 'bouta go."

"Baby, I need to talk to you about somethin' before you leave," Ke'yoko said nervously.

"What is it?" Ja'Rel asked, sensing the hesitation in Ke'yoko's voice.

"Ummm, never mind, it can wait until tonight," she replied.

"Naw, tell me now!" Ja'Rel said in a somewhat raised tone, hoping Ke'yoko hadn't found out about any of the other chicks he'd been messing around with.

"Hold on, nigga! Don't be yellin' at me!" Ke'yoko frowned.

Realizing he was being defensive, Ja'Rel calmed himself down. "I apologize, but you know I hate when you do that to me. Now what you wanna talk to me about, baby?"

"Ummm, okay, well," she stammered. "I know it's only been about a month since the last miscarriage I had, but I think I'm ready to try again."

"Ke, I don't know, baby. I don't think we ready just yet," Ja'Rel said.

"How you figure that we ain't ready?" she snapped.

"Look, I don't like sittin' back watchin' you go through all these miscarriages. Baby, we've had four already. When God is ready for it to happen, it'll happen," Ja'Rel said, hoping his wife understood where he was coming from.

"You act like you don't want a baby by me!" Ke'yoko said.

"You know I want a baby just as bad as you do. I would give anything to be a father, but it tears me up on the inside to have to sit back and watch you cry for days after you miscarry. I feel like less of a man knowin' there is nothin' I can do to erase or ease your pain. That's all I'm sayin', Ke'yoko, damn!"

"Whateva," Ke'yoko said, waving her husband off as tears began to fill her eyes.

"Don't do this, Ke," Ja'Rel said sadly.

"Do what, Ja'Rel? All I wanna do is have my husband's firstborn. Is it somethin' wrong wit' that?" she asked sarcastically.

"Naw, not at all, but damn, baby, ya body ain't even healed all the way from the last miscarriage you had," Ja'Rel said.

"Oh, so that's what the real problem is? It's my body, huh? Since I've picked up some weight you ain't attracted to me no more!"

"Come, on, baby, I love your body," Ja'Rel said. "So, what, you done picked up some weight. I still love you!"

"Yeah, a'iiiight, that's why you always checkin' out all them other bitches while we walk through the mall, 'cause you love my body!"

Ja'Rel had been caught. He'd thought he'd been discreet about all the women he'd been checking out while out with his wife. He knew Ke'yoko was feeling some type of way about the twenty pounds she'd gained since they'd been married. It didn't matter to him; he still loved her the same. "Now, how did we get on the subject of your weight? We was just talkin' about us havin' another baby," he said, hoping to steer their conversation away from his reckless eyeballing.

Hip to what Ja'Rel was trying to do, Ke'yoko gave up. "I'll see you at the office in a few," she said as she brushed past her husband with a straight attitude.

"Where you 'bouta go?" he asked, grabbing her by the wrist.

Ke'yoko snatched her arm away from Ja'Rel's grasp and continued toward their bedroom. "To get dressed for work, where else?"

"Come on, baby, I don't wanna fight," Ja'Rel said as he followed his wife.

"Neither do I! I'm done wit' the conversation," she said and continued into the bedroom.

Ja'Rel stood still and watched as his wife got dressed. He could tell by the way she aggressively put on her clothes she had an attitude. As bad as he needed to get to the office, Ja'Rel knew he couldn't leave the house without making up with Ke'yoko first.

"Okay, baby, you win," Ja'Rel said.

Ke'yoko turned to face her husband with a huge smile on her face. "What?" she questioned to make sure she heard right.

"Take ya clothes off," he demanded in a sexy tone.

Ke'yoko didn't hesitate to strip down to her birthday suit and lie in their king-sized bed. She then spread her legs and watched anxiously as Ja'Rel began removing his clothes.

"I'm 'bouta tear that pussy up!" he said as he watched his wife run her fingers up and down her clitoris.

"Come tear it up, *chichi*," Ke'yoko said seductively.

It drove Ja'Rel bananas when Ke'yoko spoke Japanese to him during sex. Even though he could only make out a few words that she'd taught him, listening to her made him want to knock the bottom out of her caramel cave.

Ja'Rel walked over to the bed and replaced Ke'yoko's fingers with his face.

"*Oyamaa,*" Ke'yoko moaned loudly.

"You like that, baby?" he asked.

Ke'yoko shook her head yes, grabbed the back of her husband's head, and tried her best to push it all the way up inside of her dripping wet cave. "I wanna feel you inside of me," Ke'yoko said.

"Let me hear you beg," Ja'Rel stopped what he was doing and said.

"Please, *chichi,*" Ke'yoko said.

Ja'Rel got up on his knees, grabbed Ke'yoko by the throat, and put just the right amount of pressure on it. "That wasn't good enough! Now beg for this dick, bitch!" he demanded.

"Fuck me, please, *chichi!* I need it," she replied all while trying to breath.

Ja'Rel took his free hand and slapped Ke'yoko across the face as hard as he could, making his wife moan in ecstasy. "Now that's more like it," he said before sliding his fully erect manhood inside of her soaking wet cave.

After giving his wife what she was looking for, Ja'Rel climbed out of bed and jumped in the shower.

Ja'Rel smiled at his wife as he walked out of the en suite bathroom.

"What you smilin' about?" Ke'yoko asked as she still lay in the same spot Ja'Rel had left her.

"You," he replied as he got dressed again for work.

"What about me?" Ke'yoko asked, sitting up.

"I love you and I feel like I'm one of the luckiest men in the world. I got a beautiful wife, a nice-ass crib in one of the nicest neighborhoods in Cleveland, I own my own business; what more could a nigga ask for?"

"Besides a baby, nothin'. Our life is perfect," Ke'yoko said, thinking about where she came from.

"It sure is, baby," Ja'Rel said while fixing his tie and walking over and kissing his wife on the lips.

"Enjoy your day. I'm callin' off work," Ke'yoko said, smiling.

"Shit, you betta get yo' ass up and get dressed before I fire you," Ja'Rel said jokingly, while slapping his wife's ass.

"I don't care nothin' about you firin' me. Shiiiit, you been tellin' me for months that you was gon' hire the neighbor's daughter, Tamika, as your secretary," Ke'yoko said.

"I already did. She starts tomorrow . . . now! Shit, you know ya husband is a busy man and I be forgettin' to do shit sometimes." Ja'Rel smiled.

"Busy my ass. Well, you ain't gon' be too busy to be at the shop answerin' all them calls if Tamika *don't* start tomorrow."

"Oh, so you too good to work for me?" Ja'Rel looked at his wife and asked with a smile.

"It's not that I'm too good to work for you. I just know you ain't payin' enough." Ke'yoko smirked.

"Whatever." Ja'Rel laughed while squeezing his wife's soft ass.

"Whoa, *chichi,* don't start nothin' you ain't prepared to finish," Ke'yoko said.

"You a freak." Ja'Rel smiled.

"Only for you, baby," Ke'yoko said.

"You better be," Ja'Rel said as his cell phone began to ring. He looked at the number and pressed the IGNORE button. "I gotta go, I'll see you in a few."

"Okay." Ke'yoko wondered who the call was from. "Who was that callin'?" she inquired.

"That was Bo. I'll hit him up later. I'm sure he don't want shit but to borrow some more money. The nigga already owe me."

"Ummm," Ke'yoko replied.

"See ya," Ja'Rel said, kissing Ke'yoko again before walking out of the room.

She watched as Ja'Rel walked out of their bedroom before getting up to get dressed for work, still wondering which one of Ja'Rel's bitches was calling his phone, knowing for a fact it wasn't Bo.

Ja'Rel waited until he pulled out of the driveway to return his missed call. "Talk to me," he said as he headed to the bakery.

"Man, I need you to get down to the office quick," Ka'yah said.

"What's goin' on?" Ja'Rel asked.

"Not over the phone," she replied.

"Say no more," Ja'Rel said, busting a U-turn on East Fortieth and Payne and heading to his office.

Ja'Rel could tell by the sound of Ka'yah's voice that whatever news she had for him couldn't be nothing nice. He floored his new chocolate brown Buick LaCrosse, hoping he didn't get pulled over in the process, knowing good and well that the Parma police didn't play no games!

Ja'Rel busted a quick right onto Broadway, turned up in Barne's Pest Control, and hopped out of the car.

"What's the matter?" he asked, rushing through the front door. Ja'Rel looked around the front office and saw the look on the face of his right-hand man, Jonesy, before looking over at Ka'yah, Mitch, Redd, and Mad Dog; and he knew it was all bad.

"Talk to me, man," Ja'Rel said.

"They found Bo's body early this mornin'," Jonesy said.

"What?" Ja'Rel asked, confused, while trying to process the news.

"I called his chick this mornin' to send him out on a call and she told me they found him in the Walmart parkin' lot with a single gunshot wound to the head," Ka'yah intervened.

"Wait," was all Ja'Rel could say as he continued to let the news about his lifelong friend sink in.

"I know, man, that shit crazy," Jonesy said, shaking his head in disbelief.

"Did they find anything on him? I mean, damn, I don't understand what happened. I talked to him last night and he told me he was goin' to meet somebody and put a big play down," Ja'Rel said, still dazed and confused.

"Did he say who he was goin' to meet?" Mad Dog asked.

"Nope," Ja'Rel said, trying to recall if he'd mentioned a name. "All he really said was this play was about to make us a lot of money."

"Ain't nobody talkin', either. You know it's been so many rumors goin' around already, but you know how that is," Ka'yah said. "Daria called and said she heard from some niggas on the block that it was a drug deal gone bad. I even heard it was his side chick who took him out."

"Don't Walmart got cameras in their parkin' lot?" Ja'Rel asked.

"Yeah, but where Bo was parked, the cameras wasn't workin'," Jonesy said.

"This shit is crazy," Ja'Rel said.

"It's gon' be okay, Rel. I know Bo was ya homie," Ka'yah said, trying her best to console her brother-in-law.

"Fuck Bo. I just gave that nigga over fifty thousand in product. How I'ma get my money?" he snapped angrily.

The eyes of everybody in the office grew big.

"Keep y'all's eyes and ears to the streets. Send the rest of the crew out, ASAP. We just took a huge loss; we gotta make it up," he looked at his crew and said.

"We got'chu, my nigga," Redd replied, speaking for the whole crew.

"I gotta get outta here," Ja'Rel said, walking toward the door. He stopped and turned back around. "Not a word to Ke'yoko. I'll tell her when the time is right."

Ka'yah shook her head okay and watched as Ja'Rel headed back out the door.

Chapter Four

"Heeeey, diva," Ke'yoko's best friend and beautician, Nadia, screamed as Ke'yoko walked into the crowded hair salon. Nadia was a sharp, classy woman. She wore her hair in a Mohawk with the sides shaved. Not everyone could rock this style that she dared to rock. This look had become Nadia's signature look and on occasion she changed the color. She was tall for a woman, with an athletic build and caramel-colored skin. No one was sure of her real eye color; she'd been rocking green contacts for as long as anyone could remember.

"Heeeeey." Ke'yoko smiled, giving her best friend a tight hug.

"How come you ain't at work?" Nadia asked.

"Don't get it twisted. That ain't my job. I'm just fillin' in until the neighbor's daughter start tomorrow, but I'm on my way in. I just wanted to stop by and see you before I go in!" Ke'yoko replied.

"Bitch, that purse is bad! Let me get it," Nadia said.

"It matches my outfit, but you can have it," Ke'yoko said.

"That's what I'm talkin' about!" Nadia said as the rest of her staff and clients enviously eyed the expensive purse. "What you gettin' done to your hair tomorrow?"

"I don't know. I'ma let you do you."

"I just got this new product in. Come tell me what you think," Nadia said, leading Ke'yoko back to her office.

Nadia and Ke'yoko had a friendship that went all the way back to high school. In school Nadia had believed in getting money any way she knew how. She would sleep with anyone if the price was right, male or female; it made no difference as long as her pockets were filled with money. She had the best of everything as a result. Ke'yoko, being raised in such a strict home, was instantly attracted to Nadia and her free-spirited ways, hoeish or not. Nadia was a ward of the state and was in and out of different foster homes. She lived life with no restrictions or boundaries. The more Ke'yoko's father attempted to place restrictions on her the more attractive Nadia's free lifestyle became and the more she was drawn to it. The girls became inseparable.

Ke'yoko had met Ja'Rel through Nadia and Bo. Ke'yoko was an observer and paid attention to everything. She wasn't sleeping to the fact that Ja'Rel and Bo kept money, and not just average amounts of it, either. Ke'yoko wanted more than the pocket change Ja'Rel was handing her and began watching his every move. Unbeknownst to him, Ke'yoko learned how to weigh, cook, cut up, package, and distribute all by watching him and Bo. Ke'yoko decided to bring Nadia in on her idea to make money in ways different from lying on her back. Nadia was down for whatever and agreed to help Ke'yoko however she needed. Nadia also agreed to keep this business deal between her and Ke'yoko and never mention it to Bo or Ja'Rel. Nadia grew from ho to hustler, and together Ke'yoko and Nadia secretly began to build their own empire.

"Oh, lord, you about to experiment on my hair," Ke'yoko said as she followed Nadia.

"That bitch thinks she's all that," said Connie, one of the stylists, once Ke'yoko and Nadia were out of earshot.

"She sho'll do. Every time she comes in here she thinks she own this bitch," Dana, another stylist, added. "I don't know why Nadia always let her into her office but not nobody else. Shit, she ain't special."

"They be actin' like they on some top-notch secret shit when they in Nadia's office," another stylist added.

"Maybe they bumpin' tacos," Connie's client interjected while laughing, making some of the other clients laugh too.

"Maybe they are," Connie and Dana both said, laughing.

"Here they come," Deon, another stylist, whispered as Nadia and Ke'yoko came out of the office laughing.

"A'iiiight, girl, I'll call you later. I gotta get to work before the boss man gets to blowin' up my phone," Ke'yoko said.

"I seen that purse at the outlet in Lodi," Connie said with a smirk as Ke'yoko walked past her.

Both Nadia and Ke'yoko looked at Connie like she was crazy.

"You know what, I'm not gon' even entertain you today, Connie. If you want some entertainment, I heard the circus will be in town this weekend." Ke'yoko dug in her purse and pulled out a hundred dollar bill and tossed it at Connie, hitting her in the chest with it. "Here, buy yourself some tickets to it." Ke'yoko then turned and headed toward the door.

Connie's face was beet red, knowing Ke'yoko had used class to put her in her place in front of the entire shop.

"Bye, girl," Nadia said, laughing.

"Deuces," Ke'yoko said, throwing up her two fingers and heading out the door.

Nadia looked over at Connie, shook her head, and smiled. Connie's ol' jealous ass stayed getting put in her place.

Ke'yoko pulled up in front of the shop and looked around the empty parking lot. "I wonder how come nobody is here yet," she said as she gathered her things and got out of the car. She walked up to the door, unlocked it, and walked in. She set her coffee and purse down on her desk and looked up at the TV on the wall.

"These niggas leavin' TVs on and shit like they pay bills here," she said aloud.

"Brian 'Bo' Thompson was found dead in the Walmart parking lot early this morning from an apparent gunshot wound to the head."

Ke'yoko looked up at the news and shook her head as Ja'Rel's best friend's picture flashed across the screen.

"The Cleveland police chief said there are no witnesses at this time; however, they believe they were able to lift some DNA from the body that may provide them with more leads. More news at ten," the newscaster continued.

"Sucks to be you," Ke'yoko said to the TV before grabbing the remote, turning it off, and getting herself settled. She never did like Bo. He was too sneaky for her, plus she knew he played a huge part in hooking her husband up with so many different females.

It was a busy Thursday. Ke'yoko had been sending the drivers out on calls all morning. If business kept booming like it was, she and Ja'Rel would be living in Turks and Caicos in no time.

"Barnes Pest Control," Ke'yoko said, answering the phone.

"Do you guys get rid of bedbugs?" the caller asked.

Naw, dumbass, we clean carpet! I could have sworn the sign outside said PEST CONTROL. "Yes, we do."

"Oh, that's great! I saw like fifteen hundred in my son's room. How soon can someone come out and do an inspection?" the caller asked.

Fifteen hundred? What you do, count 'em?
Ke'yoko smiled. "I'll write up the ticket and if we
have anyone available I'll send them out right
away," Ke'yoko said.

"Good. I need an inspection like ASAP."

"Okay. I'll see what I can do," she said before
gathering all of the caller's information.

Ke'yoko called Mitch's cell phone to see if he
could take the bedbug call.

"Mitch speakin'."

"Hey, Mitch, this is Ke'yoko," she said.

"Hey, boss lady. What's goin' on?"

"I got a bedbug call on Chapelside."

"Okay. What's the address? And did they say
around how many bedbugs they got?" Mitch
asked.

"He said it's like fifteen hundred in his son's
room," she replied before giving Mitch the
address.

"Cool, I'm on my way ova' there."

"Thank you."

"No problem," Mitch said before ending his
call, grabbing his Glock .42 from underneath the
seat, and heading over to Chapelside.

It was closing time and Ke'yoko hadn't seen
or heard from Ja'Rel the entire day. She had
tried calling his phone several times, but it was
going straight to voice mail. Her first thought

was he was laid up with some nasty-ass ho, and the more she called and got no answer, the more she wanted to close up shop and go looking for his ass. Ja'Rel was lucky that calls were coming in nonstop or she would have. Ke'yoko decided to handle her lying, cheating husband when she got home.

Ka'yah barely came to the shop anymore, it seemed like, and Ke'yoko was always having to fill in. She was so damn glad that Tamika would be starting work tomorrow and she wouldn't need to do this mess anymore.

Ke'yoko tallied all the tickets up for the last time, gathered up her things, locked up the shop, and hurried to her car, jumping in and speeding off, heading home.

Chapter Five

Ke'yoko pulled into the driveway, parked behind Ja'Rel's car, and quickly got out. She was fussing the entire way up the walk.

"This nigga got me fucked up! I've been callin' his black ass all day. I wonder what lie he about to tell," she continued fussing as she unlocked the front door and walked in.

Ke'yoko looked around the dark, quiet house. There wasn't a light nor a noise coming from the TV, nothing. Ke'yoko was hesitant about going farther than the foyer. She stood in place, flipped on the light switch, and called out to her husband.

"Ja'Rel," she said in a loud whisper and waited for him to answer. She took her cell phone out of her purse before setting it down on the floor. When she got no response, she called his name a couple more times before turning to walk back out the door to call and get somebody to come check out the house for her. She wasn't taking no chances on investigating herself, just

in case somebody was waiting for her or Ja'Rel
to come in. They lived in a nice, safe neighbor-
hood, but Ke'yoko was no fool; they did still live
in Cleveland.

"I'm in here," she heard Ja'Rel finally call out
from the dark kitchen.

"Well, why didn't you answer me the first
time I called your name?" she snapped as she
made her way to the kitchen, flipping on lights
along the way just in case it wasn't Ja'Rel in the
kitchen but someone who sounded just like him.
Ke'yoko flipped on the kitchen light. "Why you
sittin' in here in the dark?"

Ja'Rel was sitting at the kitchen table with a
half-empty bottle of Ketel One, and smoking on
a blunt filled with some killa-ass White Widow
weed. He was trying to figure out how he was
going to make up for the huge loss he'd taken
with Bo and at the same time keep his other
workers from catching cases while doing so.

"Thinkin'," Ja'Rel replied, wanting to leave it
at that before taking a pull from his blunt and
putting it out in the ashtray that sat in front of
him.

"Thinkin' about what?" Ke'yoko asked, not
satisfied with her husband's one-word answer.

Ja'Rel slowly blew the smoke from his mouth
before responding. "I got a lot on mind, Ke'yoko,"

Ja'Rel said, hoping that was enough to shut his wife's mouth.

"Just this mornin' you was one of the luckiest men in the world without a care in the world; now not even twenty-four hours later you got ninety-nine problems? I'm confused," Ke'yoko said sarcastically.

"You know Bo just got killed! It's been plastered all over the news all day," Ja'Rel snapped, fed up with his bickering-ass wife.

"Noooo, baby. I didn't have the TV on at the shop today," Ke'yoko said, acting surprised. "What happened?"

"Don't nobody know," Ja'Rel said, shaking his head, trying to make sense of what had happened to his best friend.

"Awwww, baby. I'm so sorry," Ke'yoko said, walking closer to her husband, wrapping her arms around his neck, and pulling his head into her stomach all while rolling her eyes into the top of her head.

"I don't know what I'ma do," Ja'Rel said, shaking his head.

Keep livin' ya life, Ke'yoko wanted to say so bad but didn't. Even though she didn't like Bo, she knew that he'd been Ja'Rel's best friend since they were kids and knew how he must have felt. She wouldn't know how to cope with life if anything ever happened to Ka'yah or Nadia.

Even though Ja'Rel was going through it right now, Ke'yoko still wanted to know why the hell he hadn't been answering his cell phone all day. Deciding to put that on her "things to flip about on a later day" list, Ke'yoko let go of her husband and was about to prepare dinner.

"You hungry?" she looked down at Ja'Rel and asked.

"Naw, I'm good," he said, not having an appetite at all. Ja'Rel picked up the Ketel One bottle, put it to his lips, and took a long drink.

"Okay, well, let me know if you change your mind. I'm about to go shower and put on some pajamas," Ke'yoko looked at her husband and said.

"Okay, baby." Ja'Rel picked up the lighter and blunt and relit it.

Ke'yoko kissed the top of Ja'Rel's head before walking out of the kitchen and heading upstairs to shower. Being in the shop made her feel dirty every time she went to work. How can working around a bunch of men out in the field killing mice, bedbugs, rats, roaches, and fleas have you feeling any other way? As she walked into her bedroom her cell phone began to ring.

"Wassup, ma?" she asked Nadia.

"What you doin'?"

"Nothin', about to get in the shower. What you doin'?" Ke'yoko asked as she stripped off her work clothes before walking into the bathroom.

"About to tackle ya goddaughter's thick-ass hair."

"That child does have some thick hair." Ke'yoko chuckled as she grabbed a towel out of the bathroom linen closet. "I need to come and get my baby."

"When, girl, when?" Nadia asked, laughing.

"I'ma get her and Aiko and take them to the park and get some ice cream in about a week or so."

"Girrrrl, I can't wait, 'cause when you try to bring her back, I'ma treat y'all like some straight Jehovah's Witnesses. When y'all get to knockin' I'ma be all in the closet hidin' and shit." Nadia laughed.

Ke'yoko laughed too. "Girl, you a damn fool."

"Well, I was just callin' to see what you were doin'. I'ma let you g'on and take ya shower."

"Okay. I'll call you back later on," Ke'yoko said, turning on the water to the shower and adjusting the temperature.

"Hey," Nadia called out before Ke'yoko could get off the phone.

"Wassup, chick?"

"What you doin' for ya twenty-fifth birthday?" Nadia asked.

"Girl, I don't know. I don't have any plans. And wit' Bo passin' away I don't think Ja'Rel will be up to celebratin' either."

"Yeah, girl, I seen that shit on the news today! That fucked me up! I was gon' call and tell you, but I had so many heads today I didn't have time to. But I guess that's the chances you take when you livin' the life, huh?" Nadia replied, hurt.

Ke'yoko rolled her eyes and changed the subject back to her birthday plans. "Anyways, so maybe me, you, and Ka'yah can go out to eat and get a coupl'a drinks or somethin'," Ke'yoko suggested.

"Ummmp, how about me and you go to dinner and get some drinks and then you and Ka'yah can go do somethin' by yourselves," Nadia said, twisting up her face.

"Are you and Ka'yah gon' ever get along? Damn! I don't even know what y'all beefin' for. Dammit, what is the beef between y'all two bitches?" Ke'yoko asked, wanting to get to the bottom of why her sister and best friend didn't get along.

"Man, I just can't do yo' sister," Nadia said, irritated by the thought of Ka'yah.

"And why not?"

"For one, she sneaky as fuck. She phony and I know that's ya sister but you need to watch her around Ja'Rel 'cause they a li'l too buddy-buddy for my likin'," Nadia said, putting it all out on the table.

"Come on, Nadia, that's my twin sister you talkin' about like that." Ke'yoko frowned, not feeling what Nadia had to say about Ka'yah. "And as far as her fuckin' my husband, girl, please, now you just graspin'! I know Ja'Rel is a ho to his heart, but he my ho and I love him. He would never fuck my sister. I do know that much."

Knowing she was out of place and had possibly crossed the line, Nadia recanted her opinion. It was Ka'yah she didn't like, so she had no business trying to hurt Ke'yoko in the process of spitting venom on Ka'yah's name.

"I'm sorry, Ke'yoko. Girl, I was wrong for sayin' what I said. I know Ja'Rel wouldn't do no foul shit like that. I said that shit out of anger. Do you forgive me?"

Ke'yoko was hesitant at first because the words Nadia had just said about her sister and husband stung. She knew that Ja'Rel was a low-down, cheating bastard, but him fucking her sister had never once crossed her mind.

"Ke, I'm sorry," Nadia repeated, not wanting her best friend to be mad at her for talking stupid. Nadia wasn't really sorry, just sorry she'd upset Ke'yoko. Something was off about Ka'yah and Nadia didn't like her point blank.

"It's cool," Ke'yoko finally said, still feeling some kind of way, though. "Look, I'm about to get in the shower. I'll holla at'chu later."

"A'iiight, ma."

Ke'yoko pushed the END button on her cell phone, laid it on the bathroom sink, and climbed in the shower. The thought of how close Ja'Rel and Ka'yah were and how much time they spent together started playing in her mind. She thought back to all the times she went through Ja'Rel's phone and saw Ka'yah's number all through it, but never thought anything of it because Ka'yah constantly called Ja'Rel when she needed something fixed around her house. Ke'yoko had never thought anything of it until Nadia had the audacity to put that thought in her head. She then started thinking about how touchy-feely they seemed to be when they were around each other.

Shit started popping up in Ke'yoko's head as the water beat down on her body, shit she had brushed off as being a brotherly relationship between her sister and husband. Ke'yoko shook her head in disbelief and quickly shook the foolish thoughts from her head and continued to shower. But like she always said, momma didn't raise no fool; and even though she didn't believe that stuff about Ka'yah and Ja'Rel, from here on out she would definitely keep an eye on them two, just in case there was some truth to Nadia's speculations.

Chapter Six

The day of Bo's funeral, Ja'Rel had a hard time getting motivated. Laying his best friend to rest was the last thing he thought he'd be doing. As much as Ke'yoko didn't want to attend the funeral she knew she had to be there to support her husband and to make sure them thirsty bitches knew and understood that she carried the "wifey" title, not them. Ke'yoko put on a short black tight-fitting scoop-neck dress with long sleeves. Every curve on her body showed through the dress. Ja'Rel came out of the en suite and looked over at his wife.

"Damn, baby, you look good as fuck, but you look more like you goin' to the club and not a funeral," he said, walking over to the closet and pulling out his black notched-lapel Canali suit.

Ke'yoko walked over to the standing mirror and looked at her attire feeling a little silly. She had to admit she did look more like she was going out for a night on the town instead of to her husband's best friend's funeral. She was so engrossed in proving to them thirsty hoes that she was number one in Ja'Rel's life, she'd forgotten all about keeping it classy and at the same time paying her respects to Bo. She couldn't stand him, but he did deserve some respect; he was a human being.

Ke'yoko walked over to the closet and grabbed a little longer black lace-trimmed, sleeveless, ruched cocktail dress and changed into it instead. Even though she'd changed into something a little more presentable, Ke'yoko was still killing the game.

After changing her outfit, Ke'yoko went into the bathroom and twisted her hair into a bun and stuck two kanzashi hair sticks into her hair. Ke'yoko wanted nothing to do with her Japanese side, but she still couldn't help sometimes reverting to her heritage. It was still instilled in her whether she wanted it to be or not. She was double-checking herself in the mirror and applying finishing touches when she heard Ja'Rel's cell phone ringing.

"Hello?" he answered.

Ke'yoko eased her way to the doorway and tried her best to be discreet as her husband spoke on the phone.

"The wake starts at ten a.m. and the funeral is at eleven a.m.," he said. "If I feel up to it I will. Don't forget I'm 'bouta go bury my right-hand man. A'iiiight, I'll talk to you later."

When Ja'Rel hung up the phone, Ke'yoko walked out of the bathroom as if she hadn't been eavesdropping on her husband's conversation. "Who was that?" she asked nonchalantly, pretending her dress was too high and pulling on it to make it come down some, just for something to do.

"Ka'yah," Ja'Rel replied with a nonchalant attitude as he stood in the standing mirror, straightening out his tie.

"What she want?" Ke'yoko snapped before she knew it with a straight attitude.

Ja'Rel stopped messing with his tie and turned to face his wife, looking at her like she'd just lost her damn mind. "Dang, what you say it all like that for?" he asked, confused.

"Like what?" Ke'yoko asked, trying her best to play it off.

"Like it's a problem that my sister-in-law called me to find out what time Bo's funeral is," he answered.

"It ain't no problem, nigga. You trippin'." Ke'yoko chuckled, wondering why Ka'yah called Ja'Rel to find out Bo's funeral information and not her.

"A'iiiight then," Ja'Rel said before turning back toward the mirror.

After getting themselves ready, Ja'Rel grabbed his Roberto Cavalli sunglasses off the dresser, before he and Ke'yoko headed to the car. Ja'Rel opened the door and waited for his wife to get in before walking around to the driver's side and getting in himself.

"I hate funerals," Ja'Rel said as he backed out of the driveway.

"Who does like 'em?" Ke'yoko asked while buckling her seat belt.

"You'd be surprised. I know a couple of muthafuckas who be at everybody's funeral, whether they know 'em or not." Ja'Rel smiled. "I think they just go so they can go to the repast to eat."

Ke'yoko smiled and shook her head. "That's crazy."

"Tell me about it."

Ke'yoko looked over at her handsome husband as he drove. She loved this man with all her heart and had known since the first time she'd laid eyes on him that she would marry him. Even after all the affairs she'd found out about, Ke'yoko still refused to leave and let another woman have him. Ja'Rel's ambition and determination had been what attracted her to him in the first place. Ke'yoko loved how he had taken a small exterminating company that he'd built from the ground up and turned it into something huge. When he first came to Ke'yoko with the idea of starting his business, she wasn't too excited about it, fearing it would fail because of all the competition in the area. She was grateful that she'd kept her mouth closed and supported her husband's dream, and because of that support they could afford the finer things in life. She deserved this life and had put up with a lot to live it.

Ja'Rel pulled up in front of the already crowded church and looked for a parking space. "Damn, this church is packed," he said as he scouted the parking lot.

"There's one right there," Ke'yoko said, pointing.

Ja'Rel whipped his car into the empty parking space, put the car in park, and turned the engine off.

"You okay?" Ke'yoko looked over at her husband and asked.

He shook his head yes.

"You ready?"

"As ready as I'm gon' get," Ja'Rel replied as he opened up his car door.

"Come on," Ke'yoko said, opening her door as well and getting out, waiting for Ja'Rel.

Ke'yoko grabbed Ja'Rel's arm as they walked through the church's parking lot and into the church. All eyes were on the power couple as they headed up to the casket. Ke'yoko's mind was steady wondering how many of these basic-ass females watching them had Ja'Rel slept with. She knew of at least three of these hoes for a fact.

Ja'Rel looked down at his friend and shook his head in disbelief. He fought back tears as he looked down at the man who'd helped him turn his business into the empire that it was today. He didn't know what he was going to do without his right-hand man. Yes, he had plenty of other workers on his team, but none of them was cut quite like Bo. Bo was loyal and a true friend indeed. His other partners were loyal but he couldn't give the "friend" title to any of them, for several different reasons. Bo had never given Ja'Rel a reason not to trust him, while the others had made him second-guess their loyalty a time or two.

"What's up, man?" Jonesy walked up to him and spoke, breaking his train of thought. "How you doin', boss lady?"

Ke'yoko nodded.

"Wassup, man?" Ja'Rel asked, glad he was interrupted before the tears could fall.

"Let me holla at you for a minute."

Ja'Rel, Jonesy, and Ke'yoko stepped away from the casket and let everyone else pay their respects. "Wassup?"

"Man, I heard last night that an eyewitness told the police it was a bitch who robbed and killed Bo," Jonesy said.

"Hold on, man," Ja'Rel said, stopping Jonesy from going on with what he'd heard in the streets.

"A'iiiight," Jonesy said.

"Baby, go find us a seat," Ja'Rel looked over at Ke'yoko and said, not wanting his wife to hear any more than what she'd already heard.

"Okay," Ke'yoko said, before turning to walk away. She combed through the crowd of people, looking for Ka'yah and Nadia. There were so many people packed inside the church she couldn't spot either of them. She walked to the back to find herself a seat. Just as she spotted a seat and turned around to sit down her eyes met with Ross's as he came through the door. Ke'yoko smiled, and Ross smiled back, nodding his head before heading up to the casket to view Bo's body.

Ke'yoko didn't know what was about to go down, being that Ja'Rel and Ross were in each other's presence. She watched as Ja'Rel and Ross stared each other down. Ross nodded his head in Jonesy's direction before going to find himself a seat. Ja'Rel looked over at her. Ke'yoko didn't know if it was to make sure she didn't acknowledge Ross or what; if so, it was too late. She already had.

"Damn, man, why you say that shit in front of my wife? Nigga, you know I keep her all the way out of my business just in case somethin' goes down. She can't tell the police shit 'cause she don't know shit! How many times have I told y'all asses that?" Ja'Rel said, trying to keep his anger discreet. Yet again, one of his workers was testing his loyalty. Ja'Rel loved and trusted his wife with his life, but kept what he did in the streets a secret from her just in case he got caught up. It was for her own protection, too, but more for his. He didn't for one minute believe she'd ever turn on him if push came to shove, but he wasn't taking any chances, either. Pressure had been known to bust pipes. Far as he was concerned she'd never know about his business for real.

"My bad, man, I wasn't thinkin'," Jonesy apologized.

"Well, start thinkin'. Stupid shit like that is what's gon' get all of us fucked up!"

Jonesy wasn't feeling the chastising he was getting from Ja'Rel. "I said my bad, man, damn."

"Anyways, what else was said?" Ja'Rel asked, cutting him off.

"What I just told you was all that was basically said," Jonesy snapped.

Ja'Rel shook his head. He couldn't give a damn about Jonesy's attitude right now. "I need more information. Find out who that bitch is and, when you do, bring her to me 'cause she owe me, big time. I'ma make her pay for takin' my money and my brother. I might even fuck the shit outta the bitch before I kill her." With that being said, Ja'Rel walked away.

Ke'yoko was getting restless as the funeral seemed like it would never end. She was getting tired of hearing all the different chicks get up in front of the church, reminiscing about the times they'd spent with Bo as if his wife wasn't there. Ke'yoko caught several females staring at Ja'Rel as if he was a piece of meat. One chick was so bold, when Ke'yoko caught her looking she didn't even blink or turn her head; she kept on eyeing Ja'Rel as if Ke'yoko didn't exist. It was like a breath of fresh air when the pastor announced that he was finished. Ke'yoko quickly stood up and waited for Ja'Rel to stand up as well.

He looked at her wanting to ask what the hurry was, but kept his mouth closed instead.

Some arguments weren't even worth it. Ja'Rel got stopped numerous times as they made their way out to the car.

"I didn't know Bo was so well liked," Ja'Rel said as he and Ke'yoko pulled out of the church's parking lot to head to the cemetery to say his final good-byes.

Me either, Ke'yoko thought, but kept her comment to herself.

"It was a nice funeral, don't you think so?" he asked.

"Yeah, it was nice," Ke'yoko answered.

"He woulda done the same for me. I had to make sure my homie went out in style."

After leaving the cemetery, Ke'yoko was dreading going back to the church for the repast. All she wanted to do was go home, lie across the bed, and catch up on her TV shows.

She sat at a table watching as Ja'Rel continued talking with all these different niggas and females.

"There you are. I've been lookin' all over for you," Ke'yoko heard a familiar voice say.

She turned around and smiled. "I was lookin' for you at the funeral," she said, standing up and giving Nadia a tight hug.

"Girl, you know I'm always runnin' late for everything. When I got to the funeral it was damn near over." Nadia laughed.

"Yo' ass shoulda started gettin' ready last night." Ke'yoko laughed too as she sat back down in her seat.

"I know, right," Nadia agreed, sitting down in the chair next to Ke'yoko. "Bo's funeral was packed."

"I know, I can't believe it. I didn't think nobody liked him." Ke'yoko laughed.

"Yeah, he was an asshole," Nadia said.

"Don't talk about him now. You used to be in love wit' that asshole." Ke'yoko laughed.

"For real, bitch? That was back in high school." Nadia laughed too.

"So? It don't matter when it was, you was still in love wit' him."

"I was, wasn't I? Girl, we used to skip school wit' Ja'Rel and Bo and have so much fun," Nadia said as she stared off in space, reminiscing about the good ol' days.

"We sho'll did. Who woulda thought me and Ja'Rel would still be together all these years later?" Ke'yoko asked rhetorically.

"Shit, if Bo wasn't such a big-ass ho, we probably woulda still been together too."

"You was a ho too." Ke'yoko laughed.

"Oh, yeah, I was, wasn't I?" Nadia laughed too.

"Ummmm huh." Ke'yoko smirked.

"Shit, I shoulda stayed wit' Bo 'cause every nigga I messed wit' after him wasn't no different; they was all hoes too."

"Lance wasn't no big-ass hoe," Ke'yoko said.

"Naw, he wasn't, but the nigga didn't have no dick. Only thing good came outta fuckin' wit' him was he bought the hair shop for me."

"What about Twan?"

"Only good thing came from messin' wit' him was A'Niyah. Other than that, he wasn't shit either. But the dick was good, bitch!"

Ke'yoko busted out laughing. "Bitch, you nasty! When that nigga get out?"

"Girl, he went to the board last month and they flopped him. They gave him another five years. Shit, 'bout time he get out, A'Niyah will be grown wit' kids of her own," Nadia joked.

Ke'yoko shook her head and laughed. "You a fool."

"Shit, I'm serious."

Ke'yoko and Nadia watched as Ka'yah entered the church's basement, walked straight over to Ja'Rel, and whispered something in his ear. Ja'Rel smiled and nodded his head okay before Ka'yah turned and walked away. Nadia cut her eyes over at Ke'yoko, trying her best to keep her mouth closed. She still felt bad for the stuff she'd said about Ka'yah and Ja'Rel already.

Ke'yoko's blood was boiling. Her heart was racing as all the shit that Nadia had said to her on the phone the other day came rushing back into her head. Even though she tried her best to brush it to the side, the fact still remained that Ja'Rel and Ka'yah could very well be messing around. It was no mystery that Ja'Rel was a ho and, quiet as kept, Ka'yah had been around the block a time or two her damn self. There was no telling. All Ke'yoko knew was if there was some truth to the accusations, they better not let her find out about it. If she ever did she would turn both of their worlds upside down, family or no family. Ke'yoko had to draw the line somewhere.

"Wassup, sis?" Ka'yah said, walking over to the table where she and Nadia sat.

"Sup," Ke'yoko responded, trying her best to hide her attitude from Ka'yah and Nadia.

"Nadia," Ka'yah spoke in one of the driest tones.

"Ka'yah." Nadia reciprocated the same tone.

"Girl, Bo's funeral was packed," Ka'yah said, sitting down on the opposite side of her sister.

"I know. Me and Nadia was just sittin' here talkin' about that," Ke'yoko said, forcing herself to talk to her sister without flipping out.

"What you gon' do after the repast?" Ka'yah asked Ke'yoko.

"Goin' over to Nadia's house," Ke'yoko quickly answered.

"Oh, okay, I was gon' see if you wanted to come over for some tea and my good ol' home-made green tea cookies," Ka'yah said.

"I'll take a rain check," Ke'yoko said with a forced smile.

"A'iiight. Well, I'll call you later," Ka'yah said, standing up.

"Okay," Ke'yoko replied before her twin walked away from the table.

"Now why you tell that girl that lie?" Nadia asked, already knowing the reason why.

"I don't feel like bein' bothered wit' her today. And I really ain't up to drinkin' no tea and eatin' them dry-ass green tea cookies. Shit, every fuckin' time I get pregnant she bring me a cup of tea every day. I'm tired of tea, bitch, bring me a Coca-Cola or somethin'." Ke'yoko laughed.

"I'm hip," Nadia agreed. "But y'all Japanese folks know y'all love tea."

"Yeah, but damn, she brought me a cup every single day."

"You gotta admit, that was nice of her to think about you, though," Nadia said.

"It was," Ke'yoko agreed. "The worrisome heffa wouldn't leave until I drank it, talkin' about it was good for the baby."

"You ready, baby?" Ja'Rel walked over to Ke'yoko and asked. "Wassup, Nadia?"

"Been ready," Ke'yoko replied with a slight attitude. She was still stuck on the fact that Ka'yah had acknowledged Ja'Rel before even looking for her and she was taking it out on him.

Ja'Rel could sense the attitude and brushed it to the side. He'd just buried his brother. He was in no mood for his wife's mood swings.

"Wassup, Ja'Rel," Nadia spoke.

"Okay, girl, I'll call you later," Ke'yoko said, standing up.

"Okay, well, I'm about to pull out too." Nadia stood as well.

Ke'yoko gave Nadia a hug before following Ja'Rel out to the car. She couldn't wait to get home to lie across her bed and watch television.

Chapter Seven

Ke'yoko was in the kitchen fixing herself some breakfast. Ja'Rel had left hours ago for the gym and the house was completely quite. Her cell phone started ringing, startling her. She walked over, grabbed her phone off the kitchen table, and checked the caller ID. She hated answering restricted calls. She knew they weren't behind on any bills so it couldn't have been a bill collector, so she answered the call. "Hello?"

"Ke'yoko?"

"Yeah, this is she. Who this?" she asked, not recognizing the man's deep voice.

"Kailo," he replied.

Ke'yoko was speechless. She didn't know what to say. She hadn't seen or heard from her little brother since the day her father put her out nearly seven years ago. He'd forbidden Ka'yah and Kailo to ever have any contact with Ke'yoko and had made it known if they did, they would have to leave his house and be removed from his will as well. Ka'yah had missed her twin sister so much she'd sneak on the phone and call her when her mother and father were asleep. Ke'yoko could still remember the harsh words her father had said the night he'd caught Ka'yah on the phone talking to her. He told Ka'yah she would never amount to anything and that she was just like her worthless sister. That night, their father had thrown Ka'yah out of the house and cut her off too. Ke'yoko and Ja'Rel had picked her up and let her come live with them until she'd gotten on her feet. Kailo had been young at the time and had no choice but to obey their father. So until now neither sister had heard from or seen Kailo.

"Damn, bruh, you sound like a grown-ass man," Ke'yoko finally said.

"I am a grown man." Kailo laughed.

"You're almost eighteen," Ke'yoko said, wondering where the time had gone. She remembered when he used to run around the house thinking he was Superman.

"Yep, I sure am."

"Wow, Kailo! What have you been up to, baby brother?"

"I graduated high school a year early and I'm taking pre-law classes right now."

"I shoulda known. You were always studyin' yo' ass off. Shit, ya father wouldn't have it any other way. Speakin' of your father, where is he? Does he know you on the phone wit' me? He must don't 'cause I don't hear no yellin' and screamin' in the background," Ke'yoko said smartly.

"I'm in my dorm room," he replied.

"Oh, okay. How's Mother?" Ke'yoko asked, not knowing if she really cared.

"She's good. You and Ka'yah should really call her. She misses you guys. Shoot, I miss you guys," Kailo said sullenly.

"I miss you too, baby brother. But if you missed me so much, how come it took you so long to contact me?" Ke'yoko inquired.

"I was afraid to contact you. I didn't know how you would respond to me calling you out the blue. I was sitting here thinking about you and Ka'yah while I studied and just decided to take my chances. Either you were going to talk to me or not," Kailo explained.

"What were you afraid of?" Ke'yoko asked.

"Afraid that you didn't want anything to do with me because of how Father treated you guys. I don't want you to think for one minute that I approved. I was young and didn't know what to say or do. Plus, I knew if I reached out to y'all and got caught he would put me out and wouldn't pay for my college tuition. Please don't blame me," Kailo said.

"Baby brother, I could never blame you for the way that bitch-ass nigga treated me and Ka'yah. I'm sorry to talk about your father like that but that's how I feel about him. You were young and in my eyes you didn't have a choice; you done the right thing. I just wish so much time wouldn't have passed by before you decided to reach out to me," Ke'yoko said.

"I'm sorry, Ke."

"No need to be sorry. Please, just promise me that we gon' get together and catch up. I really would like to know what my baby brother has been up to. Do you have a girlfriend? Do you have your license? I mean, I wanna know everything about you."

"I promise we can get together. I would love to come see you during my summer break if that's okay with you."

"Yes, I would love for you to come see me," Ke'yoko said happily. "But what you gon' tell your father?"

"I don't know. I guess I'll just tell him I'm staying at school for the summer to catch up on some schoolwork. Shoot, I'll come up with something to tell him by then."

"That's wassup, baby brother."

"Okay, sis, tell Ka'yah I said hello and I'm about to finish studying and I'll talk to you later."

"Kailo, please don't be a stranger," Ke'yoko said, not wanting to let her baby brother go.

"I won't," he replied.

"I love you," Ke'yoko said.

"Ewwww, that's gross." Kailo laughed.

"Shut up, boy! Bye!" Ke'yoko laughed too.

"Bye, sis, and I love you too," Kailo said before hanging up.

Ke'yoko had one of the biggest smiles on her face as she laid her cell phone back down on the table. She was so glad that Kailo had decided to reach out to her. She missed him so much. It hurt her to her heart that she hadn't been able to watch him grow up into the young man he'd become.

"What you smilin' for?" Ja'Rel walked into the kitchen and asked.

"Guess who just called me?" she asked happily.

"Nadia?" he guessed.

"No, guess again." She smiled.

"Ummmm, your dad?"

"Yeah, right. That nigga bet' not ever call me." Ke'yoko frowned.

"Well, I don't know, baby. Who called you?" Ja'Rel asked, tired of playing the guessing game.

"Kailo!" she said, excited.

"Word?" Ja'Rel asked, happy for his wife. He knew that she'd been wanting to talk to him for years.

"Yes. I'm so glad he decided to call me!"

"He about sixteen now, ain't he?" Ja'Rel asked.

"Naw, he seventeen. He about to be eighteen soon."

"Damn! Where did the time go? When we first got together he was a little boy," Ja'Rel said, shaking his head.

"I know, man, I said the exact same thing. He's in college majorin' in law! He doin' his damn thang! I'm so proud of him." Ke'yoko smiled.

"That's wassup!"

"I'm about to call Ka'yah and tell her Kailo called," Ke'yoko said, reaching for her phone.

"Ka'yah ain't home," Ja'Rel said.

"How you know?" Ke'yoko grimaced, not able to hide her irritation this time. Maybe what Nadia said was true.

"Because when I was leavin' the gym, she was pullin' up. That's how I know," Ja'Rel said.

"Oh," Ke'yoko said, embarrassed.

"Baby, you been trippin' lately. What's wrong wit' you? You need some of daddy's dick?" Ja'Rel said, wrapping his arms around his wife's waist, pulling her into his sweaty chest.

"I would love some of daddy's dick, but not before you wash it." Ke'yoko laughed.

"Shit, ain't nothin' wrong wit' my sweaty dick. You can eat a meal off this bitch. It's clean," Ja'Rel said while grabbing it.

"I'd rather not! Go wash it," Ke'yoko said, pushing her husband off of her.

"Okay, well, what if I'm not in the mood no more when I get out the shower?" Ja'Rel asked.

"I know how to get you back in the mood, trust me." Ke'yoko smirked.

"What that mouth do?" Ja'Rel joked.

"Go shower and I'll show you."

"Don't go nowhere. I'll be right back," Ja'Rel said, rushing out of the kitchen and upstairs to shower.

"He a damn fool." Ke'yoko laughed before fixing herself a plate.

Chapter Eight

Ke'yoko woke up bright and early and got dressed. She had some business to tend to before going to her standing hair appointment. She made sure her outfit was on point before grabbing her cell phone off the nightstand. She looked over at Ja'Rel, who was sound asleep, shook her head in disgust, and eased out of the bedroom. Ja'Rel had been out half the night doing God knows what. She knew as his wife she loved him and wanted nothing more than to be with Ja'Rel forever, but she didn't know how much more of his lies and cheating she could take. The last thing Ke'yoko wanted was to be weak-willed like her mother, but she had to face it: up until this point she'd been acting like her mother's child.

Ke'yoko was jamming to some old-school Ready for the World that was playing on her satellite radio. She pulled up into the Circle K gas station, parked, and turned the engine off.

She picked her Anna-Karin Karlsson sunglasses up off the passenger's seat and put them on. She watched as the morning crowd walked in and out of the store to get coffee, gas, newspapers, or whatever their morning fix was in between looking for Ross's black Charger to pull up. Ke'yoko was scared and anxious all wrapped into one. She knew Ja'Rel would kill her if he knew that she was anywhere around his number one enemy.

Ja'Rel had demanded that Ke'yoko never speak to Ross again. When she'd asked why, Ja'Rel never did tell her, but she already knew. Ke'yoko could remember a time when Ross and Ja'Rel had been inseparable, but when they both starting making money and one thought they was being outdone by the other it had caused a huge rift in their relationship. The beef they had between each other had almost turned deadly several times. Ke'yoko had always liked Ross: his mannerisms, his personality, and the way he always treated her with the utmost respect even after the fallout between him and Ja'Rel. This was one of the main reasons she still communicated with him and trusted him. Shit, the beef was with Ja'Rel, not her, so Ke'yoko didn't see anything wrong with still meeting up with Ross from time to time to catch up on life and to get his advice on how to make some extra money.

Ke'yoko kept glancing at the clock on the dashboard. She picked up her phone to see if the time on the dashboard matched the one on her phone. Just as she was getting tired of waiting, she started her car back up. As she grabbed the gear shift, the black Charger pulled into the parking lot. Relieved, she smiled, turned the engine back off, and waited for Ross to get out of his car. She watched as he got out with a black duffle bag in his hand, looking like a buffer and sexier version of Jeremih. He wore a pair of crisp khaki shorts, a plain white tee, and pair of brown Bacco Bucci slide-in sandals. His locks were neatly pulled back into a ponytail while he sported a pair of Gucci sunglasses on his face.

Damn, he sexy, she thought as he got closer to her car.

Ross opened her car door, got in, and pulled the door closed behind him.

"About time," Ke'yoko looked over at Ross and said with a smile. She quickly glanced down at his feet; she was impressed because his feet were in order for a man. His heels weren't hard and crusty and his toenails were cut and clean.

"Stop bein' so damn impatient. I told you I was comin'." He smiled back.

Ke'yoko loved when Ross smiled, showing off his deep dimples. "I'm not bein' impatient. I got other things I need to get done," she said, rolling her eyes.

"Other things like what?" he pried while removing his sunglasses, laying them on his lap.

"My hair for starters," she replied.

Ross looked at Ke'yoko's hair. "Yeah, you do need to get that shit done," he joked.

"Whatever." Ke'yoko laughed, play slapping his big, buff arm. Ross gave Ke'yoko a tingly sensation between her legs: one she'd never felt for anybody other than her husband.

"Naw, I'm just playin'." Ross laughed too.

"I know you are, shoot. Anyways, how you been?"

"You know me, sis. I'm livin' life like it's supposed to be lived," Ross said with a smile.

"And how's Sharae and the baby?"

"Sharae is a'iiight. She still tryin'a get her business off the ground. And my baby girl, Rayna, is doin' great. Man, she done got so big now, she walkin' and everything." Ross's face lit up like a Christmas tree as he talked about his baby girl. "She gettin' bad, too. Always pullin' shit off the coffee table and followin' me everywhere. She's a daddy's girl."

"That's what I'm talkin' about." Ke'yoko smiled back, feeling a twinge of jealousy.

"And what about you? How's life been treatin' you?" Ross asked, sensing the enthusiasm he had when he spoke about his baby girl had Ke'yoko feeling some type of way, being that she was unable to have children of her own.

"I'm happy," Ke'yoko replied.

"You sure?" Ross asked, knowing Ke'yoko wasn't telling the truth. He knew she couldn't be satisfied, not with all the women her husband was sleeping around with.

"Yeah, I'm sure," Ke'yoko said, forcing a smile, knowing damn well she was miserable as fuck.

"Okay," he looked at her with a mischievous smile and said and left it at that.

"What's the deal wit' the duffle bag?" she asked, trying to quickly change the subject.

"It's a little somethin' for you to show my gratitude for putting me up on that lick you hit," Ross said.

"Awww, man, you didn't have to do that."

"Yes, I did. I respect you for that. You could have given it to somebody else or kept it for yourself, but you gave it to me instead. But don't open it up until you're someplace safe."

"Besides my sister and Nadia, you're the only person I can trust. And I knew you could put yo' cut on it and get rid of it a lot faster than me. I wasn't even tryin'a fuck wit' it for real for real," Ke'yoko said.

"You trust yo' sister?" Ross asked, surprised.

Out of everything Ke'yoko had just said, why would Ross pick out the part about her trusting her sister? "Yes, Ross, I trust Ka'yah. Why wouldn't I? Do you know a reason why I shouldn't? You know somethin' I don't know?" Ke'yoko asked, skeptical.

"I don't know nothin'. All I'm sayin' is ain't nobody to be trusted, not even family," he said.

"Do you trust me?" Ke'yoko asked.

Ross looked into Ke'yoko's beautiful face and studied it for a brief second before answering. "Yeah, I do trust you," he replied with a serious look on his face; and he continued staring, feeling his manhood start to rise. Ross wanted to taste Ke'yoko's lips so bad it was making him sick to his stomach that he couldn't.

Ke'yoko began to feel uncomfortable. It felt like her and Ross's eyes were literally making love. Ross could sense Ke'yoko's uneasiness and decided to get out of the car while he still had a little sense of respect for the game.

"Well, I better get goin'. I'm sure Nadia gon' be fussin' if I'm late for my appointment," she said, quickly turning her head.

Ross picked his sunglasses up off his lap. "A'iiiight, baby girl. If you come across anything else, hit me up."

"You know I will," Ke'yoko replied.

"Say no more. Enjoy your day." He winked, put his sunglasses on his face, and opened the car door.

"You do the same," Ke'yoko replied, smiling back.

"Oh, and, by the way, you do look nice today," Ross said, getting out of the car and closing the door behind him.

Ke'yoko bit down on her bottom lip and shook her head as she watched Ross's sexy ass head back to his car. It had been a long time since she'd gotten a compliment from a man. She couldn't remember the last time Ja'Rel had given her one. Actually the day of Bo's funeral had been the last time. A woman shouldn't be able to pinpoint the last time her husband had given her a compliment. Ross stopped and looked back over at Ke'yoko with a smile on his face. She threw her hand up and waved.

Ross nodded his head in an upward motion, got in his car, and pulled off. "Ummmmp ummmmp ummmmm."

Chapter Nine

Ross couldn't get Ke'yoko off of his mind as he weaved in and out of traffic. He knew her worth and wanted nothing more than for her to be happy. He knew Ja'Rel was dogging her and had been since they'd been together. Who was he to hate on how another nigga treated his bitch? He knew she deserved better though. She deserved him. Even though he couldn't stand the ground Ja'Rel walked on and didn't care if he lived or died, messing around with his ex–best friend's wife was a line he definitely wouldn't cross. Ross still respected the game enough not to cross that same line. He knew in the end he'd be getting the last laugh.

Ross pulled up in front of his house and had one of the biggest smiles on his face as he looked at Sharae and Rayna standing in the front yard talking to their freaky white neighbor, Holly.

"Look at Daddy's baby girl," he said, getting out of the car.

Both Sharae and Holly had huge smiles on their faces as Ross made his way up the walk.

"Dada," Rayna babbled with a smile as Sharae held her in her arms.

"Hey, baby." Ross smiled, making his way over to them.

"Hey, baby." Sharae smiled, leaning in for a kiss.

"Come here, baby," he said, holding out his hands and waiting for Rayna to come to him. Without hesitation she leaned over toward her daddy's arms.

"I said hey," Sharae said with an attitude.

Ross shot Sharae a dirty look and continued playing with his daughter. "What ya doin'? You happy to see Daddy?" Ross asked in a baby's voice before giving Rayna two big, sloppy kisses on the cheek.

"Hi, Ross," Holly spoke.

"What's up, Holly," Ross spoke back before turning to walk away.

"He's so fuckin' rude." Sharae frowned as she and Holly watched him walk up the front porch stairs.

Ross walked into the house with his daughter in hand and headed straight to the kitchen. "You want a Popsicle?" he asked his baby girl, walking over to the freezer and grabbing her one.

"Why you give her that? She gon' be sticky and I just got her outta the tub," Sharae fussed as she walked into the kitchen.

Ross ignored Sharae while opening up the Popsicle, placing it in Rayna's hand.

"You didn't hear me?"

"Yeah, I heard you." Ross frowned. "All you gotta do is wipe her off when she's done eatin' it. How hard can that be? You don't do shit else 'round here," he said, handing the baby back to Sharae.

Sharae hesitated a little before taking the baby from Ross's hands. She didn't want to get that sticky red Popsicle all over her white sundress. Ross peeped the hesitation and shook his head in disgust.

"What?" she snapped. "I'm wearin' white."

"You need to get yourself together."

"I am together," Sharae snapped angrily, hating when Ross told her that.

"Yeah, okay," he replied sarcastically and chuckled, getting deeper under Sharae's skin.

"You get on my fuckin' nerves!" She frowned.

"Get the fuck out then," Ross snapped. "What's keepin' you here? I ain't gon' be around a nigga who gets on my nerves."

"Gimme the money and we'll get the fuck on!" Sharae walked over and placed Rayna inside the Pack 'n Play that sat beside the kitchen table.

"We? Bitch, please, Rayna ain't goin' nowhere! You can take yo' raggedy ass on, though." He grimaced.

"Shit, I ain't goin' nowhere without my daughter," Sharae said, knowing damn well she couldn't have cared less about Rayna for real, because she knew she would be well taken care of. Sharae's biggest fear was Ross moving another bitch up in the house after she was gone and then he wouldn't give her no more money if she didn't have their daughter.

"Rayna gon' be straight."

"How can I afford to move out anyway?"

"I give yo' money-hungry ass a thousand dollars a month for you and Rayna's needs. You think you slick. You shop at Walmart for her clothes while you all up at Saks and them little boutiques for yourself."

Sharae had been caught. "No, I don't," she lied.

"Bitch, you pitiful." Ross frowned. "All I can tell you is you better start savin' some of that money that I give you."

"Where I'ma go, Ross?"

"I don't know and I don't give a fuck. You betta ask one of them niggas you fuckin' if you can move in wit' them," he said calmly.

"Why you always accusin' me of fuckin' some-body?" Sharae asked, confused.

"Go wipe Rayna off and get the fuck outta my face! You act like somebody stupid," Ross fussed as he turned and walked out of the kitchen.

Sharae grabbed the baby out of the Pack 'n Play and followed Ross out of the kitchen. "Let's talk about the bitches you fuckin'," Sharae fussed.

"Let's talk about 'em," he said as he headed up the stairs.

"You a fuckin' asshole!"

"Now you know it's a written rule that what's good for the goose is without a doubt good for the gander," he said as he walked into their bedroom and lay across the bed.

"Whatever, Ross," Sharae said, waving him off as she headed into the en suite bathroom to wipe off Rayna.

"Good comeback," he replied facetiously.

Sharae was so worked up over Ross's accusations she could barely contain herself. Sharae finished wiping the baby off, walked back into the room, and looked over at Ross, who was on his cell phone texting someone. She instantly got an attitude. Sharae wanted to make their relationship work so bad, truth be told, but she didn't know how. It seemed like every time she was breaking Ross down he would throw something up in her face and put his wall back up. Sharae wasn't squeaky clean. She had messed around on Ross a few times and it wasn't because she didn't love him or wasn't satisfied; she couldn't help it. She was a cum freak. And, plus, why shouldn't she be allowed to fuck around on him when he was clearly messing around on her every chance he got?

Ross stood up from the bed and kissed his daughter on the cheek. "I'm out. Don't wait up," he said, putting his cell phone in his pocket.

"Where you 'bouta go?" Sharae asked.

"Who pays the bills around here? That's what I thought." Ross laughed as he headed out of the bedroom.

"Bitch-ass nigga," Sharae said quietly, while sitting down on the bed with the baby still in her arms.

Chapter Ten

Ke'yoko hit the button on the garage door opener before pulling in. She shut the engine off and hit the close button before getting out of the car. She looked around as if somebody could have been watching. She then walked over to an old box of clothes and dug all the way to the bottom, pulling out about ten pictures. She flipped through the photos as if she hadn't seen them a million times. Tears fell from her eyes as she slowly studied the flicks, studying everyone's faces. She shook her head, lifted the clothes up, and placed the pictures back into their hiding place.

Ke'yoko wiped her eyes before walking into the house. She walked straight upstairs, removing her clothes at the same time. She walked into the en suite and turned the shower on. She finished removing the remainder of her clothes, reached into the linen closet, and grabbed a washcloth before stepping into the walk-in shower. She continued to cry as the water beat down on her weary body. She cried so hard she could barely breathe. Ke'yoko was tired, her nigga had finally risen, meaning she was sick and tired of everything. She thought about her life and how she wished it was different.

She was fed up. She couldn't take it no more. She couldn't take not being happy. The pictures flashing back into Ke'yoko's mind, along with all the women she'd caught Ja'Rel cheating with, and especially her not being able to have children, was all coming out in her cry.

"Baby, you a'iiiight'?" Ja'Rel stuck his head in the bathroom and asked.

Ke'yoko quickly wiped her tears away. "Yeah, I'm good. Why you ask me that?" she asked, sounding all clogged up from crying.

"It sounded like you were in here cryin'," he said.

"Naw, I was singin'," she said, playing it off.

"Oh, shit. You might wanna keep ya day job," Ja'Rel joked as he walked out of the bathroom.

"Forget you, nigga." Ke'yoko laughed too, even though there was nothing to laugh about.

Ke'yoko finished washing up, got out of the shower, and walked into the bedroom. She looked at Ja'Rel. He was sitting up against the headboard, completely naked. The sight of him made her sick.

"Come sit on it," he said, lifting his member up and stroking it.

"I'm kinda tired, Ja'Rel," she said, not wanting to be bothered with him at all; and she continued finding something to put on.

"So you mean to tell me you gon' pass up a chance to get some of this good dick?" he asked as he continued stroking until it became brick hard.

Even though Ke'yoko was mad at her husband, she wasn't about to pass up a chance to bust a much-needed nut. She opened her bath towel and let it hit the floor.

"Oooooh, damn, baby," Ja'Rel said, admiring his wife's body. "Come here."

Ke'yoko walked over to the bed, climbed in, and sat on her throne. She rode Ja'Rel as if her life depended on it, driving him wild. It didn't take long for her to work her magic before Ja'Rel was about to bust.

"I'm 'bouta cum," he moaned loudly.

"Let me get up," Ke'yoko said, trying to get off of her husband's manhood. She was at the point that having a child with Ja'Rel was the last thing she wanted.

"Nooooo," he replied, holding her hips down, not allowing her to get off as he pumped vigorously.

"Let me up, Ja'Rel," Ke'yoko said, fighting to get up.

"Not yet, ahhhhhh," he said, busting all up inside of his wife's wet cave.

"I told you to let me up," Ke'yoko fussed, quickly climbing off her husband with an attitude. She hadn't thought she would ever get to a point where she didn't even want to have a baby by her husband. Sex was good with Ja'Rel, but she'd never been with anyone other than him to compare it. She was quite sure there had to be better out there and just maybe she should find out.

"Man, you was feelin' too good," he said as he jacked the remaining semen out of his member. "And, plus, I thought you was tryin' to get pregnant."

"I was, but I changed my mind," she said, walking into the bathroom to wash up.

"Bring me a towel," Ja'Rel yelled from the bedroom, too worn out to get out of bed. "And what made you change your mind?"

"I thought about what you said and I agree, it is too soon," she said, walking back into the bedroom with a warm, soapy towel and handing it to Ja'Rel.

"It's up to you, baby," he said, laying the towel on his Johnson. "I wanna make you happy and if you're not ready I can't do nothin' but respect it." Ja'Rel finished wiping himself off and threw the wet towel on the nightstand.

"Thanks, but I'm good. It'll happen when it's supposed to," Ke'yoko said as she slipped into some pajama bottoms and a T-shirt.

"Whatever makes you happy, baby," Ja'Rel said, lying down. "Hand me my cell phone."

As Ke'yoko picked the phone up off the dresser it began to ring. Ka'yah's name popped up on the screen, and Ke'yoko got one of the biggest attitudes. Nadia's and Ross's comments popped into her head again. She wanted to split Ja'Rel's head wide open with the phone but she tossed it on the bed instead.

"I'm goin' to cook dinner," Ke'yoko said.

"A'iiight, well, I'm about to take a nap," Ja'Rel said while yawning and looking at the caller ID.

Ke'yoko looked at Ja'Rel and felt disgusted. She forced a fake smile and headed down to the kitchen to prepare dinner.

"I'm tellin' you, Nadia, I'm starting to believe what you and Ross are sayin' about Ka'yah and Ja'Rel," Ke'yoko said, literally feeling sick to her stomach as she paced the kitchen floor.

"Girl, stop it! I keep tellin' you I was sayin' that bullshit outta anger. I don't really think . . ." Nadia stopped in midsentence. "Hold up! Did you just say Ross?"

"Yes." Ke'yoko smiled as she opened up the refrigerator to find something to cook. She was starving.

"Are you smilin', bitch?" Nadia asked, hearing it in Ke'yoko's voice.

"No," Ke'yoko lied, while grabbing the ham and Miracle Whip out, and closing the refrigerator. She needed a quick snack before cooking dinner.

"Ummmm huh. And just when did you talk to Ross?" Nadia inquired.

"Damn, is this an interrogation?" Ke'yoko joked.

"You damn right it is!" Nadia laughed.

"Well, if you really must know, I ran into him about two weeks ago." Ke'yoko continued to smile as she grabbed the bread and fixed herself two sandwiches.

"Bitch, you still smilin'?" Nadia asked, smiling as well.

"No." Ke'yoko giggled.

"Okay, sis, all I gotta say is be careful, 'cause if Ja'Rel finds out you communicatin' with that nigga, it's gon' be curtains for both of y'all's asses."

"Anyway," Ke'yoko said, twisting her lips and rolling her eyes. "You know what, I'm to the point where I'm startin' not to give a fuck no more. I can't half stomach Ja'Rel."

"What he do now?"

"The usual. Stayin' out all night, laid up with this bitch and that bitch," Ke'yoko replied angrily.

Nadia just shook her head. She had been listening to her best friend complain about the same shit for the past seven years and had yet to do anything about it.

"Then the nigga gon' hold me down on his dick so he could cum inside of me," Ke'yoko continued to fuss.

"I thought you wanted to try for another baby."

"I do, but I don't want one by his ass. I gotta get away from him."

Nadia was shocked. She'd never heard Ke'yoko talk about leaving Ja'Rel before today and she was in even more shock that as bad as she wanted a baby, she didn't want one by her husband.

"Just know, whatever you decide to do, I gotcha back," Nadia assured her.

"I know you do. Hang on, I got another call comin' in," Ke'yoko said, clicking over to the other line.

"Hello, sis?"

"Oh, wassup, baby brother?" Ke'yoko asked.

"Hey."

"Hang on, let me get off the other line." Ke'yoko clicked back over before Kailo could respond. "Let me call you back. This my brother."

"A'iiiight. Don't forget, 'cause I wanna know what all you and Ross talked about," Nadia said.

"Okay, nosey." Ke'yoko clicked back over to her brother. "Okay, I'm back," Ke'yoko said to Kailo. "Wassup?"

"I was just calling to let you know that it's almost summer break and I told you I wanted to come see you and Ka'yah," he said.

"Okay, and?"

"And I was calling to see if it was still okay," Kailo replied.

"Of course it's still okay! Why wouldn't it be?" Ke'yoko asked while taking a bite of one of her sandwiches.

"Okay, I was just making sure, that's all."

"When are you comin'?" Ke'yoko asked, anxious to see her baby brother.

"I'm flying out next Tuesday."

"Okay, great. Do you need me to pick you up from the airport?"

"No, thank you. I'll have a rental car while I'm in town," Kailo said.

"Look at you all grown up, you drivin' and shit," Ke'yoko said, happy and sad at the same time because she was robbed of the chance to watch her baby brother grow up. "Okay, well, since you not comin' until Tuesday, that'll give me enough time to get the guest room together."

"Okay, great."

"I can't wait to see you," Ke'yoko said as she continued to smack on her food.

"I can't wait to see you either, sis. Oh, before I go I need to ask a favor."

"Wassup?" Ke'yoko asked.

"Is it okay if I bring a friend with me? He doesn't want to go home for the summer either so I told him it would be okay to come to my favorite sister's house with me," Kailo said, laying it on thick.

"Favorite, huh? Whatever." Ke'yoko laughed. "Is this *friend* your girlfriend?"

"No." Kailo laughed. "Didn't you hear me say *he* didn't want to go home?"

"Oh, well, where do you know this nigga from? He don't be stealin', do he?" Ke'yoko asked.

Kailo couldn't help but laugh. "No, sis, he doesn't steal. He has more money than I can ever imagine having, and I know him from school, and he's not a nigga."

"Oh, well, what is he then?"

"He's white," Kailo answered.

"White?" Ke'yoko asked, surprised. "What you doin' hangin' wit' a white boy? They're weird as fuck!"

"Yeah, most of them are, but not Chad. He's pretty cool."

"Chad? That's a straight white boy name," Ke'yoko said.

Kailo busted out laughing. "Sorry his parents didn't name him Tyrone, Jaleel, Jawaun, or Cephus."

"Shut up, smart-ass." Ke'yoko laughed too. "I hope he eats soul food. Just know I ain't gon' be makin' no green bean casserole or no shit like that, you hear me?"

"Yes, I hear you," Kailo said, shaking his head.

"Okay, well, I'll get the other guest room together as well. I love you and will see you Tuesday."

"Okay, sis, I love you too," Kailo replied before hanging up.

Ke'yoko shook her head. She instantly became dizzy. This was the second spell she'd had this week. She had been meaning to make an appointment with her nurse practitioner, David, but never got around to it. If she kept feeling like this she would definitely have to get in to see him, but right now all she wanted to do was finish her sandwiches and quick; she was starving.

Chapter Eleven

Ke'yoko pulled up in front of Nadia's hair shop, turned the engine off, and sat for a brief second. The thought of the pictures that she kept tucked away in the garage invaded her mind. She shook her head, reaching over and grabbing a saltine cracker out of the pack and putting it in her mouth. She then grabbed her oversized Alexander McQueen purse and got out of the car. She looked around before heading into the shop.

"Can I talk to you for a minute?" she said to Nadia and made her way toward her office before Nadia could reply.

"Sure. I'll be right back," Nadia said to her impatient client who had already spent the past three hours in the shop. Nadia made her way to her office as well. She unlocked the door, walked in, and waited for Ke'yoko to come in behind her, locking the door behind them.

"See, I told you that bitch acts like she run shit when she comes up in here," Connie said, twisting up her lips. The other stylists couldn't do anything but shake their heads in agreement as the chick whose hair Nadia had been working on cut her eyes.

"What's good?" Nadia asked.

"This." Ke'yoko pulled two bricks of pure powder blue cocaine out of her purse, laying them on Nadia's desk.

Nadia picked a rattail comb up off her desk and poked a small hole in one of the packages. She then put her pinky finger on top of the hole, sweeping a small amount of product on her finger, and stuck it in her mouth. Ke'yoko waited impatiently for the verdict.

"This is some good shit," Nadia said, smiling and shaking her head in approval as she stuck her finger into the hole a second time. "Here, taste it."

Ke'yoko shook her head no. "I'm cool."

Nadia shrugged her shoulders and stuck the product into her own mouth. "So what's the plan?"

"I got Harvey comin' to get a quarter kilo," Ke'yoko said.

"Why you gotta get all technical and shit? All you had to say was nine ounces." Nadia laughed.

Ke'yoko laughed too. "Anyways, I got two sells for two big eighths or, in layman terms, 250 grams."

"Cool. I need like four Os and we gon' cook the rest and slow roll the rest," Nadia said.

"I'm down wit' it," Ke'yoko said. "I wanna take Ja'Rel's custos so bad, but I know they'll run their mouths and I can't take that chance."

"I know, man. Damn, we would make a straight killin'. But it's all good; we got our own custos. We makin' money, too. We can't go gettin' greedy. That's when muthafuckas start gettin' caught up and shit," Nadia said.

"You right." Ke'yoko shook her head in agreement. "What I really wish is we could get Mitch on our team. That nigga be makin' major moves."

"We good. We don't need Mitch. Harvey be makin' major moves too."

"True, true."

Nadia looked over at Ke'yoko. "How long we gon' stay in this dope game?"

"You tired of it?" Ke'yoko questioned.

Nadia looked around her plushed-out office before answering. "Hell naw. I was just askin' a general question."

"We gon' stay in this shit as long as we can or at least until we get caught up."

"The way we stick and move it's gon' be a long-ass time before we get caught up," Nadia said. "We just gon' have to continue to move the same way we've been doin' for the past four years."

"You right. We got this shit under control."

"A'iiight, sis, I'll holla at'chu later on. I gotta go in there and finish my client's nappy-ass head. She already been here all day. I don't wanna have to check her ass for having no attitude. I'll meet back up wit' you later on," Nadia said.

"I gotta go too. I got a doctor's appointment," Ke'yoko said.

"You still havin' them dizzy spells?" Nadia asked, concerned.

"Yes, girl, and they gettin' worse."

"Well, let me know what the doctor says and I'll meet you and Harvey around ten o'clock."

"Say no more," Ke'yoko said, exiting the office and the shop. Ke'yoko opened her car door, tossed her purse in and climbed in, then pulled off.

Chapter Twelve

Ke'yoko walked out of the doctor's office with tears in her eyes. She looked over the paperwork that her doctor had given her and shook her head in disbelief. Of all the things that could have been wrong with her, being pregnant again was the last thing she expected. Under any other circumstance, she would have been ecstatic about expecting another child. But this baby couldn't have come at a worse time, at a time when she had enough nerve and planned to leave Ja'Rel for real this time. Ke'yoko thought about having an abortion but quickly brushed that idea out of her mind. If anything, she was definitely gon' let nature take its course, and as crass as it may sound, hopefully she'd end up having another miscarriage.

Ke'yoko started up the car and pulled out of the parking lot. All she could think about was the baby and what she was going to do. She knew she was financially stable enough to raise a child, but being pregnant would definitely complicate her plans right now.

Ke'yoko pulled up in the driveway and parked next to Ka'yah. "What the fuck this bitch doin' here while I ain't at home?" Ke'yoko fussed as she gathered her things and got out of the car. She pushed the proof of pregnancy papers to the bottom of her purse. She had to find the right time to tell Ja'Rel the news or, better yet, decide if she was even gon' tell his ass. Right now just wasn't the time. The only thing she wanted to talk about was what the hell Ka'yah was there for.

Ke'yoko walked in the house looking and breathing like a deranged pit bull. She heard laughing from the kitchen and went straight into attack mode.

"Stop it. Ke'yoko ain't gon' like this." Ka'yah laughed, slapping Ja'Rel on the arm.

"Like what?" Ke'yoko asked with a straight attitude, mugging Ka'yah first and then Ja'Rel. She watched as Ka'yah quickly rolled up a sheet of paper and placed it in her purse.

Ka'yah and Ja'Rel both looked like they'd been caught with their hands in the cookie jar.

"What's up, baby?" Ja'Rel asked.

"What's up, sis?" Ka'yah asked with a smile.

"What's goin' on up in here?" Ke'yoko asked, not beating around the bush. She couldn't hold it in anymore. She needed to know what was going on between her twin and her husband and she was going to find out today.

"What you mean?" Ka'yah asked, confused.

"What the fuck you mean, what I mean? What the fuck is goin' on here between you and Ja'Rel?" Ke'yoko snapped.

"You trippin'," Ja'Rel cut in.

"Am I?" Ke'yoko asked.

"Hell yeah, you are," Ka'yah asked.

"It's quite obvious y'all fuckin' around! Y'all must think I'm a fuckin' fool! Everybody sayin' it!"

"Are you fuckin' serious?" Ka'yah asked, appalled.

"Man, Ke'yoko, I don't know what the fuck is wrong wit' you but you really been trippin' around here a lot lately! You need to go to the doctor and get whatever's wrong wit' you handled!" Ja'Rel snapped.

Ke'yoko had been trippin' lately and didn't know why. But finding out she was pregnant explained why her hormones were all out of whack and why she stayed in her feelings so much lately, other than Ja'Rel being a ho. Hell, that wasn't anything new.

"Ain't shit wrong wit' me. Y'all the ones fucked up! But it's cool; y'all can have each other. Both y'all bitches deserve each other," Ke'yoko said.

"I can't believe you," Ka'yah said, shaking her head in disbelief.

"You can't believe me? You fuckin' my husband! I ain't fuckin' yours," Ke'yoko yelled.

"So you honestly think I would stoop that low and fuck your husband?" Ka'yah asked, hurt.

"Yep. I sure do. Ever since we were kids you've been jealous of me. So, yes, I think you would stoop that low. Shit, you always callin' him all times of the night. Your number in his call log more than mines and I'm the one married to his no-good ass. Always whisperin' all up in his ear and shit. Y'all meetin' up behind my back thinkin' I don't know! You foul, Ka'yah!" Ke'yoko couldn't help her words or her rage as tears filled her eyes.

Ja'Rel shook his head in disbelief.

"I don't know why you shakin' yo' head, nigga! You just as foul," Ke'yoko shouted.

Ka'yah looked at her sister as tears filled her eyes. She couldn't find any words to address Ke'yoko right now. Ke'yoko had always had it easy, always had the good things. Ke'yoko was just spoiled and Ka'yah was sick of it and her.

Ke'yoko didn't feel an ounce of remorse about her sister's fake tears.

"If you really must know, I've been callin' Ja'Rel and meetin' up with him behind ya back tryin' to get your surprise birthday party together along wit' helpin' him design the layout of the new house he bought you for your birthday," Ka'yah said, digging the blueprint out of her purse and throwing it at Ke'yoko.

Ke'yoko was speechless, watching the paper fall to her feet. Should she believe this shit? She wasn't ready to admit there was a chance she was wrong. How in the world could she have let her mind get the best of her? Was her mind playing tricks on her? She knew what Nadia thought and she knew what she'd been seeing herself. Could her instincts be this damn wrong? Ke'yoko looked over at Ja'Rel and then at Ka'yah. Had she really messed up this time? She bent over and picked the paper up, looking at it. She didn't know if her relationship would be repairable with her sister this time. She'd said and done a lot of mean things to Ka'yah growing up, but this she knew she may have taken way too far.

"I'm sorry, y'all," Ke'yoko said, embarrassed.

"You should be," Ka'yah said before turning to walk out of the kitchen.

"Ka'yah, wait!" Ke'yoko called out.

Ka'yah didn't respond. She continued to her car.

Ke'yoko looked over at Ja'Rel hoping he'd console her and maybe understand her outburst, but instead he just looked at her as if she was scum before walking out of the kitchen and out the door, slamming it behind him.

"Damn!" Ke'yoko screamed before sitting down at the kitchen table and crying her eyes out.

Chapter Thirteen

For the next few days all Ke'yoko did was mope around the house. She still felt stupid about how she'd accused Ka'yah and Ja'Rel of messing around. She had tried calling her sister several times since the incident, but kept getting sent straight to voice mail. She wasn't going to give up. Ke'yoko had never meant to hurt Ka'yah. If Ja'Rel, on the other hand, was hurt behind it, he deserved to be because of all the hurt he'd put her through for the past seven years. He acted like he hadn't ever done anything to her for her to think he would cheat on her. He had to have been feeling some type of way too because he was barely speaking to her.

Ke'yoko woke up and quickly jumped out of bed, dashing into the bathroom to throw up. This morning sickness was really taking its toll on her. She rinsed her mouth out with water, walked back into her bedroom, and noticed Ja'Rel was gone. She shook her head and headed out of the bedroom and downstairs to get herself something to eat. She walked into the kitchen and saw a huge bouquet of 250 fresh red roses sitting on the kitchen table. Ke'yoko smiled as she walked over and smelled the flowers. The smell of the flowers was so strong it almost made her throw up. She picked up the card, took a step back from the smell, and read it:

Happy birthday, baby. These roses are a symbol of my love. This is just the beginning. Wait until later on. I have so much more to give. I had a few last-minute party preparations. I've already paid Nadia to do your hair. Your outfit is hanging in the bedroom closet. Be ready at seven o'clock.
Love always, Ja'Rel

Ke'yoko couldn't help but smile. Her day couldn't get any better, she thought, as she headed out the kitchen to go upstairs to see what Ja'Rel had bought her to wear. Her only thought was she hoped she could fit into it. The doorbell rang as she headed up the steps.

"Damn! Who could be at the door this damn early in the mornin'," Ke'yoko said as she turned around and headed back down the stairs. "Who is it?"

"Me," the deep voice responded.

"Me who?" Ke'yoko asked, not in the mood to be playing no games. She had a party to get ready for.

"Open up the door and see."

Ke'yoko quickly unlocked the door so she could give this smart-mouth muthafucka a piece of her mind. "Who the fuck—" she started.

"Happy birthday!" Kailo yelled with a huge smile.

"Oh, my goodness!" Ke'yoko squealed as she looked her brother in the face for the first time in almost seven years. Tears of joy rolled down Ke'yoko's face as she wrapped her arms around her brother's waist. He had grown so much since the last time she'd seen him.

Kailo embraced his sister as well, not wanting to let her go. All the memories of her playing army with him, reading him bedtime stories, teaching him how to ride a bike, and helping him with his homework came rushing back to him as he hugged her.

"Look at'chu." Ke'yoko smiled, taking a step back. "Boy, you gotta be at least six foot."

"Six foot one," Kailo corrected her.

"Damn, boy! I thought you wasn't comin' until Tuesday," Ke'yoko said as she continued to smile.

"I wanted to surprise you on your birthday so I came early! Sis, this is Chad. Chad, this is my big sister, Ke'yoko," Kailo introduced them.

Ke'yoko looked at Chad. He was handsome for a white boy. He had those dreamy blue eyes just like Paul Walker. If he weren't so young, Ke'yoko would have tried to shoot her shot.

"Nice to meet you," Chad said, sticking his hand out.

"We give hugs around here; we don't shake hands," Ke'yoko said, wrapping her arms around Chad, pulling him into her. The smell of his cologne had her not wanting to let him go.

"Okay, sis, you can let him go now." Kailo laughed.

"Oh, sorry." Ke'yoko laughed. "Your cologne smells so good."

"Thanks." Chad smiled.

"So are you gon' invite us in or do we gotta stand on the porch?" Kailo asked sarcastically.

"Shut up, boy, and come on in." Ke'yoko laughed before moving out of the way so her brother and his friend could enter the house.

"This is a nice-ass house," Kailo said, looking around as he followed his sister into the living room.

"Thanks." Ke'yoko smiled, taking a seat on the loveseat. Kailo and Chad both sat on the sofa.

Ke'yoko looked at her brother and all she could do was keep smiling.

"What?" Kailo asked.

"Nothin', I'm just so happy to see you. This is the best birthday present ever."

"What you doin' for it?"

"Oh, Ka'yah and Ja'Rel is throwin' me a surprise birthday party," Ke'yoko responded.

"Well, if it's a surprise how do you know about it?" Kailo asked, laughing.

"It's a long story. One that I don't feel like gettin' into right now. We'll talk about it, though," Ke'yoko said, trying to stay in a positive mood. "Have you spoken to Ka'yah?"

"Nope, not yet."

"Well, good, don't call her. We're goin' to surprise her at the party tonight," Ke'yoko said, hoping that all three of them being together again would help Ka'yah get over her anger.

"Okay, cool. So what should we wear?" Kailo asked.

"Dress to impress," Ke'yoko said.

"That's not hard to do," Kailo replied.

"Okay, well, I have to go get my hair done in a few. Would y'all like for me to fix y'all some breakfast or somethin' before I go?" Ke'yoko asked.

"No, we stopped at McDonald's before we got here. We had a long flight. All we wanna do is get some rest before the party, so can you show us to our rooms?" Kailo asked.

"Oh, okay, yeah, follow me," Ke'yoko said, standing up from the loveseat and leading Kailo and Chad up to the guest rooms. "Make yourselves at home. I'm about to get dressed and head over to the shop."

"Thanks, sis," Kailo said.

"Thank you," Chad said before entering his room.

"He's cute," Ke'yoko whispered to Kailo.

Kailo shook his head before going into his room to take a much-needed nap.

Ke'yoko walked into her bedroom and went to the closet to see what Ja'Rel had bought her. She pulled out a Nordstrom bag and removed it from over the garment. He had bought her a light blue, Oscar de la Renta poppy-print, silk-blend mikado fit-and-flare dress. Ke'yoko grabbed the price tag and checked it.

"$2,190 for this?" she said aloud. She liked the dress and all, it was so her, but she would have never paid $2,000 for it. Hey, why complain? It wasn't her money.

Ke'yoko hung the dress back up and grabbed another Nordstrom bag with a pair of shoes in it.

She quickly lifted the lid off. She picked one of the navy blue Valentino Rockstud pumps out of the box and instantly fell in love.

"These bitches are to die for," Ke'yoko said excitedly. She didn't know how she would walk in them, being that her feet had been swelling up. She had to at least wear them for a few hours so everybody could see them on her feet. Ke'yoko put the shoe back in the box and set it back in the closet before going to jump in the shower. She was going to make the best of her birthday, whether or not Ka'yah forgave her. She was going to her party and she was going to enjoy herself. She had Kailo by her side if nothing else.

Chapter Fourteen

Seven o'clock rolled around and Ke'yoko was dressed and ready to go. Nadia had cut her hair into a short style that she'd been eyeing forever. She'd never had enough nerve to get her hair cut that short. Ke'yoko had been growing her hair since she was a child, also another custom she decided it was time to do away with. Nadia's sister, Raya, had Ke'yoko's face beat. Ke'yoko felt and looked like a million bucks.

At five after seven Ke'yoko's phone rang. She looked at the caller ID and saw Ja'Rel's name. "Hello?" she answered with a smile.

"Come to the door," he said.

"Okay." Ke'yoko grabbed her house shoes and Ka'yah's gift just in case she showed up, and threw them in her purse before heading down-stairs.

She opened the door and smiled from ear to ear as Ja'Rel stood there with a ring box. "Damn, baby, you look good," Ja'Rel said, admiring his wife. He was shocked she'd cut her hair but he loved it. It flattered her face and gave her even more sex appeal. Standing there looking at her he wondered how and why he constantly stepped out on her. He blamed it on the dog in him.

"Thank you." She smiled.

"This is for you," he said, handing her the ring box.

Ke'yoko quickly took the box and opened it up. "Oh, my goodness," she said with big eyes, pulling out a platinum deluxe double-halo wedding ring.

"It's an upgrade," Ja'Rel said, removing her old ring and replacing it with the new one.

"Damn, baby," she said, admiring the huge rock on her finger. If Ja'Rel kept this up, he would surely make Ke'yoko fall back in love with him.

"You like it?" he asked with a smile.

"Like it? Shiiit, I love it," she said, leaning in and giving Ja'Rel a kiss on the lips. For the first time in a long time she felt something other than hate for her husband.

"Oh, before I forget, I came home earlier. You were gone so I gave Kailo and Chad the address to the party, so they'll be there."

"Cool," Ke'yoko replied with a smile. She had been wondering where her brother had run off to.

"You ready?"

"As I'm gon' ever get," Ke'yoko said.

Ja'Rel led Ke'yoko down the walk to a white Hummer H2 stretch limo. The driver waited outside of the door and opened it for them to get in. Ke'yoko and Ja'Rel both climbed in. Ja'Rel picked up a bottle of Patrón and poured a shot in a cup and tried to hand it to Ke'yoko.

"No, I'm good," she refused.

"What's wrong, baby? This yo' drink and, plus, it's yo' birthday," Ja'Rel said.

"I know. I'ma eat somethin' first before I start drinkin'. You know how I get when I drink on an empty stomach."

"Freaky." Ja'Rel smiled deviously.

"Shut up." Ke'yoko laughed.

"Well, it's true." Ja'Rel took the shot himself and poured himself another one, taking it to the face.

For the first time in a grip, Ke'yoko and Ja'Rel held a meaningful conversation. Twenty minutes later, the driver pulled the limo into the venue parking lot. A couple minutes later he opened up the door, helped Ke'yoko out, and waited for Ja'Rel to exit. Ke'yoko couldn't believe all the cars in the parking lot. She could hear the DJ's music playing; he was jamming.

She threw her purse on her shoulder before straightening out the invisible wrinkles in her dress. Ja'Rel pulled out his phone and began texting. All Ke'yoko could do before exploding was take a deep breath. He couldn't hold off on texting one of his thirsty hoes. It was her birthday, not theirs.

"Did I tell you how good you look, baby?" Ja'Rel said while grabbing Ke'yoko's hand and leading her up to the venue.

Ke'yoko had a straight attitude but didn't want it to show. She forced a smile and shook her head yes.

"Surprise!" everybody yelled as Ja'Rel and Ke'yoko walked inside.

"Oh, my goodness!" Ke'yoko smiled widely as if she didn't already know about the party. "Thank you."

"Say cheese," the photographer said and began snapping pictures of Ke'yoko and Ja'Rel.

Nadia walked up and gave Ke'yoko a hug. "Happy birthday, sis," she said.

"Thank you," Ke'yoko said, shaking her head in awe at how beautifully decorated the venue was. Ja'Rel had really outdone himself. She had never had a birthday party before; and if she had this would have definitely been the best one out of them all.

The venue was truly beautiful. There had to be at least a thousand or more white and light blue balloons on the ceiling. It was like walking into something straight out of a magazine. The tables were decorated with lighted center pieces and white flowers. The food smelled so good, all Ke'yoko wanted to do was go fix her a plate and throw down, but everybody kept coming up to her and wishing her a happy birthday. When she finally got a break from everybody, she looked around the room to see if Ka'yah was there. Ke'yoko was disappointed when she didn't see her sister. She walked up to the food table and stood there trying to decide what to eat. There was every type of soul food known to man on the table. Ja'Rel had even had the caterers throw some Japanese dishes on the menu as well.

"Happy birthday, twin," Ke'yoko heard a familiar voice say.

She quickly turned around and smiled when she saw Ka'yah and her nephew, Aiko, standing there. "Happy birthday, twin," Ke'yoko said. Tears flowed from her eyes. She couldn't believe she was crying. It felt good to have her sister show up for her special night.

"Don't cry. You gon' make me cry," Ka'yah said, but it was too late; tears began to flow from her eyes as well.

"I'm so sorry." Ke'yoko bawled as she and her sister held on to each other.

"It's okay, twin. I forgive you and we'll never speak on it again," Ka'yah assured her.

Ja'Rel walked over and grabbed Aiko's hand and walked him away from the crying sisters.

"Is Mommy and Auntie Ke-Ke okay?" Aiko looked up at Ja'Rel and asked sadly.

"Yeah, they okay." Ja'Rel smiled.

"Well, why they cryin' then?" Aiko inquired.

"Those are happy tears. They are happy to see each other," Ja'Rel explained.

"Oooooh," Aiko said and smiled.

The guests were standing around watching as the two sisters made up. They didn't have the slightest idea what they were crying about and didn't care. All they knew was it was a sentimental moment. Some even shed a few tears with them as they watched the two.

"Okay, okay, break it up and give me some," Kailo walked up and said.

"Kailo!" Ka'yah screamed loudly as more tears flowed.

"Surprise!" Ke'yoko smiled.

The three siblings hugged for what seemed like an eternity. Ke'yoko didn't want to let go. She wanted this feeling to last forever.

Ja'Rel even shed a tear as he watched the three cry. Nadia stood beside Ja'Rel, wiping her tears away as well.

"Say cheese," the photographer said.

"Oh, my goodness, look at'chu," Ka'yah said, wiping her tears only to have more follow.

"Ain't he handsome?" Ke'yoko asked with a smile.

"Yes," Ka'yah replied.

"Okay. Come on, y'all, this is a birthday party. Y'all got everybody standin' around here cryin' like it's a funeral," Ja'Rel said.

"Right." Nadia laughed while drying her face.

"DJ, turn it up," Ja'Rel yelled.

Ke'yoko really enjoyed herself. This was the most fun she'd had in years. All the ill feelings she harbored toward Ja'Rel were gone for the time being, or until the next time he stayed out all night. Right now, all Ke'yoko wanted to do was bask in the moment.

She had eaten and danced so much all she wanted to do was sit her tired butt down. She smiled as she watched Ja'Rel and Aiko on the dance floor, dancing together. It dawned on Ke'yoko at that particular moment how much Aiko looked just like Ja'Rel.

All Ke'yoko could do was shake her head. *See, that's the bullshit I be talkin' about. That's why I almost lost my sister the first time*. The resemblance was uncanny, though.

"What you over here shakin' yo' head about?" Ka'yah walked up and asked.

"Nothin'. Just laughing at Ja'Rel and Aiko out there dancin'," she lied, trying to keep the peace.

"Neither one of 'em got no rhythm." Ka'yah laughed as she looked out on the dance floor.

Ke'yoko discreetly looked upside her sister's head. *Nope, not gon' believe it.*

"How come you ain't drinkin'? I ain't seen a drink in ya hand all night. It's our birthday!" Ka'yah said.

"I'm cool. I don't feel like drinkin'. I got a slight headache," Ke'yoko lied.

"More for me." Ka'yah laughed, and taking her drink to the head.

As the party began to wind down Ja'Rel walked up to the DJ's booth and grabbed the mic. "Can I get everyone's attention?" he asked. "I'm a li'l tipsy so bear wit' me."

"A li'l?" Mitch yelled out.

The crowd began laughing.

"Okay, I'm a lot tipsy," Ja'Rel said, waving Ke'yoko and Ka'yah over to him. "But, I wanna wish my lovely wife and her twin sister a happy twenty-fifth birthday. I wanna thank everyone for comin' out to celebrate this joyous occasion wit' us. I also wanna give a special shout out to Ka'yah for makin' all this possible, because if it weren't for her this party would have been a disaster."

Ka'yah smiled while lifting up her glass.

"Thanks, sis," Ke'yoko leaned over and said.

"No problem."

"I have one last gift for my wife." Ja'Rel pulled some keys from his pocket and handed them to her.

"What's this to?"

"To our new house. Happy birthday, baby," Ja'Rel said, leaning over and giving her a kiss on the cheek.

Ke'yoko smiled so hard her face hurt. This by far was the best birthday ever.

"It's not quite finished yet, but it will be in the next six months or so. You'll have your heated floors throughout the entire house, just like the ones you fell in love wit' in Turks and Caicos. It's 4,500 square feet and has four bedrooms, three full baths, a three-car garage, a huge swimmin' pool . . . You name it, it's in there."

Ke'yoko couldn't believe Ja'Rel had still decided to go ahead and give her the house she wanted even after she accused him and her sister of messing around. This was like a straight dream. "Thank you, baby," Ke'yoko said, giving Ja'Rel a long kiss.

The crowd cheered as they locked lips.

"Get a room," Ka'yah joked, making everyone laugh.

Ke'yoko took the microphone from Ja'Rel's hand. "I wanna thank everyone for comin' out and celebratin' wit' me but, before you go, I want to give my sister and my husband gifts from me."

Ja'Rel and Ka'yah both looked confused. Ke'yoko handed Ka'yah an envelope. She opened it up and smiled.

"A twenty-five hundred dollar gift certificate for Saks," she announced with a huge smile.

"And this," she said, pulling out a cute, decorated watch box and handing it to Ja'Rel, "this is for the both of y'all."

Ja'Rel took the top off the box and pulled the positive pregnancy test out and smiled. "We're pregnant," he announced, while holding up the test.

The crowd went wild with cheers, whistles, and screams. Ja'Rel leaned over and kissed his wife.

"Oh, my goodness, sis, this is the best birthday ever. I'm finally gon' get my li'l niece or nephew," Ka'yah said and began to cry again.

Nadia, Kailo, and Mitch walked up to Ke'yoko and began rubbing her belly. All Ke'yoko could do was smile. She was on such a high. This was truly the happiest she'd been in a long time and she decided maybe, just maybe, she and Ja'Rel could work things out for the baby's sake. She felt like nothing and no one could bring her down at this moment. She had her sister, her brother, her best friend, and most of all her husband. Life was great. What more could she ask for?

Chapter Fifteen

Ke'yoko and Ja'Rel were just getting back from going to dinner and a movie. Since the news of the baby, Ja'Rel had really been stepping up to the plate and making sure he went out of his way to take care of his wife. He had been coming home every night, and he'd cut back on all the cheating he'd been doing. He told his tricks that he couldn't and wouldn't do anything to upset his wife; he was determined not to do anything that would cause Ke'yoko any stress. If they couldn't understand that, then he didn't know what to tell them. He knew in the past that he'd been a big part of the reason why she'd had all those miscarriages. He would never admit that to her or anyone else. Ja'Rel knew he'd done so much dirt to his wife. He really wanted to make sure at any cost that his wife had the family she'd always desired.

"So did you enjoy the movie?" Ja'Rel asked Ke'yoko as he unlocked the door.

"Yeah, it was good. The endin' was sad. I still can't believe Paul Walker is gone," she said, shaking her head while walking into the house.

"It's quiet in here. Kailo and Chad musta gone to bed early," Ja'Rel said, tossing the keys on the table in the foyer.

"They was probably tired. I did have them workin' all mornin'. I had them packin' up the truck and takin' the stuff we're not movin' into the new house down to the Goodwill," Ke'yoko said, yawning.

"Shoot, I'm tired too." Ja'Rel yawned as well. "I'm about to go to bed. You comin'?"

"I'll be up. I'ma fix me some ice cream first."

"Okay." Ja'Rel yawned again before heading upstairs.

Ke'yoko walked into the kitchen and grabbed the ice cream out of the freezer. The next thing she knew all she could hear was Ja'Rel hollering profanities at the top of his lungs. Ke'yoko dropped the ice cream on the floor, ran out of the kitchen, and darted upstairs as fast as she could.

"What's wrong?" Ke'yoko asked, scared and out of breath. She looked over at Kailo, who was wrapped up in a comforter, then over at Chad, who was lying in the bed with the covers pulled up to his chin. "What's goin' on?"

"I came upstairs and heard moanin' comin' from the guest room and shit. I walked in and these two fags was in here fuckin' like two jack-rabbits," Ja'Rel said, disgusted.

"What?" Ke'yoko asked, confused. She looked at Kailo as if he were a stranger. "You a fag?"

"No, I'm not a fag. A fag is a British word meaning a tiring or unwelcomed task," Kailo said sarcastically. "Now if you wanna know if I'm gay, the answer is yes."

"Gay?" Ke'yoko frowned. All she could do was shake her head. She was speechless.

"I'm sorry," Chad said.

Ke'yoko looked over at him and rolled her eyes. "I can't believe this shit," she said.

"Y'all gotta get up outta here," Ja'Rel said.

"No, Ja'Rel. Let's just go to bed and discuss this matter in the mornin'," Ke'yoko pleaded.

"These fag-ass niggas ain't stayin' up in here tonight," Ja'Rel said sternly.

"It's okay, sis. We'll get a hotel room," Kailo said.

"That's what y'all gon' have to do," Ja'Rel snapped.

"Ja'Rel, let me handle this," Ke'yoko begged.

"It ain't shit to handle, Ke'yoko. These homos is not stayin' here. Now I'm goin' to bed and they betta be gone before I get up." Ja'Rel looked over at Chad, then at Kailo, and frowned before walking across the hall to the bedroom.

Ke'yoko looked at Kailo. "I don't understand," she said, heartbroken.

"I didn't expect you to; that's why I didn't tell you," Kailo replied.

"Why?" was Ke'yoko's next question.

"Why not? I grew up in a house full of weak women. You were the strongest out of all of them. I admired you for standing up to Father. You don't know how happy I was when you flipped on him. It sickened me to look at Mother and Ka'yah; they acted so timid and scared around him all the time. Watching Mother all those years jump at his every beck and call made me sick to my stomach. I promised myself when I got old enough to move out that I didn't want a woman. I wanted someone strong and controlling. I wanted a man. I never had a desire to be with a woman at all; you can thank your mother for that. She turned me off from women. I can't stand a sorry, weak, sniffling-ass female."

Ke'yoko couldn't believe what she was hearing. She couldn't believe her mother was the cause of her brother turning to men for love and protection. "Wow, Kailo, I don't know what to say."

"There's nothin' to say, sis. It is what it is," Kailo replied.

"Look, you guys don't have to leave. I'll go talk to Ja'Rel and we can smooth this over in the mornin'," Ke'yoko said, not wanting to take a chance on losing her brother again. Gay or not, she still wanted her brother in her life. It would take a lot of getting used to, but she was willing to do so in order to keep him from disappearing for good.

"No, sis. It's cool. I'm not about to cause conflict in your household. Plus, you're pregnant and you don't need any added stress. We gon' be good."

"Kailo, promise me you'll stay in touch," Ke'yoko said desperately.

"I promise you I will stay in touch. Plus, I wanna be around for my niece or nephew," Kailo said, rubbing the top of Ke'yoko's head.

Ke'yoko wrapped her arms around her brother's waist and nearly squeezed the breath out of him as she held on to him for dear life. "I love you, Kailo. Do you need any help finding a room?" Ke'yoko asked.

"I love you too, sis; and, no, we will just get our things packed and be gone shortly. Go to bed. You need your rest," Kailo replied while kissing his sister on the top of her head.

Ke'yoko let go of her brother, took a step back, and looked over at Chad. "I really don't know what to say right now, Chad. We're just surprised, I guess. It was nice meetin' you though."

Chad was afraid to respond; instead he just smiled.

Ke'yoko shook her head. She couldn't believe her brother was gay. She turned and walked out of the room and joined Ja'Rel in the bedroom. He was already asleep. Ke'yoko lay down and cried herself to sleep.

Chapter Sixteen

Ke'yoko had to fill in at the shop for Tamika because she had called off once again. It had become quite frequent that she missed work every payday. Ke'yoko sat at the desk, deep in thought. She couldn't get her mind off of Kailo. There were so many unanswered questions about the night he'd left. She wanted to call and talk to him, but decided to give him some time and space. She definitely didn't want to push him back out of her life so she decided for now to just leave it alone. She didn't have a choice.

"Wassup, sis," Ka'yah said, walking in the office and breaking Ke'yoko's concentration.

"Oh, hey," Ke'yoko looked up and said with a smile. Ke'yoko loved having her sister back in her life. They were tighter now than they'd been before. They'd started calling each other every day just like old times, going out to lunch, getting mani's and pedi's, and going on shopping sprees. Ka'yah had been buying the baby all kinds of gifts, and was already planning one of the biggest baby showers ever.

"Here's your mornin' cup of tea," Ka'yah said, handing her sister the hot cup.

"Thank you." Ke'yoko smiled while taking the cup from her hand and setting it down on the desk.

"Now drink up. I keep tellin' you the green tea is good for my nephew," Ka'yah said.

"Just how do you know it's a boy?" Ke'yoko asked.

"Believe me, I just know," Ka'yah said. "Plus, we got enough girls in the family."

"There's only two of us." Ke'yoko laughed.

"Three countin' Kailo," Ka'yah said, cutting her eyes and twisting up her lips.

Ke'yoko didn't even respond. She acted like she hadn't even heard her sister's snide comment. Kailo's sexual choice was a topic Ke'yoko wasn't mentally prepared to discuss yet. *Hold the fuck up.* Ke'yoko's instincts kicked in again! She wondered how Ka'yah even knew about Kailo being gay. The only people who'd known or been told were Ja'Rel and Nadia; and she knew for a fact Nadia hadn't opened up her mouth. That left no one but Ja'Rel!

"Oh, well, sis, I'm about to go pick Aiko up from his dad's house, head home, and take a nap. I'm a little tired," Ka'yah said, yawning.

"Okay. I'll call you later on," Ke'yoko said slowly. She was still trying to figure out when Ja'Rel could have told Ka'yah and why he hadn't mentioned it to her.

"Okay, and make sure you drink your tea."

"I will." Ke'yoko picked up the cup and took a sip. "Ummmm, this is so good."

"I told you. Well, I'm out. Love you." Ka'yah smiled as she headed toward the door.

"Love you too," Ke'yoko replied and continued sipping on her tea.

Ke'yoko sat for a few more minutes sipping on her tea and staring at the wall. Her mind continued racing about Kailo, and also why Ja'Rel would tell Ka'yah about their brother instead of giving her the chance to tell her. He didn't know if she was even going to tell Ka'yah or even if Kailo wanted Ka'yah to know yet. If Ke'yoko had decided to tell Ka'yah she would have done that in her own time and in her own way. She would have eventually gotten around to telling her. Ja'Rel was way out of line.

Tired of sitting with her mind idling, Ke'yoko decided she would take the rest of the day off. If Tamika could do it, shit, she could too. It was a beautiful day out and the last thing she wanted was to be cooped up in the office. Ke'yoko finished off the last of tea, and threw the cup in the trash before calling Nadia and Ka'yah and telling them to get the kids ready because she was coming to get them. Ke'yoko had been promising them for months that she would spend some time with her nephew and goddaughter, but never got around to it. What better day than today? Ke'yoko sent the calls to voice mail, put the closed sign on the door, gathered her things, and headed to the car.

Ke'yoko sat on the park bench, catching up on the latest gossip in the *Sister 2 Sister* magazine as Aiko and A'Niyah ran around like two wild geese, yelling and screaming.

"They gon' be good and tired when I drop they asses off wit' they mommas," Ke'yoko looked up briefly and said.

"Look, Auntie, no hands," Aiko yelled as he and A'Niyah played on the teeter-totter.

"Boy, you better hold on before you fall and hurt yourself," Ke'yoko warned.

"I'm a big boy," Aiko replied.

"A'iiiight, when ya big boy ass laid out on the ground don't say nothin'," Ke'yoko mumbled.

Ke'yoko had finished her magazine and looked up at A'Niyah and smiled, and then looked over at Aiko and instantly got spooked. She looked as if she had just seen a ghost. Aiko was the spitting image of Ja'Rel. Ke'yoko had tried to brush that thought aside but it had been bothering her since the night of her birthday party. She had already accused Ja'Rel and Ka'yah of messing around once before and had been wrong about it, so they made her think. She hadn't had any solid proof. This time, if her instincts were right, she would have the proof she needed. Ke'yoko threw her magazine in her purse and stood up from the bench.

"Ouch," she said as she got a sharp pain in the lower part of her stomach. She had been having slight cramps for the past two weeks. Ke'yoko closed her eyes and said a quick little prayer. "God, please don't be lettin' me get ready to have another miscarriage. Please just let it be gas or somethin'. I know what my thoughts were before but, Lord, I want and need this baby. In the name of Jesus. Amen." Ke'yoko opened her eyes and called out to the children. "Come on, y'all, let's go."

"Awwwww, do we hafta leave?" A'Niyah whined

"We not ready to go yet. Just five more minutes," Aiko whined as well.

"We're about to go get some ice cream," Ke'yoko said, hoping that would get them to calm down.

"Yeeeeeah, ice cream," the both of them cheered.

Ke'yoko got the kids into the car, buckled them in their booster seats, and pulled off. She kept glancing back at her nephew in the rearview mirror as he and A'Niyah held a conversation.

Ke'yoko pulled into the CVS parking lot.

"Hey, this ain't the Dairy Queen," Aiko said.

"Nope. It says CVS," A'Niyah said, reading the letters on the sign.

"No, it's not the Dairy Queen, but Auntie need to run in here and grab a few things. And how about when we come out I take y'all to McDonald's?"

"And the Dairy Queen?" Aiko asked.

"Yes, and the Dairy Queen." Ke'yoko smiled.

"Yessss." The children smiled as they unbuckled themselves from their chairs and got out of the car.

Both children asked a million and one questions as they headed into the store.

"Auntie, do you really got a baby in yo' belly?" Aiko inquired.

"Yes, baby," Ke'yoko replied as she scoured the aisles.

"Who put it in there?" A'Niyah asked.

"God put it there, dummy," Aiko snapped.

Ke'yoko had a surprised look on her face, wondering where he'd gotten his information from. She had to admit, he was pretty intelligent to only be five years old. He was constantly holding a grown man conversation.

"Boy, you are too much." She laughed. "And don't be callin' people dumb."

"I'm not too much. I'm only five." Aiko laughed too.

Ke'yoko laughed and continued with her search. "Here it go." Ke'yoko grabbed an at-home DNA paternity test. "Buy one get one half off," she said aloud. "Shiiiit, I don't need but one but I can't pass this up. This a good deal."

Ke'yoko read the back of the box to see how to use the test. After reading the instructions she looked down at the kids. "Y'all ready?"

"Yes, about time," Aiko said smartly.

"Boy, you betta watch yo' mouth," Ke'yoko warned as they headed toward the checkout line. "Shit! I forgot my prenatal vitamins."

"Oh, boy," Aiko huffed.

"Boy, shut up and come on." Ke'yoko laughed as she and the kids headed over toward the vitamin aisle. The smell of all the different vitamins was starting to make Ke'yoko nauseous. "Prenatal, prenatal," Ke'yoko said as she quickly searched for the vitamins.

"Look, this is what Mommy puts in your tea to help make you feel better, and this one too," Aiko said excitedly.

Ke'yoko glanced down at the two bottles her nephew held in his hand and took them from him. She nearly fainted when she read the labels. She couldn't believe her sister was putting dong quai and blue cohosh in her tea. Her grandmother told her on her deathbed that after their mother had gotten raped, their grandfather was trying to get their mother to take these two herbs. Supposedly it was used to induce a miscarriage. Some Japanese called it an herbal abortion.

Devastated, Ke'yoko gathered the kids and headed to the checkout line. She thought back to how adamant Ka'yah had been that she drink all of her tea, and how she and Nadia had thought it was so nice of Ka'yah to bring her tea every day. Ka'yah never missed a day bringing her a cup of tea during any of her pregnancies no matter what. For some reason it had just dawned on Ke'yoko that Ka'yah only brought her tea when she was pregnant. Ke'yoko was furious, but mainly hurt. Why hadn't she realized this? She felt so stupid. Once again she thought, *I really am my mother's child.*

Ke'yoko got the kids in the car. All she could think about on her way to McDonald's was killing her sister and not thinking twice about it. Tears streamed down her face as she drove. So many questions were racing through her head. How could her sister do her like that? Why? What had Ke'yoko ever done to Ka'yah to warrant such a betrayal? Was Ja'Rel involved? Over and over: what was the reason behind her doing that? Ke'yoko was thinking so much, she literally got sick to her stomach. The heavy feeling in her chest and stomach would not subside, causing her to pull over twice to throw up.

Ke'yoko felt like it hurt to even breathe she felt so betrayed. Ke'yoko wanted to go straight over to Ka'yah's house and put a bullet in her head, just as she had done to Bo; but she decided to take another approach. She was going to give Ka'yah the rope and let her hang herself.

Chapter Seventeen

After taking the children to McDonald's and the Dairy Queen like she'd promised, Ke'yoko stopped by the house to brush her teeth and put some water on her face before dropping the kids off at home. She wanted to make sure she was fully composed before seeing Ka'yah. The pain and deception of what she was feeling was going to make looking at Ka'yah hard. Her own sister was responsible for her miscarriages and the heartache she had experienced repeatedly behind the loss of each child. And each time she had miscarried and mourned, her sister had looked her in the face and pretended to console her knowing she was responsible and had intentionally inflicted this pain on her.

Ke'yoko pulled up in the driveway next to Ja'Rel's car. She stuck the CVS bag in her purse, got out, and opened the back door to let the children out. "Come on, y'all."

Ke'yoko and the children walked up to the front door. Ke'yoko unlocked the door, held the screen door open, and waited for the children to walk in, and walked in after them.

"Y'all come in here and watch TV until I come back downstairs. And don't touch nothin'," she said, turning the channel to Cartoon Network. "I'm goin' upstairs to change my shirt."

"Okay," the children said in unison.

Ke'yoko walked out of the living room and headed up the stairs. She could hear Ja'Rel snoring all the way in the hallway. It clicked in her head that this would be the perfect time to swab Ja'Rel's mouth. He had been out all night drinking and doing God only knows what else, so she knew he would be in a deep sleep. She quickly dug in her purse, pulled the DNA test out, and opened it up.

"Shit, I might as well use the other one so I can get rid of all the evidence," she said, opening the other DNA kit as well. She pulled the tops off of the oversized swabs, pushed the half-cracked bedroom door, and peeked in. She waited a few more seconds before creeping in.

Perfect, she thought as she looked over at Ja'Rel, who lay on his back with his mouth wide open. She would have rather put a .38 in his mouth than these two cotton swabs.

She tiptoed over to the bed and continued to stare down at him. She was nervous as hell. She didn't know what she would have done if Ja'Rel woke up and caught her. She quickly collected her nerves and held a swab in each hand. Then, she stuck both swabs in his open mouth, one on each side, and scraped the inside of his cheeks about ten to fifteen times. She pulled them out just in time. Ja'Rel closed his mouth and began smacking his lips.

Got it! she thought excitedly before slowly walking back and sneaking out of the bedroom. She rushed back downstairs to the living room while the kids sat quietly watching cartoons. She put the two swabs in their envelopes, sealed them so they couldn't get contaminated, and placed them in her purse.

"You got the same shirt on," Aiko looked at his aunt and said.

"You always got somethin' smart to say, li'l boy. I got somethin' for smart-mouth little kids," Ke'yoko said.

"What you got for me?" Aiko inquired.

"This," Ke'yoko said, pulling the other swab out of her purse.

"Is it candy?" he asked.

"Nope. It's better than candy. It'll help little kids with smart mouths not have them anymore. So open up," Ke'yoko said.

"How come I ain't never heard of this?" Aiko asked.

"Boy, you only five. It's a lotta stuff you ain't never heard of." Ke'yoko laughed.

"Well, is it gon' hurt?" Aiko frowned.

"Nope, it's gon' tickle."

"Okay." Aiko opened his mouth and waited for Ke'yoko to swab his jaw.

"Now, your mouth won't be smart no more." Ke'yoko laughed as she put the swab in its designated envelope.

"I don't know if I believe that, but we'll see." Aiko laughed too.

"I wanna do it too. I don't wanna have a smart mouth," A'Niyah said while bouncing up and down.

"Are you sure?" Ke'yoko asked. She didn't have anyone else to test so she might as well use the extra swab on her goddaughter for shits and giggles.

A'Niyah vigorously shook her head yes.

"Okay, open wide," Ke'yoko said.

A'Niyah opened her mouth and giggled as Ke'yoko swabbed the inside of her cheek. Ke'yoko placed A'Niyah's swab in the other envelope.

"Come on, y'all, let's go," Ke'yoko said, rushing the kids out the door and to the car. She was not trying to chance Ja'Rel waking up. Ke'yoko put the kids in the car, got in herself, and backed out of the driveway. Ke'yoko then pulled out her cell phone and called Ka'yah.

"Wassup, sis?" Ka'yah answered.

"I'm about to drop Aiko off. Be watchin' out for him."

"You don't wanna come in and talk and have cup of tea?" Ka'yah asked.

It took everything in Ke'yoko not to flip gangsta on this phone. Instead, she kept her composure. She would definitely make Ka'yah pay right along with Ja'Rel.

"Girl, naw. A cup of your green tea sure does sounds real good right about now, but the kids really wore me out today. So I'ma drop A'Niyah off to her momma and go home and get some sleep," Ke'yoko said.

"Well, do you want me to make you a cup and bring it out to the car? It might give you some energy," Ka'yah said.

Or kill my unborn child! The nerve of this dirty bitch. "Naw, I'm cool," Ke'yoko said with an attitude, not being able to conceal it any longer.

"Dang, why you say it like that? You are tired, ol' cranky heffa," Ka'yah said, laughing.

Ke'yoko laughed too to play off her anger. "My bad, girl. I am tired."

"Okay, well, just drop Aiko off. I'll be sittin' on the porch waitin' on him. You go home and get some rest. Are we still on for tomorrow for our pedicure?"

"Heck yeah, I need to be pampered."

"Okay, I'll see you tomorrow," Ka'yah said.

Ke'yoko let out a fake yawn. "Sorry. Okay, see you tomorrow," she said before hanging up.

Ke'yoko pulled up in front of Ka'yah's house. She saw red when she saw her standing on the front porch. She waited for Aiko to get out, said good-bye, waved at Ka'yah, and pulled off before she changed her mind about whooping her ass.

Ke'yoko dialed Nadia's number and told her to get the red wine on chill because she needed to talk and bad!

"Wa'mint, bitch," Nadia said, before taking a long sip of her Château De Beaucastel.

"Bitch, you heard me the first time," Ke'yoko said, still in shock.

"I've never even heard of dong quai or blue cohosh," Nadia said, still trying to wrap her mind around what her best friend had just laid on her.

"Dong quai and blue cohosh are abortifacient properties. They're both herbs used for hormonal purposes. Midwives used to use it way back in the day to induce labor or to induce an abortion. Dong quai stimulates the uterus and helps strengthen contractions and blue cohosh helps open and relax the cervix. My grandfather tried to make my mom take it when she got raped by my real father," Ke'yoko explained.

Nadia shook her head in disbelief. She'd always known that Ka'yah was a shady, jealous bitch but you could have never made her believe she would do some foul shit like this. "I don't know what to say, Ke," Nadia said, speechless. "I know Ka'yah is your sister and all, but if I was you I would kill that bitch!" Nadia became angry.

Ke'yoko broke down. She couldn't hold it in any longer. She tried her best to stay strong, but the fact that her twin sister was the reason why she was losing all these babies tore her up on the inside. And for what reason? Possibly a man?

"I could shoot that bitch right in the face and not think twice about it," Ke'yoko said angrily. "Just like I did Bo."

Nadia's mouth flew open.

"Yeah, it was me. I'm the one who killed Bo," Ke'yoko admitted, feeling no remorse at all while wiping her tears away.

"Oh, my goodness! I swear to you I thought that." Nadia smirked. "And I was gon' ask you one day, but I didn't."

"Yeah, I took that bitch-ass nigga out! I hated that nigga. He wasn't about shit! How you gon' be sellin' me dope for the low and then gon' try to triple the price on me? And then when I tell the nigga he had me fucked up, he told me if I didn't buy it he was gon' tell Ja'Rel what I had been doin'. So I had him thinkin' he had my back against the wall. I had him meet me in Walmart's parkin' lot and shot the nigga, then robbed him for Ja'Rel's dope."

Nadia began laughing. "That nigga was shady as hell!"

"Shady ain't even the word for that nigga. How you stealin' dope from yo' best friend and sellin' it to his wife behind his back?'" Ke'yoko said, shaking her head. "And then when you tell him on me what you gon' tell him about you, dumbass nigga?"

"Wow." Nadia shook her head again before finishing off her wine. "I'm sorry, sis, but I'm still on Ka'yah."

"Don't worry. I'ma make her and Ja'Rel pay dearly," Ke'yoko said with a sinister smile.

"Cut me in." Nadia smirked.

"Naw, you know I do all my dirt by my lonely. 'Cause if anything goes down I don't have to worry about nobody turnin' on me. Not sayin' you would ever snitch on me. I will never give you the chance to. Just know that once I get these two bitches out the way, me and you gon' live like two fat rats," Ke'yoko said.

Nadia's money-hungry ass couldn't wait. "That's what I'm talkin' about. Just let me know what you need me to do and it's done."

"You know I will."

"I can't wait."

"Say no more," Ke'yoko said, standing up from the table, knocking her purse on the floor.

"What's this?" Nadia asked, picking up two of the four envelopes that Ke'yoko had in her purse.

"Oh, shit. I gotta take these to the post office in the mornin' and mail 'em off." Ke'yoko took the envelopes from Nadia's hand and put them back inside her purse.

"What are they?" Nadia inquired.

"Girl, you know how I was tellin' you that Aiko look just like Ja'Rel?"

Nadia shook her head yes. She too had thought Aiko looked like Ja'Rel but never said anything just to keep confusion down.

"Well, I went to CVS today and bought a DNA test; well, two 'cause they were buy one get one fifty percent off. And you know I can't pass up a sale." Ke'yoko laughed. "Anyway, I went home and Ja'Rel was asleep, so I swabbed his mouth and Aiko's so I'm about to send them in."

"Bitch! That's why I fucks wit' you," Nadia said. "That's some shit I woulda done."

"I know." Ke'yoko smiled. "Oh, and I swabbed A'Niyah too."

"For what?" Nadia asked, confused, not knowing if she was offended.

"Shit, 'cause she wanted to be swabbed. I was swabbin' Aiko and she said, 'Do it to me too,' so I did it and, plus, I had to get rid of the evidence. You know I couldn't have a DNA box just sittin' around the house."

"That's true. Well, let me know what A'Niyah's test come back and say," Nadia said jokingly.

"Now you know I will." Ke'yoko laughed.

"Wouldn't that be some shit if Aiko did come back as Ja'Rel's?"

"Nope," Ke'yoko said. "I wouldn't be surprised at all."

"You're right," Nadia agreed.

"Oh, well, I'm about to head home."

"Okay. Call me and let me know you made it in," Nadia said.

"I will."

Ke'yoko, gave Nadia a hug for being her shoulder to cry on, and headed home with a huge smile on her face.

Chapter Eighteen

For the next couple of weeks Ke'yoko played it cool with Ka'yah and Ja'Rel as she waited impatiently for the DNA test to come back. She was finding it hard being around Ka'yah being that she was still bringing her a cup of tea every single day and Ja'Rel had started back staying out all night. Ke'yoko kept her cool because she knew it would only be a matter of time before she got some get back on both of them.

As Ke'yoko was getting dressed for her doctor's appointment her cell phone began to ring. She walked over and picked it up off the nightstand and checked the caller ID. PRIVATE flashed across the screen but she answered it anyway.

"Hello?" she answered.

"What you got on?"

Ke'yoko looked around to make sure the room was clear. "What you want, fool?" Ke'yoko giggled.

"I need to see you."

"What you wanna see me about?" Ke'yoko asked.

"Just meet me at Nadia's shop. I'll come through the back because I know the shop is packed with a buncha gossipin'-ass women," Ross said.

"Always is," Ke'yoko agreed.

"A'iiiiight, I'll be there in about a half."

"Oh, shit, that ain't gon' work," Ke'yoko said, remembering she had a doctor's appointment.

"What you gotta do?"

"I got a doctor's appointment in like twenty minutes," Ke'yoko said.

"What you goin' to the doctor for? You ain't sick, are you?" Ross asked, concerned.

"No, I'm fine."

"Are you sure?"

"Yeah, Ross, I'm sure. I'm pregnant," Ke'yoko said hesitantly.

"Oh, okay." Ross was taken off guard by the news. He couldn't believe Ke'yoko would still be trying to have this nigga's baby after all he'd put her through in the past, not to mention the shit he was still doing to her. Even though he and Ja'Rel didn't hang around each other anymore, the streets were ringing with his business. He didn't know why but he felt a slight twinge of jealousy. "Well, congratulations," he said. "I guess I'm gon' have to get the baby a gift."

"I guess so." Ke'yoko smiled.

"Well, when do you think you'll be done with your appointment?"

"I'll meet you about six," Ke'yoko said, sliding her feet into her shoes.

"Damn, where yo' appointment at, in Kansas?" Ross joked.

"Naw, fool, some of the crowd at the shop would have died down by then." Ke'yoko laughed.

Ross loved Ke'yoko's laugh. "Oh, okay. Say no more," Ross said before ending his call.

"Who was that?" Ja'Rel walked into the room, scaring Ke'yoko half to death.

"Who was who?" Ke'yoko grimaced, hoping and praying Ja'Rel wasn't listening in on her call.

"On the phone, where else?"

"Oh, that was Kailo," she said nervously.

"Ummmp." Ja'Rel frowned while sorting through the stack of mail he got from the mailbox. "What that fag want? Some beauty tips?" Ja'Rel laughed.

Ke'yoko instantly began to sweat as she watched Ja'Rel sort through the stack of mail. She couldn't remember the last time he'd gotten the mail out of the mailbox. Now that she was waiting for the DNA results he wanted to get it out.

"Bills, bills, bills," Ja'Rel said before tossing the mail onto the bed. "Where you 'bouta go?" he looked at Ke'yoko and asked.

"I told you the other day I had a doctor's appointment today. You supposed to be goin' too," Ke'yoko said.

"I'll go to the next one. I'm tired. Business been booming at the shop, and I been puttin' it in out there." Ja'Rel yawned while climbing in the bed. "Call Ka'yah and have her go wit' you."

Ke'yoko looked at Ja'Rel and rolled her eyes before walking out of the room. She then grabbed her keys and headed out to her car. She was so mad at Ja'Rel she could have cried. He knew he was supposed to be there for her. *Typical nigga; one day they all sentimental and family oriented and the next they all about self.* Who would console her if they told her the same thing they told her the last four times? Who would drive her home? Who would be there to hold her hand while they gave her her first ultrasound? A light went off in Ke'yoko's head and even though she knew she was dead wrong for what she was about to do, she didn't care at all. She pulled out her phone and dialed the number of the only person who she knew would have her back other than Nadia.

"Damn, that was a quick appointment," Ross said, answering the phone.

"I haven't gone yet. I'm on my way now." Ke'yoko laughed.

"Oh, well, wassup?"

"I know this might be kind of an odd request but . . ." Ke'yoko started.

"Wassup, beautiful?"

Ke'yoko loved when Ross called her that. "Ummm, well, I don't have nobody to go to my appointment wit' me. I'm kinda scared to go by myself just in case they say . . . you know . . . and Nadia is at the shop, Ja'Rel 'sleep, and I don't want Ka'yah to go so I was wonderin'—"

"Say no more," Ross said, cutting Ke'yoko off. "What doctor do you go to?"

Ke'yoko gave Ross the name and address to her new doctor's office.

"I'll meet you there."

"Thanks." Ke'yoko smiled.

"My pleasure."

Fifteen minutes later Ke'yoko and Ross both pulled up in front of the office at the same time. Ke'yoko smiled as she got out of the car. Ross shared the same smile on his face. Ross was looking good as ever.

"Wassup, beautiful?" he asked, walking over to Ke'yoko and wrapping his arms around her.

"Hey, Ross," she said, hugging him back, getting a whiff of his Tom Ford Neroli Portofino cologne. *Damn, this is what heaven has to smell like.*

"You ready?"

"Yep." Ke'yoko was nervous. She didn't know what she would do if the doctor told her she was having another miscarriage. She didn't know if she would be able to survive another one. All she could do was hope and pray for the best.

Ke'yoko and Ross sat in the waiting room laughing and talking. Ross tried his best to keep Ke'yoko calm.

"Ke'yoko," the medical assistant opened up the door and called out.

Ke'yoko felt like she had bricks tied to her legs. It was like she couldn't move.

Ross noticed the unsure look on Ke'yoko's face and her hesitation. "It's gon' be okay," he said with a warm smile.

Ke'yoko smiled without saying a word. She stood up and took a couple of steps.

"Is the father coming?" the medical assistant asked Ke'yoko.

"Naw, I'm good." Ross smiled.

"Come on, Ross," Ke'yoko said, turning back around, grabbing him by the hand, wanting him to be a part of her big day; plus, she needed him just in case the news was bad.

The medical assistant took Ke'yoko through the necessary protocols before bringing her and Ross to a room. Ke'yoko sat up on the table while Ross sat in the chair next to the bed.

"I'm so scared," Ke'yoko said as they waited for the doctor to come in the room.

"Don't be. Everything is gon' be a'iiiight," Ross said, grabbing Ke'yoko's sweaty hand.

Even though they knew it was wrong the way Ross lovingly rubbed her hand, it felt so right to the both of them.

The doctor tapped lightly on the door before walking in. Ross let go of Ke'yoko's hand and sat up straight in the chair.

"I'm Dr. Vyas," he said, sticking out his hand for Ke'yoko to shake before shaking Ross's hand.

"Where's Dr. Confalone?" Ke'yoko asked. She'd never seen this doctor before a day in her life and didn't want to now.

"Sorry, he's at the hospital. I'm goin' to be givin' you your ultrasound today," Dr. Vyas said.

Ke'yoko was more nervous than before. She didn't know the first thing about this doctor and he didn't know anything about her either.

"Okay, young lady, lie back," Dr. Vyas said.

Ke'yoko did as she was told. He lifted up her shirt and pressed around on her small belly for a few seconds. She watched closely as he walked over and hit the light switch. He walked back over to her, grabbed the petroleum jelly, and spread the cold substance all over her stomach. Ke'yoko squirmed.

"Cold, isn't it?" Dr. Vyas asked rhetorically.

Ke'yoko shook her head yes.

Dr. Vyas took the probe and rubbed it across her stomach. Ke'yoko looked back and forth at the monitor and the doctor. The anxious look on his face let Ke'yoko know everything was all bad. She laid her head back and shook it.

"There we go. You were hiding," the doctor said to the baby's picture on the machine.

Ke'yoko lifted her head back up and looked at the machine. The loud sound of the heartbeat let Ke'yoko know that her baby was still alive.

She closed her eyes and said, *Thank you, Jesus*. Ke'yoko looked over at Ross and he had a smile on his face as if the baby belonged to him.

After a few more minutes of fiddling around, the doctor turned the lights back on.

"Well, everything looks good. Y'all are about to be proud parents of a healthy baby," Dr. Vyas looked at Ke'yoko and then over at Ross and said while wiping the cold jelly off of Ke'yoko's small stomach.

"Oh, no, he's not the father," Ke'yoko said, smiling.

"Oh," Dr. Vyas said, not knowing how to respond.

"I'm the godfather," Ross interjected.

"Oh, okay," Dr. Vyas said, shaking his head. "Well, Dr. Confalone will be here at your next appointment. Nice meetin' you guys."

"Thank you, Dr. Vyas," Ke'yoko said happily.

"No problem. Check out at the front when you get ready," the doctor said before exiting to see his next patient.

"See, I told you everything was goin' to be all right," Ross said, smiling.

"Thank you so much, Ross, for bein' here for me. I owe you." Ke'yoko smiled as well as she climbed down from the table.

"Let me tell you how you can pay me back," Ross said.

Ke'yoko hoped Ross wasn't about to ask for some ass. As bad as she would have loved to give him some, she took her vows seriously even though Ja'Rel treated them as a joke.

"Let's go outside and talk," he said, not feeling comfortable enough to talk inside of the doctor's office.

"Okay."

Ke'yoko checked out, made her next appointment, and walked outside to where Ross was leaned up against his car. Ross walked over to the passenger's side and opened the door.

"Get in," he said.

Ke'yoko got in the car and waited for him to walk around to the driver's side and get in too.

"Wassup?" Ke'yoko asked.

"Look, I ain't gon' beat around the bush wit' you," Ross said. "My connect is hot. He thinks the feds is on him. I think he's just bein' paranoid, but I ain't tryin'a take no chances on gettin' hemmed up and I would never come to you if I didn't need you."

"Say no more," Ke'yoko said. "Whatever you want, I got'chu."

Ross had a huge smile on his face. "I could kiss you right about now."

"Please don't, 'cause if you do you gon' hafta take me home and help me explain to Ja'Rel why I'm leavin' him for his enemy," Ke'yoko joked.

"I don't have a problem wit' that," Ross said in a joking manner but meant every word.

"Whooo, it's gettin' hot in here," Ke'yoko said, fanning herself.

"I bet." Ross smiled. "Look, when can I come get that? I'm kinda in a desperate situation. I got so many sales on the table."

"I'll meet you at Nadia's shop around nine o'clock tonight."

"Say no more." Ross leaned over and gave Ke'yoko a kiss on the cheek.

"Whooo, I gotta go." Ke'yoko laughed while opening the door and getting out.

"You silly." Ross laughed too. He watched as Ke'yoko got into her car.

Ke'yoko looked over at Ross and waved. She giggled when he blew her a kiss. She continued watching him as he started up his car and pulled off. Ke'yoko then turned her attention back to what was more important. She closed her eyes, placed her hands on her stomach, and exhaled. She thanked God over and over for letting her baby have a heartbeat. It may have not been a strong one, but it was one. Ke'yoko also thanked God for Aiko because if it weren't for him being so smart and attentive, her baby wouldn't have stood a chance. She owed her nephew more than he would ever know and she would repay him tenfold; and she put that on her unborn child!

Chapter Nineteen

Ka'yah bathed Aiko and put him to bed before preparing herself and her bae a romantic dinner. Ka'yah was too amped about him coming over! It had been almost two weeks since they'd had any real quality time together. It was getting harder and harder for them to see each other because his chick was constantly on his head. Ka'yah wasn't proud that her dude had a woman, but the heart wants what the heart wants; she couldn't help it. Ka'yah was preparing his favorite dish, a Cajun shrimp medley, side salad, garlic bread, and a bottle of Bartenura. Dessert would be her, of course.

Ka'yah was just putting the finishing touches on dinner when she heard the key in the door. Ka'yah smiled widely, smoothed her hair down, and went to meet her baby at the door.

"Wassup, bae?" she asked with a smile.

"Wassup?" he asked, giving her a kiss on the lips.

"Ummmm," she moaned.

"What's for dinner? It smells good as fuck in here," he said and walked toward the kitchen.

"I made your favorite meal," Ka'yah said proudly as she lifted the lid off of the medley and stirred it.

"Good. I'm starvin'," he said, taking a seat at the table. "Where my son at?"

"He's asleep," Ka'yah said, turning the fire off from under the food.

"Why he in the bed so early? I wanted to see him."

"'Cause it's been a long time since me and you spent any time alone. Every time I call you to come over, you wit' her," Ka'yah said, rolling her eyes.

"That *her* is my woman." He laughed.

"Whatever," Ka'yah snarled as she began fixing their plates.

"Somebody is jealous," he said, standing up, walking up behind Ka'yah, and wrapping his arms around her waist.

"I ain't jealous. That bitch ain't got shit on me!" she snapped.

"Yes, you are," he said, kissing the back of her neck, making her wet. "I'm here wit' you now, so all that other shit is irrelevant." He continued planting kisses on the back of her neck.

"When are you gon' be here wit' me and your son for good?" Ka'yah asked.

"Soon, real soon," he said before walking back over and taking his seat.

"Yeah, we'll see. I've been hearin' that same shit for years. Shit, ever since Aiko was born," Ka'yah said, placing his food down in front of him.

"Look, I done told you I'm just waitin' for the right time to leave. She is the mother of my child," he said before shoving a forkful of food into his mouth.

"And I am too. Matter fact, I'm the mother of your oldest child," Ka'yah said. No matter how he put it or tried to explain it, Ka'yah wasn't getting it. She didn't get how hard it would be to tell his chick that he was moving out and moving in with the woman he was really in love with.

"Calm down, baby. It won't be too much longer."

Ka'yah rolled her eyes again. She was definitely tired of hearing the same old shit. "Yeah, a'iiiight. Just know I'm not gon' keep sittin' around here waitin' on you to leave her. It's not fair to me and I deserve to be happy."

"I don't make you happy?" he said, standing up from the table and walking over to Ka'yah.

Ka'yah looked him in his mesmerizing eyes and slowly shook her head yes.

"Well, act like it then," he said before kissing her neck.

Ka'yah threw her head back and her baby planted kisses all over her neck. He then wrapped his hands around her waist and picked her up, placing her on the counter.

"What you doin'? Your food is gon' get cold," Ka'yah said as he began undressing her.

"Oh, don't worry. I'm about to eat." He smirked as he struggled to pull her shorts off. Ka'yah gave him a hand and pulled them down. He grabbed them and pulled them the rest of the way off and tossed them to the side.

Ka'yah watched as he unbuttoned his pants and pulled them down to his ankles. He placed his hand on her chest, giving her a light shove, making her lie back before diving into her wetness, tongue first. After he finished sword fighting with her clit, he pulled her back up while wiping the juices from his face. He took his shirt and tucked it underneath his chin, not wanting to get any evidence on it. He grabbed Ka'yah by her waist, pulled her off the counter, and slid her on top of his manhood. Her back was still against the counter for some much-needed support.

"Baby," she moaned.

"Yes," he answered while slowly pumping in and out of her, lifting her tiny frame up with each thrust, enjoying every minute of it.

"Fuck me hard," she moaned.

He began pumping in and out of her, trying his best to rupture her spleen. He pumped hard and fast. Ka'yah watched as the sweat poured off his forehead.

"I'm 'bouta cum, baby," she squealed.

"Me too," he said as he pumped as hard as he could.

A few minutes later, they both howled like two animals. He breathed heavily as he sat her back on top of the counter.

"Wrap my plate up. I gotta go," he said while pulling his pants up and fastening them.

"You 'bouta go already?" she asked, not really stressing it because she got what she wanted.

"Yep. I hate to eat and run." He smirked.

"But you hate to run without eatin'." Ka'yah smirked back.

Chapter Twenty

Ka'yah dropped Aiko off at daycare before coming home to clean up the house. She had Ciara's "I Bet" blaring as she dusted, swept, mopped, and rearranged her living room. Her cell phone rang, interrupting her groove. She laid the Swiffer Duster on the coffee table, turned her music down, and picked up her phone. She checked the caller ID and almost laid the phone back down.

"Wassup, Kailo?" she answered hesitantly.

"Hey, have you heard from Ke'yoko?" he asked sullenly.

Ka'yah could tell by the sound of her brother's voice that something was wrong with him. But she didn't have time to ask him what, nor did she really care; she had problems of her own.

"Ummm, the last time I checked Ke'yoko didn't live with me," she answered smartly.

Kailo shook his head. He loved his sister, but he couldn't stand the ground she walked on. It stemmed from their childhood. They'd never really had a close relationship growing up. Ka'yah tortured Kailo when he was little. She used to always hit him and make him cry, and was forever destroying his toys for no apparent reason. If he told his parents, the torture only became worse, so he'd stopped telling and suffered in silence. It was like she had gotten great enjoyment out of torturing him. Once Ke'yoko had left it had only gotten worse. Ke'yoko was the one who had taken up for him, and after she'd left Kailo had become fair game to Ka'yah's mean and spiteful ways.

"I was askin' because I called her phone a few times but she didn't answer," he said.

"Oh, well, I don't know; I haven't heard from her today. Come to think of it, I haven't heard from her in a couple days," Ka'yah said.

"Well, I was calling to tell y'all that Mother called me early this mornin' and told me that Father passed away late last night," Kailo said, hurt.

"Oh, wow," Ka'yah said, completely surprised. "What he die from? I didn't even know he was sick."

"He had a massive heart attack," Kailo said, shaking his head in disbelief.

"I'm so sorry, Kailo," Ka'yah said sincerely. She knew she could be a bitch at times, but hearing the news about her stepfather really did make her sad.

"Mother asked me if I could locate you and Ke'yoko and tell y'all the news. I told her I would try my best."

"Are there any arrangements yet?" Ka'yah asked.

"No, not yet. We're on our way to the airport. We're about to fly out in a few and when we get there Mother and I will make the arrangements," Kailo said sadly.

"We who?" Ka'yah asked, wanting to hear from her brother's mouth that he had a boyfriend.

"Chad and I," he answered.

Ewwwww, Ka'yah wanted to say, but she knew this wasn't the right time. He did just lose his father and he already sounded so sad. "Okay, well, let me know all the details once y'all get 'em all together," Ka'yah said slowly, still shocked by the news.

"I will. Do you think we should tell Ke'yoko right now, being that her pregnancy is high risk?" Kailo asked.

"I don't know why we wouldn't. I think she should know. It's gon' hurt her even more if we don't tell her," Ka'yah said.

"Yeah, I guess you're right. Even though she's not gon' care, she still should know."

"Okay, well, don't worry about tryin' to reach her. I'll tell her," Ka'yah said.

"Okay, thanks," he replied.

"No problem, little brother," Ka'yah said before ending her call.

Ka'yah took a seat on the sofa and tried to let the news sink in. Even though their stepfather had been mean to her and Ke'yoko—more to Ke'yoko than her because of her sister's rebellious ways—him dying really did bother her. Ka'yah snapped out of her trance and dialed her sister's number only to have it go straight to voice mail. Any other time she wouldn't have been pressed about talking to Ke'yoko, but the news of their stepfather was something she thought she should know and she felt it should come from her. Ka'yah rushed into the kitchen and made a cup of tea before grabbing her keys and heading out the door.

Ka'yah pulled up in the driveway behind Ke'yoko's car and grabbed the cup of tea before getting out.

"I wonder why this heffa ain't been answerin' her damn phone," she fussed as she headed up on the porch. Just as she was about to ring the doorbell Ke'yoko swung the door open.

"Hey, sis," Ke'yoko said, surprised to see Ka'yah standing there.

Ka'yah's eyes zoned in on the cell phone in Ke'yoko's hand. "How come you ain't been answerin' yo' phone? Me and Kailo have been tryin'a call you all day," Ka'yah said with a slight attitude.

"Girl, my phone don't even work. I was on my way to Verizon to let them look at it. It won't ring and my screen went black," Ke'yoko said, coming out of the house and locking the door behind her.

"Oh," Ka'yah said, losing the attitude. "I thought you were ignorin' me or somethin'."

"Igonorin' you for what?" Ke'yoko asked, laughing.

"I don't know. You know how ever since you've been pregnant, you been havin' mood swings."

"Blame it on my hormones, girl, they are so outta whack. Anyways, what y'all been tryin'a reach me for?"

"I think we should go in the house and sit down," Ka'yah said.

"Okay," Ke'yoko said slowly. "Is everything all right?"

"Come on, let's go sit down."

Ke'yoko unlocked the door and headed back into the house with Ka'yah in tow. She walked into the living room and took a seat on the sofa. "What's up?" she asked impatiently as her heart beat fast. She knew the news couldn't be good.

"Here, you're gon' need this," Ka'yah said, handing Ke'yoko the cup of tea she made for her.

Ke'yoko took the tea from her hand and set it down on the coffee table.

"Father died late last night," Ka'yah said quickly, watching Ke'yoko's reaction.

"What? From what?" Ke'yoko asked, surprised.

"A massive heart attack," Ka'yah replied before sitting down next to Ke'yoko and wrapping her arm around her sister, ready to console her.

Ke'yoko sat in a trancelike state for a few minutes before speaking. "Damn, how could a heartless person die from a heart attack?" she finally said.

"Ke'yoko!" Ka'yah said in a raised tone, standing up, appalled.

"What?" Ke'yoko asked, unfazed.

"How could you say such a thing? No matter how mean and cruel he was, he was still our stepfather and he loved us," Ka'yah said, defending him.

"No, get it right: he loved you and Kailo," Ke'yoko said, standing up as well. "Where were you? You act like you didn't live in the same house as me!"

Ka'yah watched as her twin sister got riled up.

"That man never once told me that he loved me, he never even pretended like he did, so miss me wit' that bullshit, Ka'yah."

"You're wrong, Ke'yoko," Ka'yah said.

"How the fuck am I wrong? That man dogged me up until the day I left," Ke'yoko said, hurt. Tears formed in Ke'yoko's eyes as all the hurtful things her stepfather had said and done came rushing back. "What type of animal would tell a ten-year-old child that they'd never amount to anything? That the only way they would ever make money is if they ended up on a pole at some hole-in-the-wall strip club?"

Ka'yah watched as her sister broke down.

"Yes, I might be wrong, but I've been wishin' death on this man ever since he made me go outside and pick the neighbor's dog shit up outta our yard wit' my bare hands. I can remember screamin' and cryin' and lookin' over at Mother and she never once opened her mouth. And call me callous, but I don't know why it took him this damn long to die." Ke'yoko bawled.

Ka'yah was in complete shock. She knew her sister disliked their stepfather but she never knew how deep her hatred ran for him until now. "Wow, Ke'yoko," Ka'yah said, walking over and wrapping her arms around her sister.

"Just please leave me alone, okay? I need to get myself together," Ke'yoko said, moving

Ka'yah's arms from around her. Ka'yah just didn't know how close she was to getting her ass kicked.

"Okay, I'll leave you alone. Please promise me that you'll calm down. You're pregnant and you don't wanna harm the baby," Ka'yah said, taking a step back.

It had hit Ke'yoko that Ka'yah had gotten her riled up on purpose. She'd known if she protected their stepfather it would push Ke'yoko over the edge. Ke'yoko couldn't believe she let her sister take her off her square like that. Then again, she could. Ke'yoko didn't understand why her sister was trying everything she could to make her have a miscarriage. The pain of the betrayal hit her hard again as she looked at her sister.

"I promise. I'll be okay. I'll call you later," Ke'yoko said, wiping her tears.

"Okay, sis. I love you," Ka'yah said while heading to the door.

"I love you too," Ke'yoko forced herself to say.

"Drink your tea. It'll make you feel better," Ka'yah called over her shoulder.

"I sure will," Ke'yoko said with a disgusted look on her face as she watched her sister head out the door.

Ke'yoko shook her head, picked the cup of tea up off the table, walked into the kitchen, and poured it down the sink.

Chapter Twenty-one

"I don't know, Nadia. I don't know if I can even attend his funeral," Ke'yoko said before picking up her sandwich. "Maybe I'll send some flowers instead."

"I think you should go. Not for him, but to support your brother. I know it would mean so much to him if you did attend. I know your father hurt you but, Ke'yoko, you gon' have to learn how to forgive and move on. If not, you're the only one who's gon' be affected by it. Shit, he's dead and gone," Nadia explained as she and Ke'yoko sat outside on the patio at John Q's Steakhouse, enjoying their lunch.

"I don't know," Ke'yoko said.

"Just think about it," Nadia said, sipping on her wine.

"I will."

"When is it again?"

"It's tomorrow," Ke'yoko replied.

"Damn, well, you gon' have to think quick. I got a Brazilian sew in at nine a.m. If I didn't have no appointment I would go to support you," Nadia said.

"It's cool. I think I'ma go, for Kailo. Not for no other reason," Ke'yoko said.

"Good. On another note, girl, tell me why Twan's ass called me last night."

"For what?" Ke'yoko inquired.

"Talkin' 'bout when am I gon' bring his daughter to see him."

"You lyin'." Ke'yoko laughed.

"I wish that I was. I told that nigga a long time ago that I would never bring my daughter up in no penitentiary to see him. Then he gon' say well can my momma or one of his other baby mommas bring her." Nadia frowned.

"Girl, no, he didn't." Ke'yoko laughed before wiping her mouth with her napkin.

"Yesssss," Nadia said, shaking her head. "I told that nigga he had me fucked up! If he wanted to be a daddy to A'Niyah he woulda stayed his ass outta the pen. Didn't nobody tell him to pistol whip his baby momma."

"Didn't he tie her up and ride around the hood wit' her in the trunk?" Ke'yoko asked.

"Yep. And the nigga gon' try to tell me that she wasn't gon' show up and testify. I told that dumbass nigga as soon as he did somethin' she didn't like, she would take the stand in a heartbeat."

Ke'yoko shook her head as she finished off her meal.

"That bitch caught him in the bed wit' another bitch and he thought just because he had bought her an old-ass Benz and a few cheap diamonds that she would be okay. Shiiiit, fooled his ass. That bitch didn't only show up for court, she told 'em that he sold drugs, ran guns, was robbin' niggas; and the bitch even told 'em he was about eighty grand behind on his child support," Nadia said, laughing.

Ke'yoko laughed too. "Damn, that bitch was foul. She told 'em about child support? Man, that was some petty-ass shit."

"It was." Nadia continued to laugh. "As if tellin' them about all his serious crimes wasn't enough. Now the dumb bitch out here struggling for real. She didn't realize how much the little bit of help the nigga was giving her really made a difference, silly ho."

"These hoes ain't loyal," Ke'yoko sang.

"Sho'll ain't," Nadia agreed.

Ke'yoko and Nadia finished up their lunch, sharing more gossip before going their separate ways. Ke'yoko was so glad to have Nadia in her life. She'd been there for Ke'yoko through thick and thin, more than her own twin sister had been. Nadia had never given Ke'yoko a reason to question their friendship, unlike Ka'yah. They'd been loyal to each other since day one and Ke'yoko loved and respected Nadia for that.

Ke'yoko woke up bright and early the next morning. She was nervous about going to her stepfather's funeral. It had been seven long years since she'd laid eyes on her mother or her stepfather. She had wished him dead for years, but now that her wish had come true, Ke'yoko wished she could have taken back all the times she'd thought and wished death on him. He'd treated her like shit, but in the end she became a better person because of it. He had helped to shape her character to an extent and hadn't even known it. He was still Kailo's father and the last thing she wanted was to see her brother hurting as she knew he was.

She climbed out of bed and walked into the bathroom where Ja'Rel was sitting on the toilet taking a shit and smoking a blunt.

"You goin' to the funeral wit' me?" she looked over at Ja'Rel and asked, while waving the smoke out of her face.

"Naw, why would I go to a funeral for a nigga I don't even know?" he asked before taking a pull from his blunt. "I don't even know why you goin'. That nigga wasn't none of yo' real daddy. And accordin' to you, the corny-ass nigga dogged you all ya life so why waste ya time goin' to a funeral to pay respect to a nigga who didn't respect you? That's some corny shit."

All Ke'yoko could do was look at Ja'Rel like he'd lost his mind. She was so mad at him for what he'd just said she could have spit in his face. True enough she hated her stepfather and he wasn't her real father, but she refused to let Ja'Rel sit and talk bad about him. And, furthermore, she was going to support her little brother because she knew it would mean so much to him. Ke'yoko turned on the shower as Ja'Rel continued doing his business on the toilet and she began getting undressed. She then grabbed a washcloth out of the linen closet.

"Damn, you gettin' thick as fuck," he said, putting the blunt out in the ashtray that sat on the sink. "It's been awhile since I had some of that ass."

Ke'yoko looked back at Ja'Rel, frowned, and stepped in the shower. *That's 'cause you too busy out in the streets fuckin' everybody else,* Ke'yoko thought as she began washing up. *And it's gon' be even longer before you get some more of this ass.*

Ja'Rel finished his business in the bathroom and walked back into the bedroom. Ke'yoko finished showering, got out, wrapped her towel around her body, and headed into the bedroom as well. She walked over to the closet and looked back over her shoulder at Ja'Rel, who was busy texting, and frowned. She pulled her black Karen Kane scalloped lace V-neck dress out of the closet and put it on, then pulled out her simple but cute and comfortable Tory Burch ballerina flats and slid her feet inside of them.

Ke'yoko walked over to the mirror to see how she was looking. She couldn't help but smile when she noticed her small belly protruding through the dress. She walked back into the bathroom and ran her fingers through her hair, making sure it was on point before heading back out into the bedroom. Ke'yoko then walked over, grabbed her purse off the chair, and headed toward the bedroom door.

"Oh, you ain't gon' say bye?" Ja'Rel asked.

"Shiiiit, you was so deep off into textin' if I would have said bye, I don't even think you would have heard me," she said smartly and headed out of the bedroom.

Ke'yoko walked down the stairs and out the door. She got in her car and put the address that Kailo had sent her in her GPS, before starting the car and pulling off. She called Nadia but it went straight to voice mail. She then called Ross to see if he could talk to her and help her calm her nerves, and like always he answered. His voice was so soothing during their entire conversation. Ross talked to Ke'yoko for the entire drive to the funeral home.

"Well, Ross, I'm here. Thank you so much for keepin' me calm," Ke'yoko said, pulling into the funeral home's parking lot.

"No problem, sis. You know I got'chu. I'ma always be here for you when you need me, the same way you've been here for more," he replied sincerely.

"Don't just be sayin' it to say it. You better mean it." Ke'yoko smiled.

"Man, you helped me get back on my feet, so why wouldn't I mean it?" Ross asked.

"I just wanna make sure."

"Trust me, I got'chu," Ross replied.

"That's what I'm talkin' about," Ke'yoko said. "Okay, well, I'm about to get out. I'll talk to you later on."

"Okay; and remember everything will be okay. Just keep in mind you're there for Kailo and nothin' else."

"I will."

"Say no more," Ross said before ending his call.

Ross had only temporarily managed to calm Ke'yoko's nerves; she was still nervous. She took a deep breath, checked her hair, and opened the car door and got out. She slowly walked through the parking lot. She looked over at Ka'yah's car and wanted to key it, but this wasn't the time or the place. She just continued into the funeral home. As soon as she walked in, she saw Ka'yah holding a conversation and laughing and smiling with their mother, Kailo, and Chad.

"Fake-ass bitch," Ke'yoko mumbled, but quickly smiled when Kailo looked over and smiled at her.

They all turned their attention to see who Kailo was smiling at. Everybody had a smile on their face, except their mother. She quickly turned back around. Ke'yoko didn't know if it was out of anger or embarrassment for not standing up for her children like she should have. The more Ke'yoko thought about it, it could have never been out of anger; if anything she was the one who should still be mad, not her.

Kailo and Ka'yah walked over to greet their sister. "Hey, sis," Ka'yah said, wrapping her arms around Ke'yoko.

"Wassup," Ke'yoko said, tensing up but hugging her back anyway.

"Hey, sis," Kailo said, giving his sister a hug as well. "Thanks for comin'."

"Don't thank me." Ke'yoko smiled.

Ke'yoko looked back up to the front of the church. One side of her wanted to go speak to her mother; then there was the other that wanted to walk up and smack her across the face. Ke'yoko quickly remembered what Nadia and Ross had said about being the only one still suffering because of all the hatred she still held in her heart for her parents.

"I'll be back," Ke'yoko said to her siblings.

"Where you 'bouta go?" Ka'yah asked, but didn't get an answer.

Ka'yah and Kailo both looked at one another before following their sister, hoping nothing was about to jump off.

Ke'yoko walked up behind her mother, who stood holding a conversation with Chad, and tapped her on her shoulder. Her mother turned around and looked at her beautiful daughter. Tears instantly clouded her eyes. She wanted to wrap her arms around her baby girl and apologize, over and over, for not being there for her child like she should have been; but instead she waited for Ke'yoko to make the first move.

"Mother," Ke'yoko spoke.

"Rie," her mother spoke back before bowing to her daughter.

It had been so long since anybody had called her by her middle name. Hearing it brought back so many childhood memories. Memories of her, Ka'yah, and Kailo outside playing like they didn't have a care in the world. Catching fireflies in the summer, playing hide-and-seek, Mother May I, freeze tag, and hopscotch just to name a few.

Ke'yoko stared into her mother's ageless face and smiled, melting her mother's heart. She wrapped her arms around her mother's tiny body and her mother hugged her back. It felt like a huge weight was lifted off of Ke'yoko's shoulders.

"How are you?" Ke'yoko asked.

"I'm fine," her mother replied with a warm smile.

"That's good."

Ka'yah and Kailo stood and watched in awe. They couldn't believe their sister was actually holding a decent conversation with their mother.

"You got a baby in there," her mother said, rubbing Ke'yoko's small belly.

"Yep, I sure do," she said proudly, while looking over at Ka'yah.

Ka'yah had an uneasy look on her face, as if she knew that Ke'yoko was hip to her.

"How many?" her mother asked.

"This is my first one," Ke'yoko replied.

"It's gon' be a boy," Ke'yoko's mother said.

"How you know, Mother?" Kailo asked.

"I just know," she replied.

"Well, I guess Ja'Rel and I better start pickin' out boy names," Ke'yoko said.

Their mother saw one of her husband's friends walk in the funeral home. "Excuse me," she said.

Ke'yoko nodded her head and watched as her mother walked over to greet him.

"I thought we was gon' have to pull you up offa her," Ka'yah joked.

"Me too," Kailo agreed.

Ke'yoko laughed. "She is still my mother."

"Excuse me while I go rescue Chad from Cousin Naomi," Kailo said, walking away and laughing.

"I'm about to find a seat," Ka'yah said, turning to walk away, only to get stopped by one of their talking cousins.

Ke'yoko eased her way toward her stepfather's casket. It felt like she had two sumo wrestlers tied to her legs. She looked down and studied his face. He looked exactly the same, almost like he hadn't aged since the last time she'd seen him.

Ke'yoko stuck her hand inside of the casket and fixed his tie.

"He really did love you," Ke'yoko's mother walked up behind her and said.

Ke'yoko looked at her mother and didn't say a word. She shot her a weak smile, letting her mother know that she knew that it wasn't all hate and that she'd forgiven him for everything. Until that moment she hadn't realized that she'd forgiven her stepfather as well as her mother for everything in the past the minute they had hugged each other. Ke'yoko's mother smiled back before walking away.

Ke'yoko turned her attention back toward her stepfather. She didn't know if it was her hormones or what, but tears began flowing from her eyes out of nowhere, one after the other. Ke'yoko began to unfold. She had been under so much stress with everything going on in her life lately, it was all too much for her to handle.

Death was so final. Ke'yoko thought back on their final argument and wished things could have ended differently. She didn't have all bad memories of her stepfather; she just chose to block what she wanted to. There were times when they did have a lot of fun when she was younger. Family trips to the park, the long car rides every Sunday, and Wednesday night board games were memories she sure couldn't erase from her mind. Not to mention he made sure she had the best education, clothes on her back, food on the table, and a roof over her head.

"I'm so sorry," she wailed as she leaned over in the casket as far as she could, catching everyone off guard. "I'm so sorry, Father."

Kailo and Ka'yah rushed over to their sister's side.

"God, I'm sorry. So sorry," she repeated over and over as she held on to his suit jacket.

Kailo waited for a few minutes before wrapping his arms around her. "Come on, sis," he said, gently trying to pull her away from the casket. She held on so tight, Kailo had to use a little force to pull her back.

"Oh my God, Kailo," Ke'yoko bawled.

"It's okay, sis." Kailo began to cry himself.

Ka'yah attempted to console her sister as well.

Their mother couldn't stand watching her three children crying. She began crying too. She walked over and did what she should have done a long time ago. She wrapped her arms around her babies and assured them that everything would be okay.

Chapter Twenty-two

Ke'yoko had pulled up at the house after the repast. She was emotionally, mentally, and physically drained. She would have never guessed in a million years that she would be so emotional over the death of a man she'd honestly believed she'd hated for all these years. Ke'yoko was happy that she and her mother were on speaking terms, but she didn't know if she was ready to have a real relationship with her just yet. Maybe that would come later on down the road, or maybe not. She was good either way because she knew she had done her part just by walking up to her.

She got out of the car, carrying her purse and shoes. "Ouch," she said, stepping on a small pebble. Ke'yoko dug in her purse looking for her keys as she hobbled up the walk. She walked up on the porch, opened the screen door, and let herself inside the house. Ke'yoko set her keys and purse on the table in the foyer and headed straight for the sofa to rest her aching feet.

"I see this lazy nigga brought the mail in," she said, grabbing it off the table, sitting down, and beginning to sort through it.

Ke'yoko's heart began beating quickly as she saw two letters with the paternity test's name on it. Ke'yoko quickly opened the first letter. She was nervous as hell as she ripped through the paper. She quickly skimmed the first page looking for the results; not finding them, she flipped to the second page and began reading aloud.

"The alleged father is not excluded as the biological father of the tested child. Based on testing results obtained from analyses of the DNA loci listed, the probability of paternity is 99.96%."

Ke'yoko felt like she had just experienced an out-of-body experience. She felt cold, numb, and her mind was clouded. She was in complete shock. Even though her woman's intuition had been telling her that Aiko belonged to Ja'Rel, she had never fully allowed herself to believe it. After reading the results, she still didn't want to believe it, but now she had no choice. She couldn't do anything but sit there and read the test results over and over to make sure she hadn't missed anything or read anything wrong. When she finally decided to take these results to these two lowdown dirty bitches, she wanted her proof to be in order.

Ke'yoko was so hurt, she couldn't even cry if she wanted to. Her well had completely run dry. All she could do was shake her head. She stood up from the sofa, grabbed the other letter, and headed upstairs to change into something more comfortable. All Ke'yoko could think about while she undressed was how her so-called husband and twin sister had betrayed her like they did. Ke'yoko opened the other letter just for the hell of it, even though it had never crossed her mind that Nadia would ever mess with Ja'Rel. She went straight to the second page to the final results and nearly fainted when A'Niyah's results read the same as Aiko's. Ke'yoko let the letter fall to the floor as she rushed into the bathroom to throw up.

Ke'yoko turned on the water and rinsed her mouth out. She walked back into the bedroom, picked the letter up off the floor, and read the results one last time, just to make sure she had read it right, just like she'd done with Aiko's. Ke'yoko was at a complete loss. All she kept thinking about was how Nadia could cross her like that. How and when did she have time? How come she had never suspected Ja'Rel and Nadia? All these different questions kept running through Ke'yoko's head. She was so tired of trying to figure everything out. With her head spinning, Ke'yoko picked up her cell and dialed Ross. She needed somebody to talk to and bad.

"Wassup, sis?" he answered.

"Are you busy?"

"A li'l bit, why? Wassup? You okay?" he asked.

"No, not at all," Ke'yoko said, feeling herself about to break down.

"Look, let me finish handlin' this business and I'll call you and you can meet me at my condo at the Pinnacle building on Lakeside Ave.," Ross said.

"Is that in the warehouse district?" Ke'yoko asked, to make sure.

"Yep. It'll be about an hour; is that too long? If so, I can head there now."

Ke'yoko didn't have an hour to wait. She needed to speak to someone now. She needed someone to keep her levelheaded because she was on straight kill mode. She could kill Ja'Rel, Ka'yah, and Nadia, and go have a nice, juicy cheeseburger and fries after doing so.

"Ross, I know you busy right now but I need you like yesterday," Ke'yoko said desperately.

Ross could hear the urgency in her voice. "Say no more. I'm on my way."

"Thank you," Ke'yoko said, hanging up the phone, grabbing her purse, and putting the test results in it before grabbing her keys and heading out the door.

Almost forty minutes later, Ke'yoko pulled up in front of the Pinnacle building and sat in her car. She sent Ross a text and let him know that she was sitting outside his condo and to call her when he pulled up. A few seconds later, Ke'yoko received a text from Ross telling her that he was already home and he gave her instructions on how to get into his condo. Ke'yoko grabbed her purse, got out of the car, and headed into the building. Ke'yoko followed Ross's instructions, got off the elevator, and knocked on his door.

"Wassup, sis?" he asked, answering the door looking like a nice piece of chocolate cake. He had on a pair of black cargo shorts, a bright yellow shirt, and a pair of black house shoes.

"You look comfortable," Ke'yoko said.

"I am," he replied, closing the door behind Ke'yoko while holding his arms out.

Ke'yoko walked into his open arms and almost melted. The smell of Ross's cologne drove her crazy. There was nothing sexier to Ke'yoko than a man who smelled good.

"You okay?" he asked, letting her go, even though he didn't want to.

"Not all at," Ke'yoko responded.

"Come on in. I'm cookin' dinner," Ross said, leading Ke'yoko out of the foyer and into his condo.

"You have a nice place," Ke'yoko said, looking around as she followed Ross into his gourmet kitchen.

"Thanks," he said, lifting the lid off the boiling pot and stirring it.

"What you cookin'? It smells good." Ke'yoko pulled the stool out and took a seat at the counter.

"Nothin' fancy. Just a li'l chicken penne, and some asparagus with some garlic bread," Ross said, adding some seasoning to the asparagus. "You hungry?"

"I stay hungry," Ke'yoko replied.

"Oh, yeah, you are eatin' for two." Ross turned the food off and walked over to Ke'yoko, holding his hand out. "Come on, let's go sit on the couch."

Ke'yoko grabbed Ross's hand and followed him into the living room and took a seat on the nice, big horseshoe-shaped sofa.

"Okay, now what was so urgent that I had to wrap up my business to come see you?" Ross asked with a smile.

Ross made Ke'yoko feel so comfortable and secure every time she was around him that she'd almost forgotten about what her real intentions were for coming over to his condo. "I don't even know where to begin," Ke'yoko said as she fought back her tears.

"Talk to me," Ross said, concerned.

Ke'yoko grabbed both sets of test results out of her purse and handed them to Ross.

"What's this?" he asked, taking the papers and beginning to read them.

After Ross finished reading the test results, Ke'yoko ran the entire demo down to him. He was in complete shock by the end of her story. He knew Ja'Rel was a grimy-ass nigga, but to have a baby by his wife's sister and her best friend was on a whole notha level.

"Wow," he said, shaking his head in disbelief.

"You can say that again." Ke'yoko laughed as she cried.

"Sis, you know I'ma keep it all the way real wit' you. All three of 'em is foul as fuck, but Ka'yah takes the cake. She's not your husband, she's not your best friend; that's your twin sister, man."

"I know. I know," Ke'yoko said.

"What you gon' do? You can't sit around and keep cryin' about it. You're carryin' a baby; you don't need all that stress. I know you hurt right now, but you gotta make this your last time cryin' over this bullshit. It's time to take action," Ross said sternly.

"What can I do?" Ke'yoko asked.

"That's for you to figure out. You're a smart woman. I got faith that whatever you do, it'll be worth it." Ross winked at Ke'yoko.

"I hope so." Ke'yoko continued to cry.

It hurt Ross to his heart to see Ke'yoko crying. He wished he could take all her pain away. He always had a warm spot in his heart for her and wished like hell that he'd met her first. He would have definitely treated her like the queen she was. Ross leaned over and gently wiped her tears away.

Ross couldn't take seeing Ke'yoko cry any longer so he stood up from the sofa. "Come on, let's go eat," he said, holding out his hand for her to grab.

"Sounds like a plan to me." Ke'yoko wiped the remaining tears away, took Ross's hand, and got up from the sofa.

"We gon' sit out on the balcony and enjoy this beautiful weather," Ross said as they walked into the kitchen. He then grabbed two plates out of the cabinet.

"That sounds nice," Ke'yoko replied, taking a seat on the stool.

Ke'yoko watched as Ross fixed two plates and grabbed a bottle of wine, some napkins, and two wine glasses.

"You need some help?" she asked.

"Please. Just grab the bottle of wine and the glasses." Ross placed two forks on their plates and headed toward the door with Ke'yoko following.

Ke'yoko grabbed the wine and the glasses, walked in front of Ross, pulled the balcony door open, and waited for Ross to walk out before walking out behind him. She set the bottle and glasses down on the table and took a seat. She set her purse on the ground beside her. Ross set their plates down before taking a seat across from Ke'yoko.

"This is a beautiful view," Ke'yoko said, looking out at city skyline.

"I thought so too. That's one of the main reasons why I moved here." Ross looked out at the beautiful view as if this was his very first time ever seeing it.

"I could wake up to this view every mornin'," Ke'yoko said and began eating.

"Well, I would let you move in wit' me but I don't know how Ja'Rel would feel about that," Ross joked.

Ke'yoko shook her head and laughed.

After laughing, talking, and drinking the entire bottle of wine, Ross was starting to feel a little tired. He stood up, stretched out his arms, and let out a loud yawn.

"You tired?" Ke'yoko asked.

"A little," he replied.

"You ready for me to go?" she asked, hoping he would say no.

"Nope, not yet. Come on and let me give you a tour of my condo," he said.

"Okay." Ke'yoko stood up without hesitation and followed Ross as he led her back into the house.

She was amazed at how beautiful and contemporary his place was. It was actually more spacious than what she thought it was. He had floor-to-ceiling windows with a breathtaking panoramic view that overlooked the lake and the city. The Aspen maple hardwood floors were shining like new money throughout the entire condo. And whoever he hired to decorate knew exactly what they were doing. All the different colors throughout accentuated one another. The eighty-inch TV that hung neatly over the fireplace like a portrait was to die for.

Ross ended the tour in his large master suite. Ke'yoko walked in and looked around. Ross picked the remote up off the end table and pointed it at the huge TV on the wall, and Maxwell's "This Woman's Work" came on. He put the remote in his back pocket and looked over at Ke'yoko and smiled.

How convenient, Ke'yoko thought as she stood in the middle of the room, waiting for Ross to make the next move.

Ross grabbed Ke'yoko's hand again and led her over to his Cosmopolis platform bed. It was so low to the floor, Ke'yoko hoped she could get back up. Ross noticed the hesitation and helped her down. He removed Ke'yoko's shoes, walked over to the other side of the bed, kicked off his house shoes, and climbed in. He took the remote out of his back pocket and dimmed the lights, not too dark but just enough to set the mood, before laying the remote on the nightstand.

Ke'yoko was nervous and didn't know what was about to go down; all she knew was everything was happening so fast. She knew that whatever was about to happen, it was long overdue and she was ready. Her heart beat quickly as Ross scooted up right behind her. He was so close she could feel his warm breath on the back of her neck. Ross wrapped his arm around Ke'yoko's waist and kissed the back of her neck, sending electricity through her entire body. That was a feeling she hadn't felt in a long time. He then began rubbing her belly, hoping to sooth Ke'yoko and the baby before drifting off to sleep.

Chapter Twenty-three

Ke'yoko drove home from Ross's house at six o'clock the next morning prepared for a fight that she was more than ready for. She had taken Ross's words to heart. She wasn't about to shed another tear about her situation. Ke'yoko also wasn't about to explain shit to Ja'Rel. She was about to do him just like he'd been doing her for years. She was going to go in the house and climb in the bed and go to sleep, without saying a word to him.

Ke'yoko pulled up in the driveway and wasn't surprised that Ja'Rel wasn't home. She grabbed her purse and got out of the car. The birds were chirping loudly as she unlocked the door. She threw her purse down on the foyer table, kicked her shoes off, and headed upstairs. She walked into her bedroom and looked at the bed. It was still neatly made from yesterday morning, letting her know that Ja'Rel hadn't been home all night. Ke'yoko removed her pants and climbed in bed. She could still smell Ross's cologne on her shirt.

Ke'yoko already had mad respect for Ross but after spending the evening with him and him not touching her, her respect for him literally went through the roof. She was happy and sad at the same time that he hadn't tried to sleep with her. Ke'yoko yearned to have Ross in between her legs, but understood why he didn't try to make a move on her. Either way, she had mad love for him. She let her mind run wild on what she wished would have happened between her and Ross until she drifted off to sleep.

Ke'yoko woke up three hours later feeling new and refreshed. She sat up and stretched before getting out of bed. She walked into the bathroom, turned the shower on, and began getting undressed. She put her shirt up to her nose to see if she could still smell Ross's cologne. "Ummmm," she said, smiling as she laid it on the sink before stepping in the shower.

After a quick shower, Ke'yoko got out, brushed her teeth, and got dressed in a pair of blue Under Armour yoga pants, an all-white T-shirt, and her blue and white Saucony tennis shoes. She walked back into the bathroom and pulled her growing hair back into a little ponytail. Ke'yoko then walked downstairs to grab herself some quick breakfast before getting her day started.

She walked into the kitchen and frowned at Ja'Rel, who was sitting at the kitchen table counting money. Ke'yoko wanted to ask him where he'd been, but he'd never told the truth in the past so she knew he wasn't about to start now, so she just left it alone.

Ja'Rel looked up from his money over at Ke'yoko. "You look like you 'bouta go fight."

"I might be," she said, turning to walk back out of the kitchen. The sight of Ja'Rel spoiled her appetite. Ke'yoko grabbed her purse and headed out the door.

She got in the car, pulled out her dying cell phone, and plugged it into the charger before pulling off. Ke'yoko drove like she was on a straight mission. She was about to go to Nadia's house. Normally she would have called first, but today she was just popping in. She needed answers and wasn't going to leave until she got them.

Fifteen minutes later, Ke'yoko pulled up in front of Nadia's house, grabbed her cell phone, and checked her messages. She smiled when she read a message from Ross telling her he enjoyed her company last night and they needed to do it again soon.

Ke'yoko got out of the car and headed up to the porch. She slowed her breathing and before ringing the doorbell she remembered the promise she had made to Ross.

"Who is it?" she heard Nadia yell.

"It's me, Ke'yoko."

"Hey, pretty lady," Nadia said, smiling as she opened the door for her bestie.

"We need to talk," Ke'yoko said, walking straight in, getting right to the point.

"What's wrong?" Nadia asked, concerned. "Is everything okay?"

"Heeeeey, Auntie Ke'yoko," A'Niyah ran over to Ke'yoko and said, wrapping her arms around her waist.

"Hey, baby." Ke'yoko leaned down, giving her stepchild a kiss on the forehead.

"My tooth fell out and the Tooth Fairy gave me five dollars," A'Niyah said, showing off her missing link.

Ke'yoko studied A'Niyah's face to see if she could see Ja'Rel in her but couldn't. She'd always been the spitting image of Nadia. "Good." Ke'yoko smiled.

"Go to your room and play, 'Niyah; me and Auntie Ke'yoko are about to talk grown folks' business," Nadia looked at her daughter and said.

"Okay."

Ke'yoko and Nadia watched as A'Niyah skipped out of the living room.

"Let's go sit down." Nadia headed over to the sofa with Ke'yoko on her heels.

Ke'yoko sat down next to Nadia and looked at her for a brief second and wanted to haul off and slap the fever out of her body.

"What's goin' on, sis?" Nadia asked anxiously.

Ke'yoko pulled Aiko's DNA test results out of her purse and handed it to Nadia. Nadia skimmed through the mumbo jumbo before reading the second page. Her eyes grew real big as she read the results out loud.

"That dirty bitch! Wow, Ke. This is some foul shit, baby girl," Nadia said, astonished by the results. "I don't even know what to say. Are you okay?"

"I'm copin'," Ke'yoko said, one wording her.

"I know that Ka'yah is your sister, Ke, but that bitch is grimy as fuck!" Nadia snapped.

"She ain't the only one." Ke'yoko frowned.

"Yeah, you right; Ja'Rel foul as fuck too!"

The longer Nadia acted innocent, the madder Ke'yoko got. How in the fuck did this bitch have any room to call Ja'Rel or Ka'yah foul? Ke'yoko was furious at how calm Nadia was acting knowing damn well she had a baby by her husband too.

"Don't worry, sis. Like I've been tellin' you from the beginnin', whatever you decide to do,

I got'cha back. And I know you pregnant right now, but if I were you I would stomp a mud hole in Ka'yah after I have the baby." Nadia was still shaking her head in disbelief.

Ke'yoko couldn't stand it anymore. She was not about to let Nadia keep talking about what her sister had done and not own up to her own bullshit.

"I got A'Niyah's test results, too. You wanna see 'em?" Ke'yoko said, pulling them out her purse.

"Yeah, why not? I know who my baby daddy is and it sure the hell ain't Ja'Rel." Nadia smiled as she took the papers from Ke'yoko's hand and turned to the back page to the results.

"You wanna bet?" Ke'yoko grimaced, wanting to spit on her for sitting there lying to her face.

Nadia's smile quickly faded as she read and reread the results. Nadia finally looked up at Ke'yoko with tears in her eyes. "Oh my God," Nadia said as tears escaped her eyelids.

Nadia appeared to be dazed or she was a damn good actor; Ke'yoko was unsure of which one. "How could you of all people do me like that?" Ke'yoko asked Nadia. Ke'yoko had promised Ross that she wouldn't shed another tear but she couldn't help it. She was hurt. It was bad enough that she had suspicions about Ka'yah and Ja'Rel, but Nadia sleeping with her husband behind her back never once crossed her mind.

Nadia reached out for Ke'yoko.

Ke'yoko scooted over. "How could you?" Ke'yoko asked again. "Me though, Nadia?"

"It's not what you think, Ke," Nadia cried.

"I can't fuckin' tell! You got the test results in your hand, so what the fuck do you want me to think? That I'm crazy?" Ke'yoko yelled while standing up.

"Let me explain," Nadia said as she collected her thoughts, standing up as well.

"I'm waitin'," Ke'yoko said impatiently.

"Look, Ja'Rel came over to the house one night to bring Twan some work, but Twan wasn't home yet and he asked me if he could wait for him. Me not thinkin' nothin' of it, I told him yes. So I was sittin' on the couch drinkin' some wine and asked him if he wanted some. He told me yes, so I got up and went to the kitchen to get him a glass. And all I can really remember is us sitting on the couch, laughing and talking, and I started feeling dizzy and next thing you know I woke up the next mornin' on the couch wit' my pants off, sore, with an incredible headache." Nadia cried as she had flashbacks of that very night.

"So you're tellin' me that Ja'Rel drugged you?" Ke'yoko asked, making sure, not knowing if she believed Nadia's story.

"He had to have," Nadia said, wiping her tears away, still trying to piece together the events of that night so many years later. "Ke'yoko, you know I would have never slept wit' Ja'Rel willingly. I would never cross you like that. You my best friend."

Ke'yoko studied Nadia's face to see if she could sense if she was lying. Something told her deep down that Nadia was telling her the truth.

"How come you never told me this before now?" Ke'yoko asked slowly.

"I didn't have any real proof so I couldn't confront him. I wanted to say somethin' to you, but I couldn't because I had no evidence," Nadia continued. "Who wants to believe let alone admit their best friend's dude is capable of that? That's some Lifetime shit!" Nadia was devastated. Why would Ja'Rel do that to her?

"Well, we have all the evidence we need now," Ke'yoko said, referring to the test results.

"Yeah, we do," Nadia agreed, still in awe. Here she was thinking the entire time that Twan was A'Niyah's father, and come to find out she belonged to her best friend's husband. Nadia couldn't get over the fact that Ja'Rel would take what wasn't his. And why her? She'd never done anything to this nigga but be cordial to him because he was married to her best friend. She searched her memory hard and for the life of her she could not remember ever leading Ja'Rel to believe she wanted him. Ja'Rel had never shown any signs of wanting anything to do with her! Again, all she could think was why would he do this to her?

She had been able to wipe the memory and thoughts from her mind for so many years, convincing herself she'd been tripping; but now with her best friend hitting her with this hard proof, so many feelings were rushing at her. She realized how easy it was to take away someone's sense of security, and that hers had been a false sense of security for so many years. It was scary and sickening. Ja'Rel had treated her like the ho everyone had called her back in the day, making her feel dirty and unclean all over again. Her hate for him at that moment was scary.

"Ja'Rel has been known to do some foul shit, but to drug and rape somebody . . . That dirty bastard," Ke'yoko said, trying to wrap her head around the news.

"I'm so sorry, Ke." Nadia began crying all over again.

"It's not your fault." Ke'yoko walked over and wrapped her arms around her friend to let her know that everything would be okay.

"I should have told you what I thought," Nadia bawled angrily. "How can I face or even look at A'Niyah? Do this nigga understand or even care what he has done to us? To me?" Nadia knew these questions were hypothetical questions that she would never have an answer to, and very obviously Ja'Rel didn't care because he had looked her and her daughter in the face all these years after knowing what he had done to her with no remorse.

"It's okay, Nadia," Ke'yoko said. It was all she could think to say as she watched her friend's anguish and turmoil.

Ja'Rel was pure evil and was carelessly touching lives with no regard for the outcome. Ke'yoko was ashamed at how blinded she had been by Ja'Rel and felt partly responsible. Once again, she thought maybe she was more like her mother in ways she didn't want to be. All these years of calling her mom a weak, sniveling woman behind her father. Well, she had closed her eyes to all of her own husband's ways and the infidelity out of a twisted sense of need and wanting to be the "The Mrs. Barnes." Wanting to show these bitches in the streets she had something and someone special at home, and in reality she didn't have anything all these other hoes didn't have or couldn't have access to anytime they wanted. No wonder these bitches looked at her and laughed. Ja'Rel had made it possible with blatant disrespect by allowing it.

"Now what? What do we do now?" Nadia looked at Ke'yoko and asked. Ke'yoko could see the pure hatred in Nadia's eyes. The need for revenge, the need to make Ja'Rel understand what he had done and taken from her so many years ago.

Ke'yoko looked Nadia dead in her eyes and said, "I don't know yet; just know he gon' pay dearly for everything he has done and all the pain and turmoil he has caused. I promise this, Nadia!" With that being said, Ke'yoko got herself together and headed for the door. She needed to be alone to think. Ke'yoko had to get a plan in order; only thing was she wasn't quite sure what.

Chapter Twenty-four

Ke'yoko was at the stove finishing up dinner when Ja'Rel walked in.

"Ummmm, what you cookin'?" Ja'Rel walked up behind Ke'yoko, wrapped his arm around her waist and asked, before kissing her on the cheek.

"I'm makin' your favorite." She smiled while lifting the top off the Cajun shrimp medley. "The garlic bread is in the oven cookin' and the salad is in the fridge."

"That's wassup." Ja'Rel smiled happily, while rubbing Ke'yoko's belly. "You've been cookin' a lot lately. What did a nigga do to deserve this?"

"Shoot, I haven't cooked in such a long time. And I was lookin' at you one day and you looked like you was losin' weight so I said I better start feedin' my baby," Ke'yoko said, smiling.

"Yeah, 'cause I'm kinda' gettin' tired of eatin' fast food."

"Shit, I bet. Now go upstairs and get washed up for dinner," she looked at her husband and said.

"I can't wait to eat." Ja'Rel turned around, walking out of the kitchen to go change out of his work clothes.

"I can't wait for you to eat either," she said deviously.

Ke'yoko waited until she heard Ja'Rel walking up the stairs before pulling two pills out of her apron pocket. She opened up the kitchen drawer and grabbed the pill crusher and finely crushed the pills up into tiny pieces of dust. She quickly fixed Ja'Rel's plate. She then sprinkled the powdery pills on top of his food before grabbing the parmesan cheese out of the cabinet and shaking some on top to disguise the medicine.

"It's time to eat, Ja'Rel," Ke'yoko yelled while placing his plate on the kitchen table before getting him a glass of Kool-Aid.

"I'm comin'," he said on his way down the stairs.

Ke'yoko stood at the stove, fixing herself a plate. She looked back and smiled as Ja'Rel devoured his food.

"Damn, this is the bomb!" he said as he scarfed down his meal.

"I'm glad you like it," Ke'yoko said, sitting down across from her husband, watching. "You want some more?"

"Naw, I'm full right now. I'll eat some more when I get back," Ja'Rel said, taking the last little bite of his garlic bread and driving it around the leftover sauce on the plate before sticking it in his mouth.

"Where you 'bouta go?" Ke'yoko asked, not really caring.

"I got some business to handle. I won't be gone too long," he said, finishing off his Kool-Aid and letting out a loud belch.

"Should I wait up for you?"

"Naw, don't wait up 'cause I don't know how long I'll be gone," he said, getting up from the table and walking out of the kitchen.

You'll be back much sooner than you think.

"Damn, you coulda put your plate and glass in the sink," she yelled, but Ja'Rel was already out the door.

Ke'yoko shook her head and smiled as she cleaned off the table before going upstairs to shower.

"Again?" Ka'yah frowned.

"Look, I don't know what's wrong. It's gotta be stress," Ja'Rel said, lying on his back as Ka'yah was in between his legs on her knees with his limp dick in her hand.

"Stress?"

"Yeah, stress," he said, irritated.

"What the fuck you gotta be stressed out about?" Ka'yah asked with an attitude.

"I got a lotta shit to be stressed out about. I got a baby on the way, my wife stay on my fuckin' neck about me stayin' out all night, not to mention I'm fuckin' her twin sister! As if that alone ain't enough to be stressed out about!"

"Whatever," Ka'yah said, climbing out of bed. "This the third time this week you couldn't get it up! I mean, what the fuck, Ja'Rel!" Ka'yah snapped while grabbing her pack of cigarettes and a lighter off the dresser and lighting one up. Ka'yah took a couple pulls from the cigarette and blew the smoke out before putting it out in the ashtray. She looked over at Ja'Rel and shook her head. "Are you fuckin' her?"

"Fuckin' who?" Ja'Rel asked, already knowing who she was talking about.

"Ke'yoko, nigga!" she snapped.

"Naw, baby." Ja'Rel climbed out of bed, walked over to Ka'yah, wrapped his arms around her waist, and pulled her into his body.

"Are you sure?" she questioned.

"Baby, I promise I ain't fuckin' her. You the only person I fuck wit'," Ja'Rel lied with a straight face.

"Ummmm huh," Ka'yah said, skeptical. She didn't know why Ja'Rel thought she was so naïve. She knew that he was out there laying more pipe than a little bit.

"This yo' dick," Ja'Rel said, grabbing a handful of his limp manhood.

"If you don't fix yo' little problem it won't be too much longer," Ka'yah said while staring at his pitiful-looking member.

"You gon' let all this good dick go to somebody else?" He smirked.

"Ja'Rel, I need some dick! I can't keep goin' through this wit' you. A sista got needs," Ka'yah said, disgusted.

"Come on back over to the bed and try to suck it again. I think it's about to get hard," Ja'Rel said, grabbing Ka'yah by the hand.

Ka'yah looked down at Ja'Rel's Johnson and smiled as it looked like it was about to come back to life. "Come on," she said, walking over to the bed.

"Let me go pee first," Ja'Rel said, turning toward the bedroom door.

"Damn! This is like the tenth time you done pissed since you've been here," she snapped while rolling her eyes.

"Calm down. I'll be right back," he said, heading across the hall to the bathroom.

"Uggggh, I don't know what's wrong wit' this nigga." Ka'yah grimaced as she waited for Ja'Rel to get back.

Ja'Rel walked over to the bed and lay back. Ka'yah positioned herself between his legs again, anxiously grabbed his manhood, put it into her mouth, and went to town. She pulled every trick she had out of the bag, trying her best to get his dick hard. After about ten minutes of putting in work, Ka'yah gave up.

"Look, it ain't no use. Ya shit ain't gettin' hard!" Ka'yah said angrily.

"Just keep tryin'. It's about to get hard," Ja'Rel said.

"Keep tryin'? Shiiiit, nigga, my jaws hurt! Just face it, ya shit ain't gon' get hard," she said, irritated.

"Come on, one more time," Ja'Rel said.

"No, nigga, I'm done!" Ka'yah was fed up as she climbed out of bed with a straight attitude. "Uggggh, this nigga's dick won't even get hard!" she said aloud to herself.

"Come on, baby, just one more time!" Ja'Rel begged as he climbed out of bed.

"No! Just go home to ya wife," she said, bending down, grabbing his clothes, and pushing them into his chest.

"Are you serious?" Ja'Rel asked.

"Hell yeah, I'm serious!" she snapped. "And don't come back until you get some Viagra, some Cialis, or somethin'! Shit, I coulda had a V8!"

"Okay, I see how you are," Ja'Rel said as he got dressed.

"Naw, you ain't seen shit yet," Ka'yah said, still frowning.

"I ain't fuckin' wit' you no more," he said, putting his shirt on.

"I don't give a fuck, nigga! Take yo' limp-dick ass on up outta here and don't worry about comin' back!" she yelled.

"It's cool. I won't." Ja'Rel got himself together and headed out of the bedroom. "Don't call me for shit! If it ain't about my son, it ain't about nothin'!"

"Boy, bye," Ka'yah said, waving him off. She was heated. Her hormones were on high and her body was throbbing with need in more than one place. She needed to get off point blank. The worst thing for her was to have this nigga lying next to her, unable to get the job done. Ka'yah's mind was in overdrive; she just knew this nigga was fucking her sister, or else he would be able to get that shit up.

Ja'Rel looked back at Ka'yah, shook his head, and walked out the door with both his pride and dick on limp.

***

Ke'yoko lay in the bed in her cozy pajamas, head wrapped in a scarf, while eating popcorn and watching one of her old-school favorite movies *Bustin' Loose,* cracking up laughing.

"Dakota gotta pee!" she yelled, mocking the little, chubby black girl in the movie.

Ja'Rel walked in the room looking like he had just lost his best friend.

Ke'yoko looked over at her husband. "That was quick." She smirked before turning her attention back to the TV.

Ja'Rel just looked at her, not saying a word, and walked into the bathroom and slammed the door behind him.

Chapter Twenty-five

Ke'yoko was up getting ready for her doctor's appointment. She was excited to be getting another ultrasound today. She was hoping that Dr. Confalone would be able to tell her the sex of the baby because every time he'd tried previously, the baby had its legs closed. Ke'yoko didn't care if it was a boy or girl; she was just happy to be having a healthy, living baby.

"You want me to go to your appointment wit' you?" Ja'Rel looked over at Ke'yoko and asked.

"No, thanks. I done been to the doctor about twenty times and you've never offered to go, so why now?" Ke'yoko asked.

"I don't know. I just wanna be there, that's all," Ja'Rel said.

"I'm cool," Ke'yoko said with an attitude. "You continue to keep doin' you, while I do me." She walked out of the bedroom.

Ke'yoko was tickled pink because Ja'Rel had been staying at home every night for the past month, trying to act like a husband should. It would have made her happy, if he was doing it by choice and not because she'd been crushing Xanax and Lasix in his food making him impotent.

Ke'yoko got in the car, called Ross, and told him she was on her way over to his condo. Ross had been going to all of Ke'yoko's doctor appointments with her. He made sure she ate right and exercised, and he tried to keep her as stress free as possible. Ke'yoko was grateful to have him in her life.

Ke'yoko and Ross walked out of the doctor's office with smiles on their faces.

"A boy," he said, smiling.

"A freakin' boy." Ke'yoko smiled too.

"This calls for a celebration," Ross said.

"Yes, it does. What we gon' do?" she inquired.

"How 'bout goin' back to my condo and watchin' some old movies while eatin' root beer floats, chips, and pizza," Ross suggested.

"Whaaaat? You gon' let me eat all that, Mr. Personal Trainer?" Ke'yoko asked, laughing.

"Yes, but only this one time. We celebratin' and tomorrow you'll be right back to eatin' healthy again."

"Sounds good to me. Let's go."

"Do you wanna go home first and check in wit' Ja'Rel?" Ross asked sarcastically.

"Ja'Rel ain't neva checked in wit' me, so why would I check in wit' his ass?" Ke'yoko asked, smiling.

"Okay. I just don't wanna get you in no trouble." Ross smiled as he and Ke'yoko made their way over to his car.

"Whatever." Ke'yoko laughed as Ross opened the passenger door for her to get in before walking around to the driver's side and getting in himself.

"Mommy, how come you didn't let me speak to Auntie Ke'yoko?" Aiko asked as he and his mother stood outside the Family Dollar store across the street from Ke'yoko's OBGYN office.

"Oh, don't you worry; we'll call her later on," she looked down at her son and said with a devilish grin.

Ja'Rel was blowing Ke'yoko's phone up as she and Ross watched *Black Dynamite*. She kept letting it go to voice mail. He would not let up; he kept calling back to back, just like she used to do to him. Finally getting tired of her phone ringing, she decided to answer it.

"Excuse me," she looked over at Ross and said.

"Take care of ya business," he replied while pausing the movie.

"Wassup?" she answered with a straight attitude.

"Where the fuck you at? And how come you ain't been answerin' yo' damn phone!" Ja'Rel snapped.

"Why? And you don't answer yo' phone when you busy," she said, slightly irritated that he was questioning her.

"Because I asked, that's why!" he said in a raised tone.

"Do I call and question your whereabouts or what you doin' when you not at home?" she asked.

"You used to," Ja'Rel responded.

"The key words are 'used to.' I don't do it no more!"

"Whatever, man," Ja'Rel said. "Do you want me to wait up for you?"

"Naw, don't wait up!" Keyoko pushed the END button on her phone and tossed it in her purse. "Sorry about that," she looked over at Ross and said.

"You cool," he said with a smile.

"Now, where were we?"

Ross picked the remote back up and pushed play on the DVR. "You think you gon' be okay when you get home? That nigga ain't gon' try to put his hands on you, is he?" Ross inquired.

"Naw, that nigga ain't crazy," Ke'yoko said, unfazed.

"Well, let me know if he do 'cause I'ma put that nigga in the grave," he said seriously.

"Don't worry. I'ma be good when I go home," Ke'yoko assured him.

"Okay. I'm just makin' sure. I know that's ya husband and I don't get in between people's shit, but I ain't never gon' let that nigga get away wit' puttin' his hands on you whether you pregnant or not." Ross didn't crack a smile.

Listening to Ross defend her had Ke'yoko feeling hot and bothered. "I'm good, baby, thank you." She smiled. "Calm down, tiger."

"Okay."

Ke'yoko and Ross were laughing, talking, and watching the movie. Ross stopped watching the TV and looked over at Ke'yoko and just stared at her, making her feel a little uneasy.

"What?" she asked.

Ross just shook his head as he set his root beer float on the table.

"What?" she repeated.

"You are so beautiful," he said, smiling.

"Thank you." Ke'yoko smiled back.

Ross scooted over closer to Ke'yoko, took her root beer float out of her hand, and set it on the table. He then leaned his head back on the sofa and stared up at her. He studied her entire face.

She looked down in his eyes and smiled. "How come you've never tried to sleep wit' me?" Ke'yoko asked after an awkward silence. "I think I know the reason why, but I just wanna be sure."

Ross smiled and sat up. "Where that come from?" He laughed.

"I don't know. I guess I just wanted to know. I mean, we've been spendin' a lot of time together and you've yet to make a real pass at me. I mean, you flirt but that's about the gist of it," Ke'yoko said, needing to know the exact reason.

"You really wanna know?" Ross asked, prolonging his response.

"Yes, I wanna know. If I didn't I wouldn'a asked," she said, laughing.

"Look, ma. I'ma keep it real wit' you. Every time we're around each other, I wanna make love to you so bad it's unreal. But there are some niggas who still respect the code and I'm one of 'em."

"What code?"

"Ma, you pregnant by another nigga. What I look like fuckin' you? And even though me and my baby momma ain't together, she still live wit' me so I would never disrespect you or her like that. I feel like if I can't bring you to my home in the daytime, I don't have no business makin' love to you at night, you feel me? Now, don't get me wrong, I take a cold shower every time you leave, believe that," Ross said, laughing. "But respect and honor, your honor and mine, mean more to me than all that. I don't care about what the next nigga doin' or did. I'ma always stay true to myself."

Ke'yoko couldn't do nothing but respect Ross's way of thinking. They watched two more movies and continued laughing and talking. It was almost eleven o'clock and Ke'yoko was getting tired and, even though she didn't want to leave, she definitely didn't want to wear out her welcome.

"Okay, big head, I'm 'bouta go," she looked over at Ross and said.

"A'iiight. Let me walk you to your car." Ross stood up from the sofa and helped Ke'yoko up. "Now don't forget tomorrow morinin' we back in the gym," he said as they headed toward the door.

"I know, I know. I'll be there at eight o'clock."

Ross and Ke'yoko walked into the hallway and got on the elevator. They chitchatted on their way down. Ross walked Ke'yoko over to her car, opened the door for her, then closed it once she got in. She then started the car and rolled the window down.

"You be safe," he leaned in the window and said.

"I will," she looked at him and said with a smile.

"See you in the mornin'." He leaned in and kissed her on the lips.

"Oh my God!" she said, turned on.

"Good night, Ke'yoko," Ross said, smiling before turning to walk away to go take a cold shower.

Ke'yoko wished like hell that Ross was like any other grimy-ass nigga. She wished that he would have asked her to come back up to his condo and make sweet love to her until the wee hours of the morning. Instead, she had to go home to her nasty dick-ass husband. Ke'yoko buckled her seat belt and pulled off. Her cell phone began to ring as she drove.

"This better not be Ja'Rel's ass," she said, pulling her phone out of her purse and checking the caller ID. She was shocked to see Ka'yah calling her. She thought she got the hint by now since she hadn't spoken with her in weeks. Ke'yoko started not to answer but did anyway. "Wassup?" Ke'yoko answered.

"Hey, stranger," Ka'yah replied. "How come I haven't heard from you in a minute?"

"I've been busy," Ke'yoko said, irritated already with their conversation.

"Busy doin' what?"

"Busy takin' care of Ke'yoko for once in my life," she said.

"Ummmm. I see you have time for everybody else, but you put your sister on the backburner; that's kinda fucked up, don't you think?"

"Like who?"

"Like Ross," Ka'yah spat.

Ke'yoko was mad as hell. How in the world did Ka'yah find out about her being with Ross? She must have been following her or something. This bitch was turning into a real live stalker. She should be happy Ke'yoko was with Ross and not at home with Ja'Rel.

"Me and Ross are handlin' some business together," Ke'yoko said nonchalantly.

"Ummmm, well, does Ja'Rel know that you and Ross are dealin' wit' each other?" Ka'yah asked suspiciously.

"I don't know! Why don't you ask him?" Ke'yoko shot.

"I don't talk to him," Ka'yah said.

"Since when?" Ke'yoko asked. She wanted to go all the way in on her sister and bust her dirty ass out but remembered Ka'yah would pay right along with Ja'Rel so she let up. "Anyways, girl, what you want?"

"I was just checkin' on you and the baby," Ka'yah replied.

"We good."

"Okay, well, I'll call you tomorrow. Maybe we should get together and have a cup of tea."

Ke'yoko was on fire. She couldn't believe this bitch was still trying to get her to drink that tea. "Yeah, maybe we should," Ke'yoko said through clenched teeth.

"Talk to you later," Ka'yah sang.

Ke'yoko didn't even respond, she just hung the phone up. "Biiiiiitch," she said and continued driving home.

Chapter Twenty-six

Ross stepped on the elevator and smiled the entire ride back up to his condo. He walked in and began cleaning up his and Ke'yoko's mess. He could not stop thinking about her as he filled the dishwasher with their dirty dishes. He wiped off the kitchen counter, straightened the magazines on the coffee table, turned off the lights, and headed home.

Ross pulled up into the driveway and sat for a minute thinking about Ke'yoko. Thinking about her smile, the way she laughed, the way she smelled, and most of all how soft her lips were. He couldn't believe he kissed her even though he had been wanting to for years. The fact that she was married to a nigga he was once close with bothered the shit out of him. He opened up the car door and got out. He whistled all the way into the house. He walked in and tossed his keys on the coffee table before heading upstairs to check on his baby girl.

Ross walked into Rayna's room, made sure she was covered up, kissed her on her forehead, and smiled before walking across the hall to his bedroom. He walked in and looked over at Sharae who was sitting on the bed staring at some papers. He acted as if she wasn't there and began getting undressed so he could go take a shower.

"Is it yours?" Sharae finally asked.

Ross turned around with a confused look on his face. "What?" he asked with a frown.

"I said is it yours?" she repeated slowly.

Ross was oblivious to what she was talking about. "Is what mine?"

"The baby," she said, holding up the sonogram photos.

"What was you doin', goin' through my shit?" he asked.

"Naw, I was lookin' for Rayna's birth certificate and ran across these sonogram pictures. Now, can you answer my question?" Sharae asked impatiently.

"Nope, he's not mine," he answered nonchalantly.

"You a fuckin' liar! If the baby wasn't yours then why would you have these fuckin' pictures?" Sharae yelled as she stood up from the bed and walking over to Ross, getting in his face.

"Look, man, don't be sittin' here questionin' me. I told you the baby wasn't mine."

"What the fuck ever! You foul as fuck, nigga," Sharae said, shaking her head while poking Ross in the side of his head. She knew Ross was out in the streets sleeping around with different women and had been since they'd been together, but she really must have meant something to him in order for him to have unprotected sex with her and get her pregnant.

"Whatever," he said, waving her off, while lightly shoving her away from him.

"Are you in love wit' her?" Sharae asked, bracing herself for the truth.

Ross looked Sharae dead in her eyes and slowly shook his head yes. "Yeah, I am," he admitted, feeling if Sharae didn't deserve anything else, the truth was something he owed her.

"Wow," Sharae said, hurt. She looked at Ross and waited for him to tell her that he was just playing and wanted to spend the rest of his life with her and Rayna, but he never did.

"Look, man, I'm sorry," Ross looked at Sharae and said.

"So how long you been fuckin' her?"

"I ain't never fucked her," Ross said truthfully.

"So you gon' keep standin' here lyin' to me in my face?" Sharae asked, appalled.

"Look, I don't have to lie to you about anything. I've never fucked her."

Sharae stared at Ross and wanted to swing
on him but she knew it would be a losing battle.
With what little pride and self-respect she had
left she decided at the moment she would give
Ross what he'd been asking her for for a long
time.

"Look, man, I will be out your house tomorrow. I'ma move in wit' my momma," Sharae
said.

"You can go. I've been tellin' you that shit
for the longest, but Rayna ain't goin' no damn
where!" he said in a raised tone.

"You kill me wit' that 'Rayna ain't goin'
nowhere' shit! Nigga, you don't even be home
long enough to spend no time wit' her! So miss
me wit' that shit! I'm takin' my daughter wit'
me, case closed. If you wanna see her, you know
where my momma stay!" Sharae said and meant
every word.

Ross wanted to argue, but he couldn't argue
with the truth; he was too deep off in the streets
to be raising his daughter on his own right now.
It was gon' kill him to let Rayna go, but he knew
he had to do what was best for his daughter, and
being with her mother was it. The thought of his
baby girl moving out hurt Ross to his heart, and

if Sharae wasn't all up in his face he probably would have shed a tear or two.

"You right," Ross said.

"Huh?" Sharae asked, shocked.

"You can take her wit' you. You're right, I'm not in a place right now where I can take care of her physically. But as long as I got breath in my body, financially she gon' always be straight."

Sharae knew Ross would be there for Rayna without a doubt, which was the least of her worries.

"Now when I wanna come get her, I don't want no shit," Ross said.

"It won't be none," Sharae said, forcing a weak smile.

"I love you, baby momma," Ross looked at Sharae and said before kissing her on the forehead.

"I love you too, baby daddy."

Ross smiled at Sharae before going into the bathroom to take yet another cold shower.

Chapter Twenty-seven

Ke'yoko pulled her car into the garage, got out, and walked over to the same box where she kept her hidden pictures. She dug her hand to the bottom of the old clothes and pulled the pictures out and began looking through them, just like she'd done at least once a month to keep reminding herself how no-good her husband had been since the beginning of their relationship.

Ke'yoko stared at the picture of Bo and his wife with Ja'Rel and some chick. Ja'Rel was bent over, kissing the stomach of this pregnant broad. When Ke'yoko had first hired the private investigator all she'd wanted was to find out if Ja'Rel was messing around with the woman. Ke'yoko found out a little more than what she had bargained for. She found out that not only was Ja'Rel messing around with the chick in the picture, but the baby she was pregnant with was his as well. The PI had pictures of Ja'Rel going into the hospital with balloons, teddy bears, and flowers for three days straight. Ke'yoko also got pictures of Ja'Rel taking the broad and the baby home in her car. Now of all the disrespectful things Ja'Rel could have done to her, riding your side chick and your illegitimate baby in your wife's car took the cake.

Ke'yoko was so hurt when the PI had given her the pictures because not only did this broad have his baby, Ke'yoko was pregnant as well and Ja'Rel was spending all his time with his side chick and their baby, while she was at home alone. When Ke'yoko was lying in the hospital having a miscarriage, Ja'Rel was nowhere to be found. Nadia and Ka'yah called him several times trying to reach him but couldn't. Ja'Rel didn't find out about his wife's miscarriage until the next afternoon. She had lain in the hospital overnight by herself completely emotional and mind racing. It had been almost two years to the day that Ke'yoko had found out about Ja'Rel's child. Even though the thought of Ja'Rel having another baby ate Ke'yoko up on the inside, she'd made a promise to herself that she would keep it a secret until the time was right to uncover all of Ja'Rel's bullshit; and his time was almost up.

Ke'yoko walked into the house and looked around to make sure Ja'Rel wasn't home, before walking into the kitchen and calling her brother.

"Wassup, sis," he answered, happy to hear from her.

"Wassup, baby brother? How you been?"

"I've been good. Just tryin'a get settled in our new house," Kailo said.

"Oh, you moved outta the dorm?" Ke'yoko inquired.

"Yeah, sure did. I had to get out of there."

"Well, it ain't nothin' wrong wit' that. So how's school anyways?"

"Ummm, I kinda dropped outta school," Kailo said and waited for his sister to explode.

"You did what?" Ke'yoko asked rhetorically.

"I dropped outta school," he repeated.

"What the fuck you do that for, boy?"

"Look, sis, I never wanted to be an attorney. That was father's dream, not mine. I only went to college because he was paying for it. After he passed, I decided to do what I wanted to do all my life," Kailo explained.

"And what's that?" Ke'yoko asked.

"I'm in the process of opening up my own pet store," Kailo said happily.

"A pet store?" Ke'yoko frowned. "What the fuck?"

"Yes, a pet store. It's always been a dream of mine, ever since I can remember."

"What does Chad think about you quittin' school and openin' up your own pet store?"

"Chad was very supportive of me quittin' school and startin' my own business," he replied.

"And what if your store is a flop?" Ke'yoko said, not trying to rain on her brother's parade, but trying to be realistic about the situation and see if he had a backup plan.

"We've discussed that, too. I told Chad that if my store doesn't generate money after two years, I'll sell the business and go back to school," Kailo said.

"Okay, that's smart. Well, at least you put some thought into it and have a plan. Good luck," Ke'yoko said.

"Thanks, sis."

"Maybe I can come buy your nephew some goldfish or somethin'." Ke'yoko laughed.

"Nephew?" Kailo asked happily.

"Yes, nephew."

"Another boy, huh? That's so exciting," Kailo said. "I know we better get an invitation to the baby shower!"

"Trust me, y'all will."

"Okay, sis. Well, I hate to rush you off, but I really need to get this TV mounted on the wall."

"Okay, but before you go let me ask you a question," Ke'yoko said.

"What's up?"

"Didn't you tell me you done an internship in high school at the Cleveland police department?"

"It was somethin' like an internship for one of my classes. Why, what's up?"

"I bet you know a lot of dirty cops then, don't you?" Ke'yoko inquired.

"Dirty ain't the word." Kailo laughed, thinking back on all the dirty deeds he was involved in at such a young age.

"Ummmm," Ke'yoko said. "Are you still cool wit' any of 'em?"

"Oh, yeah, I got a lot of good friends who work there. The chief and his wife flew out to Massachusetts to party with me and Chad a few times. Why you ask?"

"Ke'yoko, you home?" Ja'Rel called out.

"Shit, let me call you back, Kailo," Ke'yoko said before pushing the END button on her phone.

"Who was that?" Ja'Rel asked while walking into the kitchen.

"Kailo," she replied.

"Oh, your queer-ass brother," Ja'Rel joked, and was the only one who laughed.

Ke'yoko rolled her eyes and walked out of the kitchen.

Chapter Twenty-eight

Ke'yoko was sitting at the kitchen table flipping through a magazine while waiting for Ross to call her and it hit her that she hadn't spoken with Nadia in a couple of weeks. It wasn't unusual for them to go awhile without speaking because Nadia stayed busy in the shop while trying to keep a handle on their workers, but for her not to check in was rather odd to Ke'yoko.

Ke'yoko picked up her cell phone and called Nadia's cell phone, only to have it go straight to voice mail. She then dialed the number to the hair shop.

"Nadia's?" Connie answered.

Ke'yoko rolled her eyes. Connie was the last person she wanted to talk to. "Ummmm, yes, is Nadia available?" Ke'yoko asked, trying to change her voice.

"Naw, she ain't here, Ke'yoko," Connie said with an attitude.

"Do you know when she's comin' in?"

"Shit, do I look like her keeper?" Connie asked smartly.

"Look, Connie, I know you're not fond of me, but a lot of people aren't and I still sleep real good at night knowin' this. All I wanna know is when is Nadia due to come in?" Ke'yoko said.

"I don't know! She's yo' best friend. How don't you know where she at? How don't you know she hasn't been at the shop for well over a week? With a friend like you who needs an enemy?" Connie commented harshly.

"Fuck you," Ke'yoko said, before hanging up on Connie.

Ke'yoko got up from the table and walked out of the kitchen. She grabbed her purse and keys and headed over to Nadia's house. Ke'yoko knew something had to be going on because Nadia didn't miss work, no matter what. Money was her first true love.

Twenty minutes later Ke'yoko pulled up in front of Nadia's house. Her car was in the driveway so she knew she was at home. She got out of the car and looked at her lawn. The grass looked like it hadn't been cut in weeks. The flowers she had hanging on her front porch were all dying and withered from not being watered. Ke'yoko shook her head because this was not Nadia. She made sure everything around her stayed intact.

Ke'yoko rang the doorbell and waited for Nadia to answer. After a few minutes of waiting and getting no response she began knocking on the door. Still getting no answer, Ke'yoko began getting nervous, hoping she was okay. She began knocking on the door like the police. Still getting no answer, she began calling her name, drawing attention from Nadia's neighbors.

"Nadia, now, I know you in there. Your car is in the driveway. If you don't come open this door I'm 'bouta call the police and have them kick ya door in," Ke'yoko warned.

A few seconds later, Nadia came and unlocked the door before heading back to the sofa where she'd been for almost a week. Ke'yoko twisted the knob and let herself in. It was pitch dark in Nadia's house as she made her way to the living room.

"Nadia?" Ke'yoko called out as she felt her way through the hall and into the living room.

"Whaaaat?" Nadia asked, not wanting to be bothered.

"Why is it so dark in here?" Ke'yoko asked, walking over to the drapes and opening them up.

"'Cause I want it to be," Nadia snapped.

"Oh, my goodness! What the fuck is wrong wit' you?" Ke'yoko looked over at her friend and asked. Ke'yoko couldn't believe how Nadia was looking. Her hair was matted to her head, she had no makeup on, and had on a dirty, light blue robe. As long as she and Nadia had been friends, she had never seen Nadia looking less than flawless. Ke'yoko was at a loss.

"Ain't nothin' wrong wit' me," Nadia said while protecting her eyes from daylight.

"You must not have looked in the mirror lately, 'cause, bitch, you *thu*!" Ke'yoko said, not knowing any other way to describe what her best friend was looking like.

"So?" Nadia said uncaringly.

"And what took you so long to let me in?"

"I was hopin' you would catch on and go home," Nadia said, knowing better. She knew that she had to let Ke'yoko in because she would have called the police to kick her door in just like she had threatened.

"Yeah, right. Where's A'Niyah?"

"She's at her grandmother's house; or, should I say, the lady we thought was her grandmother up until a few weeks ago," Nadia said, hurt.

"Why you send her over there? She barely even know them folks," Ke'yoko fussed.

"I know. But I can't stand lookin' at my baby. Every time I do, all I can see is Ja'Rel," Nadia said.

Ke'yoko's cell phone began to ring. She checked the caller ID, saw Ka'yah's name, and pressed the IGNORE button. "Nadia, you can't take what Ja'Rel done to you out on A'Niyah. It's not her fault."

"I know it's not," Nadia said as tears filled her eyelids. "It's just that every time I look at her I'm reminded of what I think happened. Ke'yoko, ain't no tellin' what that nigga done to me while I was passed out." The thought alone made Nadia hate Ja'Rel even more. "And don't act like you don't blame me a little bit or feel some typa way toward me for what happened," Nadia said.

"Bitch, don't play me! If I was mad or feelin' some typa way toward you I wouldn't be over here right now tryin'a make sure you good. It's not like you asked that nigga to drug or rape you. And it's not like you enticed him. He did this shit on his own, and he's the only one I blame!" Ke'yoko replied.

Nadia felt a little relief. She had been so embarrassed ever since she'd found out the test results, she was too afraid and ashamed to face Ke'yoko; that's why she had been avoiding her. Even though she hadn't asked for what had happened to her, let alone to have a baby by her best friend's husband, Nadia felt horrible and felt like she had betrayed Ke'yoko too. She felt like she should have been more aware that night and should have never left her drink unattended. That was one of the oldest rules when in the club; but, hell, she had been in the safety of her own home, she thought. "Are you sure?" Nadia asked.

"Yes, I'm sure, Nadia. I'm not mad at you at all. I actually feel bad for you," Ke'yoko said as her cell phone began to ring. She looked at the screen and hit the IGNORE button again. If Ka'yah knew what was good for her, she would stop calling her.

"What am I gon' tell Twan? Shit, how am I gon' tell A'Niyah that Uncle Ja'Rel is really her daddy?"

"Shit, if I was you, I wouldn't say nothin' to neither one. Ain't no need to stir the pot if the shit ain't boilin'," Ke'yoko said.

"I don't know, man. You don't think they deserve to know the truth?" Nadia asked.

"I look at it like this: A'Niyah don't know Twan and probably won't ever get to know him as her daddy. Pretty soon, Ja'Rel will be history, too, so ain't no need of fuckin' the baby's head up. Introducin' this nigga as her daddy only to have him get snatched away like Twan is too much for that baby to handle."

"What you got brewin'?" Nadia inquired.

"You know I don't talk. Just sit back and watch. Ja'Rel and Ka'yah time is almost up." Ke'yoko smirked.

"Say no more." Nadia smiled, glad that Ke'yoko was finally about to take a stand against her conniving-ass sister and husband, and feeling relieved knowing her best friend really didn't blame her for what Ja'Rel had done to her.

"Oh, you know I won't. Get yo' ass up and get dressed. Let's go get somethin' to eat. I'm starvin'," Ke'yoko said.

"Gimme five minutes," Nadia said, getting up from the sofa.

"Naw, the way you got this living room smellin', I'ma give you at least fifteen," Ke'yoko joked.

"Fuck you." Nadia laughed as she headed into the bathroom to take a quick shower so she could go grab a bite to eat with her best friend.

Ke'yoko laughed too before taking a seat on the sofa. Her cell phone began to ring again.

"This better not be this bitch, Ka'yah! If it is I'ma let this bitch have it," she said, checking her caller ID again. She smiled when she saw Saks' name come across the screen. That was Ross's code name to throw Ja'Rel off just in case he decided to go through her phone.

"Hello?" she answered with a huge smile.

"Wassup? What you doin'?" Ross asked.

"Nothin' much. Just sittin' over here choppin' it up wit' Nadia, and 'bouta go get somethin' to eat," Ke'yoko replied.

"Oh, okay, that's wassup."

"You good?" Ke'yoko asked, concerned.

"Yeah, I'm cool. I was just callin' to hear your voice, that's all. I haven't talked to you all day."

"Okay, well, when I'm done hangin' wit' Nadia I'll give you a call."

"Say no more," Ross said before hanging up.

Ke'yoko was giddy as all get out. As she was about to put her cell phone back in her purse it rang again. She looked at the screen and chuckled. "This bitch just will not let up," she said to herself. Ke'yoko pressed IGNORE only to have Ka'yah call right back. She shook her head, and turned her phone off before throwing it in her purse.

"You ready?" Nadia walked back out into the living room and asked.

"More than you'll ever know." Ke'yoko smirked and followed her best friend out the door.

Chapter Twenty-nine

Ke'yoko was lying in the bed relaxing while watching TV. She was thinking about what she was going to do while Ja'Rel was out of town for the weekend at the exterminator's convention he was supposedly attending in Atlanta.

"I thought you went down to the office last night and took the deposit to the bank and set the alarm?" Ja'Rel walked in the bedroom, looked over at Ke'yoko and asked.

"I did go down there and set the alarm, but I forgot to grab the deposit. I thought about it when I got halfway home and I damn sure wasn't about to turn around and go get it," Ke'yoko replied.

"Can you go get it and deposit it for me?" he asked as he began grabbing his socks and underwear out of his drawer. "You know I hate havin' large amounts of money in the safe."

"Shiiiit, ain't that what you hired Tamika's lazy ass for?" Ke'yoko asked.

"Remember? I told you I had to fire her ass yesterday for comin' to work late every day, taking two-hour lunch breaks, and forgettin' to turn in the deposit for like three days in a row. Plus, she was lazy as hell!" Ja'Rel said as he pulled his weekender out of the closet and began packing it.

Ke'yoko did briefly remember Ja'Rel coming home ranting and raving about having to fire Tamika, but she wasn't paying him any attention while he was talking. "Oh, yeah, well, I'm tired. I don't feel like leavin' the house today. Can you have Ka'yah go drop it off at the bank?" Ke'yoko asked as she let out a fake yawn.

"Man, you done got real lazy, too, since you done been pregnant," Ja'Rel said.

"I'm entitled. Plus, I can't help that the baby is takin' all of my energy," Ke'yoko said.

Ja'Rel grabbed his cell phone and called Ka'yah.

"Wassup, daddy?" Ka'yah answered.

Ja'Rel glanced over at Ke'yoko and prayed she didn't hear her sister calling him daddy. "Can you do me a favor please?"

"Anything for you," Ka'yah replied.

"Can you run down to the shop, grab the deposit out the safe, and drop it off at the bank?"

"I can do that. But only if you do me a favor too."

"And what's that?" Ja'Rel asked.

"Come spend the night wit' me."

"I would do it myself but I'm goin' out of town."

"You can leave from my house in the mornin'," Ka'yah said.

"I can do that." Ja'Rel nervously glanced back over at Ke'yoko, who was acting as if she was interested in the TV show she was watching.

"Promise?" Ka'yah asked.

"Yep. Yep. And thanks," Ja'Rel said, before hanging up the phone.

"Is she gon' go?" Ke'yoko looked away from the TV and asked.

"Yeah, she gon' run down there," he answered.

"Good," Ke'yoko said with a devilish grin.

"I'm about to run and handle some business before I head to the airport. I'll be back in a few."

"A'iiiight," Ke'yoko said quickly before turning her attention back to her TV show.

Ka'yah walked into the shop and headed straight to the safe. She didn't have no time to be messing around. She needed to get home and get dinner on before Ja'Rel got over there. She was already running behind because she was busy arguing with Daron about keeping Aiko for the night. She walked into Ja'Rel's office, walked over to the safe, and put the combination in. She pulled it open and was surprised to see he had a gun in the safe with the deposits.

"Now, why would this nigga have this in the safe? His dumbass know he's a felon and can't be around no firearms." Ka'yah shook her head and grabbed the gun. She examined the gun, rubbing her hand across the cold steel with a silencer. "This a nice-ass gun," she said pointing it at the wall, pretending like she was shooting at someone. Ka'yah then began posing like one of Charlie's Angels, before blowing on the barrel of the gun. She began laughing at herself before placing the gun in her purse to take it back to her house to put it in a safe place.

Ka'yah grabbed the money out of the safe, walked out of Ja'Rel's office, locked the office back up, and headed to the bank to drop the deposits off before hurrying home.

Ka'yah rushed through the door, put her purse on the sofa, and headed straight to the bathroom to take a quick shower. After showering, she threw on a pair of the shortest shorts she could find in her drawer, and a wife beater, and slid her feet into her Coach flip-flops before heading into the kitchen to prepare dinner.

Ka'yah had the music blaring while sipping on some Bartenura. She grabbed her vibrating cell phone and began smiling when she noticed a text from Ja'Rel telling her that he was on his way. She turned her dinner down to a simmer, poured herself another glass of wine, and went and took a seat on the sofa and waited for Ja'Rel's arrival. Ten minutes later, she heard a knock on the door. She smiled and finished off her last little bit of wine before walking toward the door.

"How come you didn't use your key," Ka'yah said with a smile as she answered the door.

Her smile quickly faded when she noticed two detectives and some uniformed officers standing at her front door.

"Ka'yah Cho?" one detective asked, flipping his badge out.

"Yes," she replied nervously. Ka'yah tried her best to quickly think about what she had done for the detectives to be at her door. The only thing she could think of was all the bad checks she'd been writing.

"You're under arrest," he said, stepping in with his entourage behind him.

"Under arrest for what? Writin' bad checks?" she asked, unfazed because she knew that Ja'Rel would surely get her out on bond.

"No, for the murder of Brian 'Bo' Thompson," the other detective interjected.

"What?" Ka'yah asked, confused. "I ain't killed nobody!"

"Save it for the judge," one of the cops said, turning her around and placing handcuffs on her.

"This has to be a mistake! Bo was like a brother to me," she pleaded.

One of the detectives instructed the officers to look for any evidence. One of the officers went straight to Ka'yah's purse and pulled out the gun she had gotten out of the safe.

"Well, well, well, look at what we have here," he said, holding the gun up, showing Ka'yah.

"That's not mine," she said quickly.

"Well, who's is it?"

"It's not mine," Ka'yah said and left it at that.

"It was in your purse so that makes it yours," the officer said with a smirk.

"I swear the gun is not mine," Ka'yah said as tears began to cloud her vision.

"Take her down to the station," one of the detectives said.

All the neighbors were outside as they brought Ka'yah out of the house in cuffs and put her in the back of a cruiser. She was so embarrassed she couldn't even hold her head up. She quickly glanced up as she sat in the back of the police car and watched as Ja'Rel drove by real slow. She called out his name, but he couldn't hear her. All kinds of thoughts went through Ka'yah's head as they hauled her down to the police station. For the life of her she couldn't figure out why of all people to accuse of killing Bo they had chosen her. With no evidence, no eyewitness, no nothing. Ka'yah shook her head, sat back, and couldn't wait to get to the station so she could make her one phone call.

Chapter Thirty

Ja'Rel didn't know what was going on as he slowly drove by. He looked over at Ka'yah, who sat in the back of the police cruiser, and quickly turned his head. He heard her call his name, but he kept it moving. The police being there alone was enough to make him mind his own business. He wasn't about to stop to see what was going on. He loved Ka'yah but he loved his freedom even more. He wasn't about to chance the police questioning him about stuff he had nothing to do with. Besides, he was on probation and out past his curfew. Whatever Ka'yah had done couldn't have been that bad. Ja'Rel thought about rushing home to tell Ke'yoko but decided to go see his son and other side chick first.

Ka'yah was sitting in the police station trying to call everybody she knew, but no one answered their phone. She was thankful that the CO was nice enough to let her use the phone until she reached somebody. Her flirting with him helped a lot. After trying to reach Ja'Rel, Ke'yoko,

Daron, and even Kailo, Ka'yah had no choice but to call the one person she never thought she would ever have to reach out to.

"Hello?"

"Hello, Mother?" Ka'yah said slowly.

"Ka'yah?" her mother asked, surprised.

"Yes, it's me."

"Is something wrong?" her mother asked, concerned, feeling there had to be being that her daughter was calling her after not hearing from her since her late husband's funeral.

"Mother, I'm in jail," Ka'yah said as tears filled her eyes. The reality of her being locked up was finally starting to set in.

"Jail? For what, Ka'yah?" Her mother panicked.

"They tryin'a say I killed Bo," she replied as the tears began falling.

"Who?" her mother asked.

"Bo, Mother. You don't know him," Ka'yah said, annoyed.

"Well, did you kill him?" her mother inquired.

"No, Mother," she huffed.

"Well, what do you want me to do?"

"Get in touch wit' Ke'yoko for me. She'll know what to do," Ka'yah said.

"What's her phone number?" her mother asked as she looked for something to write with.

Ka'yah rambled off her sister's phone number to her mother. "If she doesn't answer, go by her house," Ka'yah said.

"Okay, but I don't know where she live at," her mother said.

Ka'yah gave her mother Ke'yoko's address.

"Time's up," the CO said.

"Look, Mother, I have to go. Do what I said and I'll try to call you back later," Ka'yah said.

"Okay," her mother said before hanging up and calling the number Ka'yah had given her for Ke'yoko.

Ke'yoko was lying in the bed still watching TV when another unfamiliar number came across her cell phone screen. Someone had been blowing her up for the past twenty minutes, but she refused to answer.

"Hello?" she answered reluctantly, thinking it might be important.

"Rie?" her mother said.

"Mother?"

"Yes."

"Wassup?" Ke'yoko asked, confused while wondering how she got her number.

"Your sister is in jail," her mother said.

"For what?" Ke'yoko asked.

"For murder. She said they trying to accuse her of killing Bobby," her mother said.

Ke'yoko took the phone away from her mouth and chuckled because her mother got the entire name messed up. "Bo," Ke'yoko corrected her.

"Bo, Bobby, it's all the same," her mother said.

"That's crazy. Is there anything I can do to help?" Ke'yoko asked, acting as if she was really concerned about her sister's well-being.

"Ka'yah asked me to call you because she said you'll know what to do."

Yeah, leave her bitch-ass right where she at until she rots to death, Ke'yoko wanted to say but didn't.

"Rie, please get your sister out of jail. I don't know what to do," her mother said, frantic.

"Calm down, Mother. I'll handle it," Ke'yoko said facetiously.

"Good. Call me and let me know what's going on. I have money if you need it."

"Okay, Mother. I'll keep you posted."

"Okay, thank you," her mother said before hanging up.

Ke'yoko couldn't believe Ka'yah had reached out to their mother. She wondered why she didn't call Ja'Rel to bond her out. Ke'yoko laid her cell phone back down, turned back on her side to try to get comfortable, and continued watching the end of her TV show.

***

"Hey, baby, you awake?" Ja'Rel stumbled in a two a.m. and asked while tapping Ke'yoko on the shoulder.

"What you think?" Ke'yoko snapped.

"I don't know that's why I'm askin'," Ja'Rel slurred.

"It's two in the fuckin' mornin'," she said, looking over at the clock on the wall. "So why wouldn't I be asleep, Ja'Rel?"

"Anyways, they said Ka'yah got locked up," he said.

Ke'yoko quickly sat up in the bed. "For what?" she asked, surprised, acting as if she didn't already know.

"I don't know. They just said she got arrested. I don't know no details," Ja'Rel said as he removed his clothes.

"Who is they?" Ke'yoko inquired.

"I don't know. I just overheard some niggas talkin' about it at the club," Ja'Rel lied as he climbed in the bed.

"I'm confused."

"About what?"

"About how my sister gets locked up and you don't call and tell me!" she said, pretending like she was mad.

"Baby, I didn't know if you was asleep or not and I didn't wanna call and wake you up if you were," Ja'Rel said.

"This is fucked up!" Ke'yoko grabbed her cell phone off the nightstand and began dialing numbers.

"Who you callin'?"

"I'm callin' to find out what's goin' on wit' my sister! Who else would I be callin'?" she snapped. Ke'yoko turned her ringer all the way down as she pretended to be talking to someone at the police department. "Okay, thank you," she said sullenly.

"What they say?" Ja'Rel inquired.

"The CO told me to call back in the mornin' and they can tell me more. I'll just go down there in the mornin'," Ke'yoko said as she lay back.

"Good. Let me know what they say. If she need some bail money, I got her, on the strength of her bein' your sister," Ja'Rel said.

You sure it ain't on the strength of her bein' ya baby momma? Ke'yoko wanted to say badly, but got herself comfortable instead. "Thanks."

"No problem, baby. You know I love your sister just like you do. Shit, she's my family too. And you know Aiko is my li'l dude. I love him like he was one of my own," Ja'Rel said.

Ke'yoko instantly got heated. She wanted to spit in Ja'Rel's face, ol' slick nigga, but decided not to because his time was about to end, just like Ka'yah's.

"Good night, Ja'Rel," Ke'yoko said while rolling her eyes before closing them and drifting back off to sleep.

Chapter Thirty-one

Ka'yah had been trying to reach Ke'yoko and Ja'Rel for the past two days, but neither one of them had been answering their phones. She didn't know what the hell was going on. Ke'yoko had already been acting funny toward her before this mess had happened, but she'd thought she and Ja'Rel were on the same page. Ka'yah was blowing her mother's phone up every chance she got. She hadn't talked to her mother this much in her entire life, but she didn't have a choice since she was the only one who would answer and accept the calls.

Ka'yah was stressed all the way out because she'd been told by her mother that when she had called the automated system, it was saying her bond was set at $1 million cash. The police weren't telling her anything and she hadn't even been to a hearing yet. The COs kept telling her there were too many people in front of her going, but she would get her turn eventually.

Ka'yah got up from her bunk and walked over to the empty phone and was about to call her mother when a big, burly female they called Bones walked up and stood real close behind her.

"I was about to use that, fresh meat," she said, putting her hand on top of Ka'yah's.

"I was here first." Ka'yah frowned, snatching her hand away.

"And what that mean?" Bones asked, while lifting up a piece of Ka'yah's hair and putting it up to her nose, sniffing it.

"Look, I don't know how you get down, but by the way you look, it wouldn't take a rocket scientist to figure it out; but I don't get down like that," Ka'yah snapped as she swung her head around.

Cell block B was in an uproar. They were cracking up about what Ka'yah had just said to Bones, the block bully. Ka'yah had said what everybody else was afraid to say. The inmates were loving it.

"Bitch, who you talkin' to like that?" Bones asked, embarrassed. She got all up in Ka'yah's face.

"No disrespect, but they do sell toothpaste in the commissary; you should try to buy you some on store day." Ka'yah took a step back, making the block laugh even harder.

"You think you funny?" Bones asked.

"I ain't tryin'a be," Ka'yah responded.

"Bitch, I will fuck you up!" Bones snarled.

"You might fuck me up; then again, you might not. Let's just say I haven't forgotten much of the twelve years I was forced to study karate." Ka'yah quickly stood in an Okinawan shiko-da-chi stance.

Bones looked at Ka'yah and thought twice. She would never live it down in here if she got her ass whooped by this little-ass girl. She knew she could fight, but she had never gone head-to-head with somebody who knew karate. Bones knew if she tried Ka'yah and lost, she'd have to give up her prison throne and reputation and she wasn't willing to do all that.

"Cho, you got a hearing. Let's go," the CO yelled into the block.

Ka'yah remained in her stance, not trying to chance Bones grabbing her from behind.

"Cho, let's go," the CO yelled again.

"Don't worry, bitch, I'll see you in prison. It's a small, revolving world in there and, when I do, I'ma make you my bitch." Bones smirked.

"Don't count on it," Ka'yah said and turned to walk away with her heart beating like two snare drums. She couldn't believe her fake stance had gotten her out of yet another ass whooping. Ka'yah didn't know the first thing about karate, but people always thought because she and Ke'yoko were part Japanese that they automatically knew karate, which had saved her from a lot of ass whoopings all through school.

Ka'yah turned around and got handcuffed, waiting impatiently as they put the shackles around her ankles too. She didn't know what was going to happen during her hearing. This was her first time ever being in trouble. She hoped Ke'yoko, Ja'Rel, or even her mom would be in the courtroom to support her as she shuffled down the long hall. Ka'yah was confused and surprised when the CO escorted her into a roomful of other inmates instead of a courtroom.

"What are we doin' here? I thought I was goin' to court," she said with a perplexed looked on her face.

"You are about to go to court. Look into the camera and smile," the CO replied.

"This ain't how it is on *Law & Order*," Ka'yah said.

"Well, this ain't TV; this is real life," the CO said smartly.

"All rise," the bailiff came on the screen and said.

Ka'yah was a nervous wreck and was sick to her stomach. Ka'yah sat quietly as the bailiff said a few more words and the judge walked in and took his seat. She watched closely as he put his glasses on and began riffling through a pile of papers. Ka'yah nearly fainted when he read her name, case number, and charge first.

"Do you have an attorney present?" the judge asked.

Ka'yah was stuck. She wanted to reply but the words wouldn't leave her lips.

"He's talkin' to you," the CO snapped.

"Ummm, no, no, sir, not yet," Ka'yah stammered.

"How do you plead?" the judge continued.

"I plead the Fifth," Ka'yah responded, remembering hearing that on one of her favorite episodes of *CSI*.

"Do you have an attorney or would you like for us to appoint you one?"

"No, thanks. My sister is gettin' me one," Ka'yah said, hopeful.

"Okay, that's fine. We'll continue court at a later date. Your bail is denied," the judge said and began reading off someone else's name, case number, and charge.

"What the hell just happened?" Ka'yah asked the CO as he escorted her back to the block.

"They just continued your case until you get an attorney and he denied your bail," the CO said, basically repeated what the judge had just said to her, but for some odd reason she understood it better coming from the CO than the judge.

"I can't believe a fine chick like you is down for murder," the CO said, checking Ka'yah out.

"I'm innocent. I didn't kill nobody!" Ka'yah snapped.

"Yeah, that's what they all say." The CO chuckled.

"You'll see when my sister and boyfriend come bail me out!"

"You look real familiar," the CO said. "Did you go to Laurel high school?"

"Yeah," Ka'yah answered slowly. "You didn't, unless you got a sex change."

The CO laughed. "Naw, my sister went there and I used to pick her up from school. Do you got a twin sister?"

"Yes," Ka'yah replied.

"Okay, damn! I always thought y'all was fine." He smiled.

"Thanks." Ka'yah smiled back.

"Damn shame you 'bouta go to prison for murder or else I woulda asked to take you out," the CO said.

"I ain't goin' no damn prison, 'cause I ain't killed nobody!" Ka'yah snapped.

"Yeah, yeah," he said, shaking his head in disgust.

"Hey, do you think you can let me use the phone to call my sister? She can't accept collect calls on her phone so I need to call her straight through," Ka'yah said, batting her eyes at the CO.

"You tryin'a get me in trouble?"

"No, I wouldn't do that. It won't take long. I'm just gon' tell her to come visit me and that's all."

The CO thought for a brief second before replying. "Look, if I do this, you gotta hook me up wit' ya sister," he said.

This thirsty-ass nigga, she thought before replying, "Bet."

The CO smiled happily. "You can go in this office right here." He looked around to make sure the coast was clear before unlocking the door. "And hurry up. You got two minutes."

"Thanks." Ka'yah shuffled over to the phone, picked it up, and quickly dialed Ke'yoko's phone number, only to have it go to voice mail. "This dirty bitch!" Ka'yah was furious as she listened to Ke'yoko's jolly voice on her voice mail.

"Ke'yoko, this Ka'yah. I don't know what your problem is wit' me, but I haven't done anything to you. Mother told me she called you to let you know what was goin' on wit' me, so I don't know why you not answerin' when I call you. I'll tell you what, if you don't want Ja'Rel to find out about you and punk-ass Ross, I expect you to be down here tomorrow to visit me," she said before hanging up the phone and shuffling back toward the door.

The CO opened the door for Ka'yah, let her out, and locked it again.

"Thanks," Ka'yah said with a huge smile.

"Well?" the CO asked impatiently.

"Well what?" Ka'yah asked, confused.

"Well, did you tell her I wannna get wit' her?" he asked, hopeful.

"Oh, yeah, yeah," Ka'yah lied.

"What she say?" the CO asked with a huge smile plastered on his face.

"She told me to give you her phone number," Ka'yah continued to lie.

"That's what I'm talkin' about." He smiled as he escorted Ka'yah back to the block. "I'ma get the number from you at dinnertime."

"Okay, I got'chu," Ka'yah said as the CO removed the cuffs and shackles.

Ka'yah walked back into the block and headed straight to her bunk, lay back, and began reflecting on her life, wondering if karma was the reason she was in this fucked-up situation. Ka'yah pushed that thought to the side. Never in her life had she done anything bad enough to deserve no mess like this. She drifted off to sleep, taking a quick nap before dinner.

Chapter Thirty-two

Ke'yoko woke up bright and early so she could catch Nadia before she headed to the shop. She was so happy that her best friend was back to her old self again. It had taken a lot of convincing for Nadia to finally believe that she wasn't mad at her and didn't blame her one bit for what Ja'Rel had done to her. Nadia was relieved but still a part of her felt in some major sort of way that she owed Ke'yoko her life. One good thing that had come out of Ja'Rel's infidelity was that it had brought Ke'yoko and Nadia even closer than before, if that was possible.

"Wassup, sis?" Nadia asked, answering the phone.

"Hey, girl, you ain't at the shop yet, are you?" Ke'yoko asked.

"Naw, not yet. Just dropped A'Niyah off at the daycare. Why, wassup? You good?"

"Yeah, I'm good. I was just callin' to tell you about the voice mail Ka'yah left me last night," Ke'yoko said as she climbed out of bed.

"How she leave you a voice mail?" Nadia inquired.

"Girl, I do not know," Ke'yoko said as she headed down to the kitchen to fix herself something to eat. "All I know is I checked my messages before I went to bed last night and here her bitch-ass is on my phone lightweight threatenin' me."

"Threatenin' you how?" Nadia inquired.

"Talkin' 'bout if I don't come down there to visit her she was gon' tell Ja'Rel about Ross," Ke'yoko said, pulling the eggs out of the refrigerator.

"Whaaaaaaaat?" Nadia asked, surprised.

"Girl, yes." Ke'yoko laughed as she grabbed a skillet off the pot rack and put it on the stove and turned on the fire.

"That bitch got a lot of nerve," Nadia said, shaking her head in disgust.

Ke'yoko grabbed a bowl out of the cabinet and began cracking her eggs. "Who you tellin'? Bitch, yo' ass in jail. You ain't in no position to be talkin' shit!"

"Right. If anything, the dumb ho should be tryin'a kiss yo' ass so she can get some money on her books for commissary," Nadia joked.

"Exactly!" Ke'yoko agreed, grabbing the butter and cutting a couple of slices off into the skillet before pouring her eggs in.

"Well, what you gon' do? You gon' go visit or nah?"

"I'ma go visit her silly-ass tonight. But not because of her threat, 'cause I can give less than a fuck about what she tells Ja'Rel. Shit, I don't even know how she gon' talk to him 'cause I went through his cell phone the other night and he got about a hundred missed calls from her," Ke'yoko said, scrambling her eggs.

"Whaaaaat? I wonder why he ignorin' her?" Nadia questioned.

"Girl, I don't know and don't care." Ke'yoko turned the fire off from underneath her eggs.

"I don't blame you. What you gon' say to her?" Nadia asked as she pulled up into the hair shop's parking lot.

"I don't even know. I'll think of somethin', though."

"I know you will. And I would give ten million dollars to be a fly on the wall," Nadia said, turning off her car.

"You know I'ma fill you in."

"I know you are. I can't wait! Call me as soon as you leave the county," Nadia said.

"Say no more." Ke'yoko hung up the phone, fixed her plate, and sat down at the kitchen table. "One down and one to go." She smirked before feeding her face.

***

Ke'yoko quickly hung up the phone as Ja'Rel walked into the bedroom before walking into the bathroom.

"Who was you talkin' to?" Ja'Rel walked over to the doorway and asked his wife.

Ke'yoko looked at him like he was crazy. "Why?" she asked while picking up her brush and brushing her hair back.

"Because I asked, that's why!" he said in a raised tone. "For the past few weeks you been hurryin' off the phone every time I walk into a room like you got somethin' to hide!"

"I ain't got shit to hide! And let's not forget I'm grown, too," Ke'yoko said, picking up her hair tie and putting her hair into a neat ponytail.

"What you bein' grown got to do wit' anything?"

"It's got a lot to do wit' it! Bein' that I'm grown, I don't have to hide shit, unlike some people I know," she said smartly, while looking at Ja'Rel like he was scum.

"I don't got shit to hide either," he said defensively.

"Yeah, a'iiiiight," Ke'yoko said sarcastically before brushing past Ja'Rel.

"What's that supposed to mean?" Ja'Rel asked while turning to follow Ke'yoko into the bedroom.

"Oh, nothin'," she said uncaringly.

"It shouldn't mean nothin' 'cause I ain't doin' shit!" Ja'Rel said.

"Okay," Ke'yoko said nonchalantly, pissing Ja'Rel off with her laidback attitude.

The way Ke'yoko had been acting lately had Ja'Rel feeling like she really did know what he'd been up to; either that or he was just being paranoid just like he had been ever since Ka'yah had gotten locked up. A few times he'd thought he was being watched by the cable guy who was parked down the street from the shop. Another time he thought he was being followed, and had pulled into the gas station to get away, and when the car pulled in behind him, Ja'Rel had been relieved to see that it was an old white lady driving. He didn't know what Ka'yah was in there telling the police. He knew she wasn't built Ford tough like Ke'yoko. Ja'Rel knew if anything ever went down, even though she didn't know his business, Ke'yoko wouldn't open her mouth. Ka'yah, on the other hand, would be talking so much the police would probably have to beat her to stop talking.

"Don't get fucked up!" Ja'Rel replied.

"Oh, don't worry. I won't," Ke'yoko said while grabbing her purse off the bed, putting it on her shoulder.

"Where you 'bouta go?"

"Damn! I'm goin' to see Ka'yah if you really must know," she huffed.

"About damn time! I would hate to be your sister. That girl been locked up for a few days and you just now goin' to check up on her!" Ja'Rel shook his head in disgust.

"She good. I've been callin' down there checkin' up on her. Shit, how come you ain't been to see her? You said she's your family too," Ke'yoko asked facetiously.

"You know I can't go down there. You know I'm on papers," Ja'Rel said.

"You do everything else while you on papers," Ke'yoko said smartly.

"What's that supposed to mean?" Ja'Rel asked suspiciously.

"Nothin'. I'll holla at'chu later." Ke'yoko walked out of the bedroom, leaving Ja'Rel standing in the middle of the bedroom wondering what all Ke'yoko really knew about him.

Chapter Thirty-three

Ke'yoko pulled up into the county's parking lot and just sat there staring at the huge building. In some sort of weird way, her womb-mate being locked up was starting to affect her. Even though Ka'yah had done so much to cross her, Ke'yoko did still feel bad that her sister was probably about to spend the rest of her life behind bars. She began thinking back to when they were growing up as kids, how close they used to be. How they used to lie in bed and laugh and talk all night, sharing their dreams and goals. She remembered how, once they'd become teens, Ka'yah would always cover for Ke'yoko, taking all the heat from their dad when Ke'yoko got caught up in her lies. And, lastly, how they'd live together in the same house with their husbands and children. Ke'yoko missed their close relationship and would have given anything to get it back. For the life of her, she didn't know what had gone wrong that had made Ka'yah turn on her the way she had.

Ke'yoko removed her license and some documents from her purse and laid them on the front seat of her car before digging in the bottom of her purse and grabbing some loose change. She placed her purse under her seat, grabbed her license and the documents, and got out of the car, closing the door behind her. She filled the parking meter with coins and looked both ways before crossing the busy street. She tossed the leftover coins into a homeless man's coffee cup before heading into the building. For some strange reason, Ke'yoko was nervous as she waited in the line.

"License," the CO behind the glass said, holding out his hand, never looking up.

Ke'yoko slid the license underneath the little hole in the glass. She looked at the other CO who stood up against the wall with a stern look on his face.

He looked at the picture on the license and quickly looked up at Ke'yoko. "So you're the other twin?"

"Yes," Ke'yoko replied, wondering how he even knew she existed.

"Y'all look so much alike," the CO said with a smile.

"Thanks, I guess," Ke'yoko said.

"Kailo always speaks highly of you. I'm Riley," he said with a smile.

Ke'yoko smiled back, realizing it was Kailo who'd told him about her. She was happy to hear that her brother had nothing but good things to say about her. "Nice to meet you, Riley," Ke'yoko said, remembering Kailo mentioning his name a few times during their many conversations.

"Nice to meet you too, Ke'yoko," Riley said, messing up the pronunciation of her name.

"You heard from Kailo lately?" she asked.

"Yes, sure have. Matter fact, I just talked to him about two days ago. He told me to be expectin' you," Riley said, handing Ke'yoko her license back.

"That's good to know." Ke'yoko took her license from his hand.

"Window eight." Riley smiled and winked.

Damn, he fine, Ke'yoko thought while smiling back and heading over to window eight.

"You know the phone in window eight is messed up and doesn't record anything, right?" the other CO leaned over and asked Riley.

"It's cool," Riley said before checking in the next visitor.

Ke'yoko sat down on the hard, metal stool and looked around the crowded visiting room while waiting for Ka'yah. She looked up on the wall and read the sign: ALL CALLS ARE SUBJECT TO MONITORING. That made her nervous, too, because now she had to choose her words carefully.

A few minutes later, Ka'yah came through the door talking loud. She walked down to window eight, looked at her sister's big, round belly, and sucked her teeth before sitting down. For a split second Ka'yah began feeling bad about all the dirty things she had done to her sister. She and Ke'yoko picked up their phones at the same time.

"What took you so long to come visit me?" Ka'yah asked, getting straight to the point.

"Hello to you too. And, yes, Aiko is doin' good. I'm goin' to pick him up when I leave here. He's goin' to stay wit' me and Ja'Rel until you get out," Ke'yoko said sarcastically.

"Yeah, yeah. Did Mother tell you what I was locked up for?" Ka'yah asked.

"Yeah, she told me," Ke'yoko replied, annoyed by her sister's uncaring attitude toward the well-being of her son.

"So are you and Ja'Rel gon' get me an attorney or what?"

"I'll get you one," Ke'yoko said.

"How can you afford to get me an attorney? Ja'Rel is the one wit' all the money," Ka'yah asked, slightly annoyed. "I need a good lawyer, not one of these court-appointed niggas, either!"

"I said I got'chu. And, furthermore, I don't even talk to Ja'Rel no more," Ke'yoko said.

"Why not?" Ka'yah asked, trying to contain her happiness. "You musta finally realized that he ain't about shit, huh?"

"I hate to say it, but yeah. You told me he wasn't about shit a long time ago, but I didn't listen to you." Ke'yoko shook her head.

"What he do?" Ka'yah asked, pretending to be concerned, knowing she couldn't have cared less.

"Check this shit out." Ke'yoko opened up one of the documents and pressed it up against the window.

"What's that?" Ka'yah asked as she skimmed through the DNA results.

"DNA results."

"For who?" Ka'yah pried, knowing the only child Ja'Rel had was Aiko.

"For A'Niyah," Ke'yoko replied.

"Nadia's daughter?" Ka'yah asked, surprised.

"Yep," Ke'yoko said, shaking her head.

"What the fuck?" Ka'yah asked, seeing red and feeling sick to her stomach at the same time.

"Yeah, that's what I said," Ke'yoko said, laying the document back down.

"Them dirty bitches!" Ka'yah said angrily.

"It's cool. They'll get theirs."

"They sure will. If that's the last thing I do, I'ma make both of them pay!"

"That's only half of it," Ke'yoko continued.

"There's more?" Ka'yah asked, not knowing if she could handle any more news about the man she was supposed to spend the rest of her life with.

"Girrrrrl, yeah! You know Kailo knows everybody. So I had him have one of his friends do a li'l snoopin' for me, and found out Ja'Rel got a whole notha family on the other side of Cleveland."

"He got what?" Ka'yah asked, shocked.

"Girl, he got another son by this broad named Kassidy and she's pregnant again. Crazy thing is we due around the same time." Ke'yoko chuckled.

Ka'yah felt like she had just been shot in the chest as she sat and took all this information in. She couldn't believe Ja'Rel was playing her like he was. He had her thinking she was the only one, but hearing the news about Nadia and Kassidy proved her wrong.

"How can you laugh about this shit? Ain't you hurt?" Ka'yah asked slowly. She was completely heartbroken by the news her sister was throwing at her.

"Chile, naw, I ain't hurt. Ja'Rel been a ho since day one."

Ka'yah couldn't believe how calm her twin sister was. She wanted to break down and cry but she had to hold it together. In order for her not to start crying, Ka'yah changed the conversation up. It was hard to converse about anything else the way she was feeling but she couldn't show any real emotion in front of her sister.

"Anyways, I gotta get outta here! You know I ain't kill Bo. I liked Bo," Ka'yah said, shaking her head. "I don't even know where they would get some shit like that from. What reason would I have to kill Bo? You was the one who didn't like . . ." Ka'yah stopped in midsentence.

Ke'yoko stared Ka'yah in the face. "Finish your sentence, sister," Ke'yoko said slowly. She gazed at her sister, never looking away.

Ka'yah stared back at Ke'yoko, unable to finish her sentence. Ke'yoko's demeanor instantly turned cold and uncaring. Ka'yah's mind began to race as she started putting things together as Ke'yoko continued to stare at her.

"You set me up?" Ka'yah finally said.

Ke'yoko smirked. "Now why would I do a thing like that, sister?"

"You dirty bitch!" Ka'yah shot.

"No, dirty is when you fuck your sister's husband and have a baby by him or, better yet, when you feed your sister poisonous tea, causing her to have not one but four miscarriages." Ke'yoko couldn't do nothing but look at her sister and shake her head.

Ka'yah's eyes got big as saucers as she listened to Ke'yoko, wondering how she found all of this out.

Ke'yoko switched over to their native language, not wanting anyone to be able to understand anything she was about to say, and continued talking. "So technically you are a killer; you just didn't kill Bo. I did," she said with a smile.

Ka'yah followed suit and began speaking in Japanese as well. "Why?" was all Ka'yah could think to say.

"Why not?"

"So you really gon' let me sit in jail for somethin' you did?" Ka'yah asked, shocked. Ka'yah never thought anything her sister did could hurt her. Of course, other than living with the man of her dreams and constantly popping up pregnant by him. She'd always thought she had the upper hand. She had so many feelings swirling inside of her she didn't quite know how to feel or what to really think.

"Why wouldn't I? All the dirty shit you have done to me, you deserve every day that they gon' give you." Ke'yoko frowned.

"It's cool. My man Ja'Rel will get me an attorney," Ka'yah said spitefully.

"Ha." Ke'yoko chuckled. "Ja'Rel won't even answer your calls, fool, and furthermore he's gon' need money for his own attorney."

"He ain't in no trouble."

"Not yet, but I'ma set him up next, so maybe y'all can be pen pals." Ke'yoko smiled.

"Bitch, you need some serious help," Ka'yah spat.

"I need help? I'm appalled," Ke'yoko said snidely. "Y'all created this monster; now deal wit' it."

"It's cool. I'll be out of here." Ka'yah smiled confidently.

"What about the spit they found on Bo's body?" Ke'yoko asked.

"What are you talkin' about?" Ka'yah was confused. This was the first time she'd heard anything about some spit.

"And what about the gun I planted in the safe? I knew yo' stupid ass would fall for that," Ke'yoko replied.

"I don't know shit about no spit. And even if they did find it, it was yours, not mine, so now what, bitch? You goin' down, dumbass ho! And as far as the gun, it wasn't mine either!" Ka'yah said victoriously.

"Did you forget we're identical twins with the same DNA? So the spit will come back as yours. So who's the dumbass ho now?" Ke'yoko asked viciously. "And they found the gun in your possession so technically it does belong to you." She looked at her sister, hung up the phone, and winked and smiled before standing up and turning to walk away, leaving Ka'yah sitting there with her mouth wide open.

The reality that she was really facing a life bid slowly sank in. "I'ma kill you when I get out of here, bitch!" Ka'yah started screaming as she began wilding out, yelling and pounding on the glass, causing a huge scene. Two COs ran over and grabbed her, trying their best to restrain Ka'yah. She continued going off.

Ke'yoko never turned around. She kept her head held high and strutted toward the door. She looked over at Riley and winked before heading out to her car.

Chapter Thirty-four

Ja'Rel was pacing back and forth waiting for Ke'yoko to come back home from seeing Ka'yah. He felt bad for not answering any of Ka'yah's calls, but he thought he'd better wait to see what was going on with her first before he did.

Ja'Rel was relieved when he peeked out the front window and finally saw Ke'yoko pulling up into the driveway. He was more anxious than a kid on Christmas Eve to hear what Ke'yoko had to say about her twin sister. He quickly grabbed the newspaper, sat down on the sofa, and pretended to read, not wanting his wife to sense his eagerness.

Ke'yoko finished up her call with Nadia before getting out of the car and heading into the house. She wasn't surprised that Ja'Rel was still at home. She knew he'd be anxious to hear what was going on with his side bitch. Ke'yoko put a fake smile on and walked in the house.

"Wassup?" she asked, looking over at Ja'Rel, who was busy pretending to be reading yesterday's newspaper.

"Oh, wassup?" he replied while looking up from the newspaper.

"Anything good in the newspaper?" Ke'yoko asked.

"Not really," Ja'Rel replied.

"Shiiiit, it's gotta be 'cause this is the second day in a row that you've read that same paper," Ke'yoko said smartly and headed into the kitchen.

Ja'Rel laid the paper down, got up from the sofa, followed his wife into the kitchen, and stared at her while she poured herself a tall glass of almond milk.

"What?" Ke'yoko asked, noticing him gazing at her.

"Well?"

"Well what?" she toyed, already knowing he wanted to know what was up with Ka'yah.

"What did they say about your sis?"

"Oh, yeah, they holdin' her on a million dollar cash bond for the murder of Bo," she said nonchalantly, before taking a drink of her milk.

"Huh?" Ja'Rel asked, confused.

"Yeah, they tryin'a say Ka'yah killed Bo," Ke'yoko said, shaking her head and taking another drink of her milk.

"Why would she do that? Ka'yah liked Bo," Ja'Rel replied while taking a seat at the kitchen table. There was no way he was going to believe that Ka'yah would hurt Bo in any kind of way, let alone kill him.

"I don't know why she would kill him. And as far as her likin' him, we all know she's one helluva actress. She sho'll fooled the hell outta me," Ke'yoko said, finishing off her milk and placing the empty glass in the sink.

"I don't believe Ka'yah would do no shit like that! Somebody tryin'a set her up," Ja'Rel said, looking over at his wife.

"Well, we'll see what they got when she goes to court."

"We gotta get her an attorney. Quick, fast, and in a hurry. A good one at that," Ja'Rel stated.

"For what?" Ke'yoko said before realizing it had slipped out of her mouth.

Ja'Rel looked at his wife like she'd lost her mind. "What the fuck you mean, for what?" He grimaced.

Ke'yoko had to clean her words up and fast. This was the first time she'd slipped since she'd put her plan in motion.

Ke'yoko looked over at Ja'Rel for a brief moment before speaking. "Look, I didn't wanna tell you this because I know you love Ka'yah like your blood run through her, and what I'm about to tell you is gon' hurt you to your heart."

"Tell me what?" Ja'Rel asked impatiently.

Ke'yoko sighed before speaking. "Look, Ka'yah wants me to help set you up so she can get out of jail," she said, looking over at Ja'Rel. "She said the detectives came and questioned her about you and your crew. She said they told her if she told them what you were into that they would cut her a deal."

Ja'Rel listened as his wife continued talking.

"She told me about all the dope you was sellin' and that you was usin' the company as a front." Ke'yoko waited for a response from Ja'Rel.

Ja'Rel couldn't believe what his wife was telling him. He knew it had to be true because there was no way Ke'yoko knew that he was selling dope and using the exterminating company as a cover-up. Ja'Rel was beyond happy that he'd avoided Ka'yah's calls. He was glad he followed his own instincts, because he had made up his mind that the next time she called he was going to answer.

"What? And what did you say?" he inquired nervously.

"Yep. And I told her hell naw! You my husband so why would I do some shit like that?" She frowned.

Ja'Rel shook his head. He couldn't believe this shit. He knew he wasn't hallucinating all the times he'd thought he was being followed. Ka'yah was trying her best to set him up. He was just happy that he'd stayed on minding his Ps and Qs.

"She said she was gon' tell the detectives everything to get her sentence reduced. She said she also told them if they would lower her bond, she would get out and wear a wire to set you up," Ke'yoko lied with a straight face.

Ja'Rel was confused as hell. It was hard to believe that Ka'yah would tell Ke'yoko all of this because he knew how she really felt about her twin sister. But it was too much of a coincidence for Ke'yoko not to be telling the truth. Ja'Rel was hurt by the fact that Ka'yah was trying to set him up, but he was more hurt because he thought she loved him just as much as he loved her. Ja'Rel's head was spinning. He had to get out and get some fresh air.

Ke'yoko looked over at Ja'Rel. She didn't know if her eyes were playing tricks on her, but Ja'Rel's face looked as if he'd just turned a few shades of green. It took everything in her not to burst out laughing.

"I'll be back," Ja'Rel stood up from the table and said. He needed some air bad. Too much was going on for him right now and he felt like he was suffocating with all of this news.

"Are you okay, baby? You look a little sick," Ke'yoko said, holding in her laugh.

"Yeah, I'm good. I'm just glad that I never answered any of Ka'yah's calls. I can't believe she tryin' to set me up! That dirty bitch." Ja'Rel shook his head, walked over to his wife, and kissed her on her forehead. "Thank you for always bein' loyal."

"Why wouldn't I be loyal to someone who's always been loyal to me? For better or for worse, baby; them was the vows," Ke'yoko replied slowly. She felt a twinge of guilt repeating that line of their wedding vows

"True," he said, smiling slowly before turning to walk out of the kitchen and heading out the door.

Ke'yoko had no words for the spectacular story she'd just come up with out the blue. All she could do was shake her head and smile before going upstairs to take a nap.

Chapter Thirty-five

Ke'yoko had just gotten comfortable after getting home from a long day at her doctor's appointment with Ross. After the stress test and drinking the nasty glucose for the second time, all Ke'yoko wanted to do was kick her swollen feet up and relax. She was getting tired of going to the doctor's three times a month, but since she was considered high risk, she had to do what was best for her son.

Ke'yoko was so ready for her baby boy to come she didn't know what to do. Two months wasn't coming quick enough for her. Ke'yoko was tired of feeling fat and drained all the time. Some days she thought she was the ugliest person walking the face of the earth, but Ross always assured her on a regular how beautiful she was.

Ke'yoko was just about to drift off to sleep when the doorbell rang. "Shit! Who the fuck at the door?" she snapped as she struggled to roll over and get out of bed. Ke'yoko made her way into the hallway and wobbled down the stairs.

She instantly got pissed because whoever was on the other side of the door was pressing the annoying doorbell over and over.

"I'm comin', shit! Stop ringin' my damn door-bell!" she shouted while snatching the door open. Ke'yoko was surprised to see her mother standing there. "Mother?"

"Can I come in?" she asked, wasting no time.

"Is everything okay?" Ke'yoko asked, letting her mother enter the foyer, all while wondering how she knew where she lived.

"Yes," she said, stepping in.

Ke'yoko and her mother both stood in silence. "Wassup?" Ke'yoko finally asked.

"I just left the county jail from seeing your sister," her mother said.

"Okay," Ke'yoko said uncaringly.

"And I came over here to see if what she told me was true," her mother asked, looking her daughter dead in the face to see if she was about to lie, just like she used to do when she was a little girl.

Ke'yoko kind of felt intimidated as her mother stared at her just like she used to do when she was younger. "To see if what was true?" Ke'yoko asked, already knowing.

"Come on, Ke'yoko, cut the shit," her mother said.

Ke'yoko was surprised because she had never heard her mother use that type of language. "What shit?" Ke'yoko asked.

"Were you the one who killed Bob and blamed it on your sister?"

"I ain't killed nobody! And his name is Bo," Ke'yoko said sternly.

"I want to believe you so bad because I know I raised you better than that," her mother said.

That statement must have struck a nerve because Ke'yoko instantly got mad. "Raised me? Did you forget I raised myself?" Ke'yoko asked.

"I did the best that I could, Rie! And you know that!" her mother said in a raised tone.

"Well, your best wasn't good enough." Ke'yoko was hurt as all her childhood memories of her mother never being there to protect her from her stepfather came rushing back.

"Look, I didn't come over here to debate nor discuss what type of mother I was to y'all. All I came over here for was to find out if what Ka'yah was saying to me was true and to tell you that if it is, make it right. She's your sister, for heaven's sake!"

"Sister? Well, sisters don't fuck each other's husbands and have babies by them!" Ke'yoko spat angrily, appalled that her mother had the audacity to come over here and tell her to do right on a situation when she didn't even know what the situation was.

Ke'yoko's mother's jaw nearly hit the floor.

"Yeah, that's right. Aiko is Ja'Rel's son. I done a DNA test on him," Ke'yoko snapped angrily. "I bet'chu she didn't tell you that while she was up there tellin' you everything else, did she?"

All Ke'yoko's mother could do was shake her head in disgust. "I didn't know," her mother said as tears filled her eyes.

"I know you didn't, but now you do so you can stay out of it! Yeah, I killed Bo and blamed it on her; is that what you wanted to hear? If so, you heard it. Now what? Are you gon' testify against me?" Ke'yoko asked, as tears filled her eyes for the first time. Finally saying the words that her nephew was really her stepson hit her like a ton of bricks.

Ke'yoko's mother was speechless as tears freely flowed down her face. She knew she hadn't been the best mother in the world, but she knew she hadn't been the worst, either. For the life of her, she didn't know where she'd gone wrong with her three children. She had such high hopes for all three of them, even after they all moved out or left on their own. She still wanted nothing but the best for them. She loved her children with all her heart, but she refused to let them disturb her peace any longer; she was done.

"Look, I'm sorry that you had to endure that. But you're a beautiful, strong young lady, and I'm quite sure you'll figure it all out. I've already told your sister about me selling the house and moving back to Japan next week. I refuse to let my children humiliate me any more than you three already have."

Ke'yoko looked at her mother with hatred in her eyes. Yet again, when she needed that motherly love the most, she gave Ke'yoko her ass to kiss.

"Get the fuck outta my house, you selfish-ass bitch! You're the main reason why your children are fucked up the way that we are anyway," Ke'yoko said harshly.

Before Ke'yoko saw it coming, her mother's tiny hand rested on the side of her face and before she realized it, she had quickly slapped her mother back. Her mother was in complete awe. Ja'Rel walked into the house as Ke'yoko's mother stood in the foyer holding her burning face. The tension in the room was thick and it had him feeling uncomfortable in his own home. He had definitely walked in on something.

"Hi," he said, speaking to Ke'yoko's mother.

"Now get the fuck out like I said and don't bother tellin' me when you leave the country 'cause I don't give a fuck. You been gone to me for years!" Ke'yoko looked at her mother and said.

Without a word, Ke'yoko's mother turned and walked out the door, never looking at Ja'Rel or responding to his greeting.

Ja'Rel was in shock as he stood wondering what he'd missed. "What was that all about?" he finally asked.

"Go to hell!" she looked at him and said, before going back upstairs and climbing in the bed, leaving Ja'Rel speechless.

Chapter Thirty-six

Ja'Rel had been walking on eggshells ever since Ke'yoko had told him about Ka'yah wanting to set him up. She had him so paranoid, he was always looking over his shoulder and thought everybody was out to get him, even Ke'yoko at times. Ja'Rel had gotten his cell phone number changed and had only given it to a couple of people. He wasn't taking any chances on somebody giving Ka'yah his new number. He'd even decided to lay low and get out of the game for a minute, just until all of this blew over, leaving room for Ke'yoko and Nadia to swoop in on his customers and they'd done just that.

"When is Mommy comin' home?" Aiko asked Ke'yoko as they sat on the front porch on an unusually mild winter day, waiting for Nadia to bring A'Niyah over.

"I already told you, baby, it's gon' be a long time before Mommy comes home."

"Why?" he asked.

"Aiko, I already told you your mommy done somethin' bad. And when you do bad things eventually you have to pay for it. And your mommy has to go to jail for what she did," Ke'yoko explained for the hundredth time, the best she knew how.

"So who gon' take care of me?"

"I'ma take care of you."

"Well, who gon' take care of me when you have the baby?" Aiko inquired.

"Again, me; who else?"

"Well, how you gon' take care of me and the baby?" Aiko asked.

"Trust me, I'm capable of takin' care of more than one child at a time," Ke'yoko assured her inquisitive nephew.

"Can I help you take care of the baby?" he looked over at his aunt and asked.

"You sure can. I'm gon' need your help. You can be somethin' like a big brother," Ke'yoko said.

"Yesss," Aiko said happily. "Can I feed him?"

"Yep, and change his dirty diapers," Ke'yoko joked.

"Ewwwww, no way." Aiko laughed while shaking his head no.

"I'll be back," Ja'Rel walked out of the house and said.

"Can I go wit' you, Uncle Rel?" Aiko looked up at Ja'Rel and asked.

"Not this time, li'l man. Unc got some business to take care of, so maybe next time," Ja'Rel said while rubbing the top of Aiko's head.

"Awwww, man," Aiko pouted.

"I'll tell you what, when I get back I'll play the game wit' you okay?"

"Okay," Aiko said happily.

Ke'yoko watched as Nadia pulled up in the driveway and parked behind her car. She had hoped that she and Ja'Rel would miss one another. Nadia hadn't seen Ja'Rel since she'd found out that A'Niyah was really his child, and Ke'yoko didn't know how she would react seeing him face to face.

"A'Niyah's here!" Aiko jumped up from his seat and said, running down the stairs to meet them.

"I'll see you later on," Ja'Rel looked at Ke'yoko and said.

Ke'yoko quickly threw her hand up and waved bye and watched nervously as he headed down the stairs.

"Wassup, Nadia?" Ja'Rel spoke.

"Hey, Ja'Rel," Nadia said, forcing herself to keep calm and continued up the walk. Ja'Rel being this close to her made her sick.

"Dang, A'Niyah, you gettin' so big." Ja'Rel smiled while touching one of her long ponytails.

Watching Ja'Rel touch her daughter made Nadia cringe. "Go play, 'Niyah," Nadia said and continued walking.

"Okay," A'Niyah replied and started chasing Aiko around the yard.

"Wassup, sis?" Nadia asked Ke'yoko as she walked up on the porch. Nadia rubbed Ke'yoko's huge belly before taking a seat.

"Nothin' much. Sittin' here miserable as hell," Ke'yoko said.

"You look like you 'bouta bust," Nadia said, glancing over at Ke'yoko's belly.

"I feel like I'm about to. Oh, and I like how you handled yourself," Ke'yoko said.

"What you talkin' about?" Nadia asked, confused.

"When Ja'Rel spoke to you. I just knew you was about to serve that bitch-ass nigga."

"Naw, he ain't even worth it. Plus, I already know what you got in store for his ass is gon' give me way more satisfaction than cussin' his ho-ass out! I did feel sick to my stomach, but I know there's a bigger picture to keep in mind."

"You already know," Ke'yoko said with a smile.

Ke'yoko and Nadia both sat in silence while looking out toward the street at the passing cars.

"When you gon' get rid of that nigga anyway?" Nadia asked out the blue.

"Trust me, I'm workin' on it. I just hope what I got in mind goes as planned. If it does, it's goin' down! Or should I say he's goin' down!" Ke'yoko replied happily.

"What plan? Fill me in," Nadia said.

Ke'yoko shot her best friend a "you know better" look.

"Well, it don't hurt to try." Nadia laughed. "Have you heard anything else from Ka'yah?" Nadia asked.

"Nope. She ain't no fool. She better not call me. I heard through the grapevine that she had her court-appointed attorney try to get the tape pulled from the phone that she and I was talkin' on when I went to visit her," Ke'yoko said.

"Whaaaat?" Nadia asked.

"Yeah, girl. She told them I admitted to her that I killed Bo. So when they pulled the tape, it was so distorted they couldn't make out none of our conversation," Ke'yoko said. "Nice try."

"Wow, that bitch is devious!"

"She'll be a'iiiight. She might as well sit back, kick her feet up, and get prepared to do her time."

"Might as well. It sho'll don't look like she gon' be goin' nowhere no time soon," Nadia agreed.

Ke'yoko looked over at Nadia with a serious look on her face.

"What's on ya mind?" Nadia asked.

"I need you to promise me somethin'."

"Promise you what?" Nadia asked, confused.

"Promise me that if I ever need you you'll always be here for me," Ke'yoko said, feeling herself getting ready to get emotional. It had to be her hormones or the fact that after Ja'Rel was gone, she was only going to have her son and Aiko to lean on.

"Sis, I promise you that I'll always have your back, no matter what! I'll drop everything to be by your side whenever you need me," Nadia assured her best friend.

Ke'yoko smiled. "Thank you."

"No need to thank me. Well, I'm about to head on home. I'll be back later on to pick A'Niyah up."

"You might as well let her spend the night with her brother." Ke'yoko smirked.

Nadia playfully shot Ke'yoko the side-eye.

"What? They are brother and sister." Ke'yoko laughed.

Nadia laughed too, before standing up from her chair. "True," she replied. She leaned over and wrapped her arms around Ke'yoko. "Call me later."

"You know I will. I'm about to go to the Redbox, order these kids some pizza, and lie back and chill."

"Okay, well, call me if you need me," Nadia said.

"I will." Ke'yoko smiled as Nadia headed down the stairs.

Nadia walked over to A'Niyah, kissed her on the cheek, hugged Aiko, and headed to her car. She opened up the door and just stood there staring up at Ke'yoko. Ke'yoko waved good-bye. Nadia waved back before getting in her car, starting it up, and pulling off.

Chapter Thirty-seven

Ke'yoko ran into the grocery store to pick up a few things for dinner. Cooking for a picky five-year-old every day was something she definitely had to get used to. After getting a cart full of junk food for Aiko, Ke'yoko headed toward the register.

"Shit, I forgot the Popsicles," she said and made a U-turn toward the frozen food section, knowing it would be a war zone in her household if she went home without Aiko's favorite snack.

Ke'yoko smiled down at a little boy who was whining to his mother about getting some ice cream while pulling on her leg. She knew her mind had to have been playing tricks on her because she swore the cute little boy was the spitting image of Aiko.

"I told you we not gettin' no ice cream, Relly. Now stop pulling on my leg," the mother said sternly.

Relly? Noooo, it couldn't be, Ke'yoko thought, quickly looking over at his pregnant mother, discreetly staring at her to make sure it wasn't who she thought she was. A warm sensation came over Ke'yoko's entire body and she felt nauseous.

Ke'yoko's heart nearly jumped in her throat when she realized this definitely was the broad from the pictures. Ke'yoko didn't know what her next move would be so she played the situation by ear.

"You got a cute little boy," Ke'yoko said to the chick while checking her out to see what Ja'Rel saw in this broad. She wasn't bad looking. Ke'yoko definitely had to give credit where credit was due, but no doubt about it, she wasn't as fine as Ke'yoko was. You could tell this chick was used to the finer things and kept herself together.

The chick looked over at Ke'yoko and smiled. "Thank you. He looks just like his daddy."

He sure does. "When are you due?" Ke'yoko asked, pointing at her huge stomach.

"I got a month left and, girl, I cannot wait!" she replied, looking like she was ready to pop as well.

"What a coincidence. I got a month left too," Ke'yoko replied.

"Oh, wow." The lady smiled. "Is this your first one?"

"Yeah, this my first one. I've had a few miscarriages in the past, so I'm kinda excited."

"I bet."

"Crazy thing is, my husband is even more excited than I am," Ke'yoko said, wanting to bust Ja'Rel's lying, cheating, no-good ass out, but didn't.

"Yeah, my fiancé is ecstatic too."

Fiancé? Bitch, please, get in line wit' the other broads, Ke'yoko thought, wanting to laugh in this naïve broad's face; but she kept it together.

"He's always wanted children but his ex-wife couldn't give him any, so you can only imagine how happy he is to be a daddy for the second time," the lady said.

Ex? Bitch, I'm still Mrs. Barnes, Ke'yoko wanted to say badly, but didn't. "Yeah, I bet," Ke'yoko said slowly.

Ke'yoko was on fire but decided to take the high road. That was the problem with this world today: bitches always wanted to attack the other female when they found some mess out, instead of dealing with the man. Ke'yoko refused to be a statistic; plus, this woman didn't owe Ke'yoko anything. Ja'Rel did. She was married to his ass not the woman in front of her.

"Well, congratulations and good luck on your delivery," the lady said, smiling.

"Same to you." Ke'yoko smirked, before turning to walk away.

Ke'yoko was happy about how she'd handled herself as she made her way to the car with her groceries. The old Ke'yoko would have confronted this chick before exposing Ja'Rel, but the new Ke'yoko didn't have time for that nonsense; she had more important things on her mind. Plus, it wasn't that chick's fault that she'd gotten involved with a fraud-ass nigga. She would find out soon enough. Ke'yoko kinda felt sorry for this broad, because she was about to be in the same boat. She was going to be a single mother and didn't even know it yet; she just hoped and prayed that the chick was strong enough to handle it like she was.

Chapter Thirty-eight

Ke'yoko was sitting on the sofa with her tablet looking at different properties while talking to Kailo on the phone.

"You sure you don't wanna go through with this?"

"How many times are you gon' ask me that question? Yes, I'm sure," Ke'yoko said, clicking on a property that had really caught her eye.

"Are you sure? I mean, even after everything you went through you want me to call my dogs off?" Kailo asked one last time just to make sure.

"I said I'm cool, big head," Ke'yoko said, laughing.

"All right, it's your call. I'm just making sure 'cause I know how pregnant people think with their hearts and not with their heads," Kailo said.

"Whatever," Ke'yoko said. "And what pregnant person have you been around?"

"Chad's sister, Lauren. All she does is cry about everything. Ugggh, she gets on my nerves.

The other day she was over here and we was sitting out on the porch and she saw a butterfly land on a flower and broke down. She said that was the most beautiful thing she'd seen in a long time," Kailo said, making Ke'yoko laugh.

"Well, not all pregnant people are like that. I gotta admit, I do get emotional over some of the smallest things, but seein' a butterfly landin' on top of a flower? Ummm no!"

"Well, Lauren's ass is sickening."

"Let me call you right back!" Ke'yoko quickly hung up the phone on Kailo and pretended like she was occupied with her tablet.

"Who was that?" Ja'Rel walked into the living room and asked.

"Why do you always ask me who I'm on the phone wit'?" Ke'yoko frowned.

"I ask what I wanna ask when I'm the one payin' the bill." Ja'Rel frowned back.

"You're right. You can ask whatever you wanna ask, but I don't have to answer you," Ke'yoko said smartly.

"You better be glad you pregnant! Just wait until after you have that baby. Every time you get fly, I'ma put my foot off in yo' ass. Something I shoulda done a long time ago. You done really got outta hand!" Ja'Rel said.

"Yeah, whatever," Ke'yoko said, waving her husband off. "Where you 'bouta go?" Ke'yoko asked for no reason at all.

"Don't worry about it, I'm grown!" he snapped.

"You get on my fuckin' nerves! I was askin' 'cause I was gon' have you pick Aiko up some Popsicles from the store. It ain't like I was checkin' for you," Ke'yoko snapped back.

"Truth be told, you get on my fuckin' nerves too and I ain't goin' near no store! Get yo' lazy-ass up and go to the store yourself," he said, grabbing his car keys.

"One of these days I'm gon' pack up and leave yo' black-ass," Ke'yoko warned.

"And, what you want me to do about it?" Ja'Rel snapped angrily. He had been hearing the shit for years and was finally tired of hearing it. "When you leavin'? You need help packin'? I can give your miserable ass a hand with that soon as I get back."

Out of all the things Ja'Rel had said and done to Ke'yoko, hearing him say those words hurt her more than anything. Yes, she had been threatening to leave him for years, but all the other times he'd assured her that he would never let her go because he loved her too much. At least when he said those words, whether he was lying or not, she could still cling to a small shred of hope that he had really loved her at one point. To have him finally respond differently was heartbreaking. Ke'yoko thought that after all the years she'd stuck by his side and all the bullshit he'd put her through she was still worth fighting for.

Ke'yoko had tears in her eyes. She was so hurt.

"Save them tears for ya new nigga," Ja'Rel spat and headed out the door.

All Ke'yoko could do was break down and cry after Ja'Rel slammed the door. This wasn't an ordinary cry; this was an earthshaking cry. After getting it all out of her system, Ke'yoko pulled herself together and made a quick call before calling Kailo back.

"Let me guess: Ja'Rel came into the room," Kailo said, answering the phone.

"Yep, you guessed right," Ke'yoko said.

"Your nose sounds clogged up. You didn't sound like that before. Have you been crying?" Kailo asked, concerned.

"Naw, I think it's my allergies," Ke'yoko lied, not wanting her brother to get all riled up.

"Okay, sis, don't make me fuck that nigga up. You know I already wanna do some damage to his bitch ass!" Kailo said angrily.

"We already are, remember?"

"Do he be putting his hands on you?"

"Naw, boy. He did threaten me before he left, though; but he never follow through wit' it," Ke'yoko admitted. She was no fool. Even if Ja'Rel was physically abusive to her, Kailo's overprotective ass would be the last person she would tell.

"What? That chump ain't no fool. He know if he puts his hands on you he won't live to talk about it." Kailo grimaced and meant every word.

"I ain't thinkin' about that nigga," Ke'yoko said.

"I mean, who that fool think he is, threatening you?" Kailo said, not letting it go.

I shoulda just kept my mouth closed, Ke'yoko thought as Kailo went on and on.

"I mean really, what's his problem? My sister ain't no punching bag. If he wanna punch somebody, tell the bastard to come punch on me," Kailo fumed. "I'll be there in a few days and let that bitch-made punk come out his face sideways if he want to. I'ma give him what he looking for! That bitch betta know I'm not soft by no means!"

Ke'yoko had never heard her brother talk like that before, so she knew he had to be mad.

"Aiko lost a tooth today," Ke'yoko said, quickly changing the subject to something more positive.

"Oh, wow, that's cool. Now you know you gon' have to put a least five dollars under his pillow tonight," Kailo said, calming down some.

"Five dollars, shiiiiit. We didn't get five dollars when we lost our teeth." Ke'yoko laughed.

"Shit is different nowadays. Haven't you heard of a thing called inflation, sis?" Kailo joked.

Ke'yoko laughed. "Right."

"Okay, sis, I'm about to get off of here," Kailo said.

"Let me guess: Chad came in," Ke'yoko said.

"Yep, you guessed right." Kailo laughed.

"A'iiiight, knucklehead, I'll talk to you later." Ke'yoko hung up the phone and continued her house hunt.

Ja'Rel was on his way to Kassidy's house to make sure she was all right. She had sent him a text telling him that she thought her water had broke. Ja'Rel was trying his best to get to his destination without breaking the speed limit; he didn't need no extra heat brought his way right now. Just as Ja'Rel put his blinker on and busted a left on Chadbourne Road, police lights started flashing out of nowhere.

"What the fuck?" he asked himself, not realizing they were even behind him.

Ja'Rel looked down at his seat belt to make sure he had it on while slowing down and pulling over on the side of the road. "Now, I know I wasn't speedin'. So I don't know why they pullin' me over," Ja'Rel said aloud, while putting his car in park and turning the engine off. "I don't got no warrants so I'm all good."

The officer took his time getting out of the cruiser, walked up to Ja'Rel's car, and tapped on the window with the blunt end of his flashlight. Ja'Rel rolled the window down and put his hands on the steering wheel. The way these police were out here killing all these black men around the world like it was a sport, he wasn't taking no chances.

"License and registration," the officer said.

"I'm about to grab my wallet out of my back pocket and then get my registration out of my glove compartment," Ja'Rel announced.

"Move slow, 'cause my trigger finger is itchin' and I'm lookin' for a nigga to help me scratch it," the officer looked Ja'Rel dead in the face and said without cracking a smile.

Ja'Rel slowly reached his hand in his back pocket and pulled out his wallet. "What you pull me over for?" Ja'Rel asked while taking his license out and reaching over, grabbing his registration out of the glove compartment, and handing them to the officer.

"I'm askin' all the questions here! You don't have a light on your license plate, that's why I pulled you over," the officer said, snatching the license and registration from Ja'Rel's hand and walked back to his cruiser.

"Fuckin' asshole!" Ja'Rel spat angrily once the officer was out of earshot.

Ja'Rel impatiently sat in the car waiting for the officer to bring his stuff back so he could get to Kassidy, who was blowing his phone up with text messages and calls.

"Hello?" he finally answered after getting tired of hearing his phone buzzing.

"Where you at, baby?" Kassidy asked, breathing heavily.

"I got pulled over by the police," Ja'Rel answered.

"For what?"

"For some bullshit! He talkin' about I don't have a license plate light. But let me call you back. He's gettin' back out of his car," Ja'Rel said, relieved.

"Okay, baby, please hurry. I'm in a lot pain," Kassidy said, trying her best to breathe just like they'd taught her and Ja'Rel in the Lamaze classes.

"Love you," Ja'Rel said.

"Love you too," Kassidy said before hanging up the phone.

"Can you step out of the car?" the officer walked back up to Ja'Rel's car and said.

"For what?" Ja'Rel asked nervously.

"'Cause I said so, that's why," the officer replied.

"What the fuck?" Ja'Rel asked, confused, knowing for a fact he didn't have any warrants that he knew of. "I gotta get outta the car for a license plate light?"

Ja'Rel watched as another cruiser pulled up as he stepped out of the car.

"Naw, you got a failure to appear," the officer said.

"Failure to appear? You must got me mistaken wit' somebody else. I've been to all my court dates," Ja'Rel protested.

"Well, when I ran your name it told me otherwise. You got like six unpaid parking tickets."

"Wait a minute, I gave Tamika the money to . . ." All Ja'Rel could do was shake his head. "That dirty bitch!" He had slipped up not checking up on the job assignments her greedy ass was supposed to have taken care of. He'd fired her ass for being sloppy and had been meaning to go back over things.

Ja'Rel voluntarily turned around and placed his hands behind his back so he could get cuffed.

Of all the times to go to jail, he had to go on the night that his chick was in labor. Ja'Rel looked down at the seat at his vibrating cell phone and shook his head when Kassidy's name kept popping up across the screen.

Ja'Rel felt real fucked up the entire ride to the county because this would be the first time he wouldn't be present for the birth of any of his children. He could still remember the proud feeling he'd had as he and Ke'yoko had witnessed Aiko being born. There was no feeling quite like that in this world.

Ja'Rel sat at the desk as the booking officer entered his information into the computer.

"Can I make my one call?" Ja'Rel asked.

"Yep, the phone is right there," the booking officer said, never taking her eyes off of the computer screen.

Ja'Rel picked up the old-style phone and dialed the one person he knew no matter what would always have his back. Even when he dogged her, cheated on her, or talked crazy to her, she would always be there for him.

"Hello?" Ke'yoko answered, half asleep.

"Baby, I'm in jail," Ja'Rel said.

"And? What you want me to do about it?" Ke'yoko shot, before hanging up the phone on Ja'Rel, giving him a taste of his own medicine and loving every minute of it.

Ja'Rel looked at the phone like it had done something wrong to him. He couldn't believe Ke'yoko had just played him like she did. "Stupid bitch," he spat. "Can I make another call?"

"Nope, you made your one call," the booking officer looked at him and said.

"You see she hung up on me," Ja'Rel replied.

"So? That ain't got nothin' to do wit' me. You musta done somethin' to her. You know how you niggas are," the booking officer said, shaking her head. "What you do, fuck her sister or somethin'?"

"Ha ha ha, very funny," Ja'Rel said, unamused by the officer's sense of humor, even though she'd hit the nail on the head. "I ain't done shit to her! You know how you black women are," Ja'Rel said, sitting back in the chair with a straight attitude.

"No, I don't. How are we?" the officer responded.

"Miserable, always bitchin' about somethin', lazy as fuck in the bed, don't wanna have sex after y'all get y'all's hair done 'cause y'all are so afraid that fake-ass shit is gon' get messed up, you know, just to name a few," Ja'Rel said.

"Ha, I see why she hung up on your stupid ass," the officer spat with an attitude.

"See, that's the attitude I'm talkin' about. Y'all always rollin' y'all's neck and eyes," Ja'Rel said, shaking his head. "I see why brothers get them a Becky and take good care of her and leave Ta'niqua, Sha'quantay, and Chardonnnay in the hood right where y'all belong. I shoulda been smart and got me one!"

The booking officer looked at Ja'Rel and shook her head in disgust. "Come get this Uncle Tom—ass nigga up outta my face before I accidently do somethin' to him," the officer yelled to one of her partners.

"I struck a nerve, huh?" Ja'Rel said as the other officer helped him up out of the chair to escort him to his cell.

"Not at all, inmate. I'm goin' home to my husband tonight; where you gon' be?" the guard asked with a smirk. "You dumbass nigga; that's why you not gon' get another phone call, and if you keep runnin' that smart-ass mouth of yours, just maybe your paperwork might come up missin' as well."

"This ain't shit. I won't be in here long. I'll be out as soon as I call my attorney in the mornin'," Ja'Rel said with a cocky attitude.

"Sleep tight and don't let the bed bugs bite, and I mean that literally." The booking officer winked with a shit-eating grin on her face.

Ja'Rel was stripped down and given an orange jumpsuit, some shower shoes, and a thin blanket before being escorted to a tiny cell. He lay there thinking about all the dirty, underhanded shit he'd done to Ke'yoko all these years and began feeling bad. He had made it up in his mind that after he got out, he was going to treat her better, just like she deserved. As Ja'Rel lay on the hard bunk thinking and damn near scratching his skin off, he looked down on his blanket and the last words that the booking officer said to him instantly hit him. He quickly threw the bed bug–infested blanket off of him and jumped up and ran over to the door.

"Guards!"

Chapter Thirty-nine

Ja'Rel was sitting at the table trying to eat the slop they fed them for breakfast while waiting for them to come get him for court; yet again, they called everybody's name but his. They had been playing him crazy ever since he'd been locked up in the county. Every time he was supposed to go to his hearing they kept spinning him, telling him they couldn't find his paperwork. And when he would call his attorney to get to the bottom of how he was being treated, his attorney acted like he was taking their side. If he didn't know any better, he would swear on a stack of Bibles that his attorney was against him too. Not giving him his mail and turning Kassidy and the kids away on visiting day took the cake. They kept coming up with different excuses why they couldn't let them in. From her clothes being too tight, to his name not being on Kennedy's birth certificate, just to name a few. Ja'Rel had even tried calling Ke'yoko a few times, but she wouldn't answer the phone for him.

"So I just ain't gon' get to go to court again today, huh?" Ja'Rel asked the CO, who was escorting another inmate back who was about to go home.

"I didn't call your name, did I?" the CO said smartly before turning to walk away.

Ja'Rel was fed up and beyond furious. He had been in jail for over a week all over some unpaid parking tickets. He had missed the birth of his daughter, didn't know what was going on with Ke'yoko, didn't know what the hell Ka'yah was saying; he was stressed the hell out! He had never heard of such nonsense his whole twenty-seven years on earth. Luckily, he had Mitch around to make sure the company and everything was running smoothly. But he was second-guessing that too now; for the past couple days, Mitch had started acting funny too and stopped accepting his calls.

"Don't worry, old man. I'll go to your house and keep your wife warm and play daddy to your kids," the young dude said jokingly.

Ja'Rel didn't find any humor in his statement. Before he knew it, Ja'Rel had pounced on the young cat and had begun beating the life out of him. Ja'Rel had lost it. He took all his built-up frustration out on this young dude.

"Stop! You killlin' him," a few of the other inmates yelled as they stood back and watched Ja'Rel nearly take this young dude's head off. There was no way they were going to try to stop that.

The COs heard the commotion coming from the block and took off running to see what was going on. There was blood everywhere when they ran into the block. The COs began yelling for the other inmates to return to their racks until they got the situation under control.

"Stop! Get off of him," the COs were yelling at the top of their lungs while hitting Ja'Rel in the back with their batons.

Ja'Rel was so gone he didn't even hear them, nor did he feel the blows. The only thing that was on his mind was killing his prey.

"Stop, stop!" the COs continued yelling, afraid to go near Ja'Rel.

Two other COs ran into the block and began using their Tasers on him. That was the only thing that seemed to make Ja'Rel pause. Ja'Rel slowly tried to stand up, staggering, and looked down at what he'd done to the young boy. He hadn't completely stood up and before he knew it, the COs had bum-rushed him, making him slip on the blood and fall backward, hitting his head on the hard, cold steel seat.

Chapter Forty

Ke'yoko was sprawled out across the bed, knocked out. It had been a long time since she had a good night's rest. Between her fuller bladder and listening to Ja'Rel snoring like a grizzly bear all up in her ear she was kept up many nights. Sleeping alone was something she could definitely get used to.

Ke'yoko was abruptly awakened by her ringing cell phone, making her jump up out of her sleep. She looked at the clock on the wall and tried to roll over as quickly as her heavy body would allow her to. Her first thought was anybody calling her at two a.m. had to have an emergency.

"Hello?" she answered without checking the caller ID.

"You 'sleep, sis?" Kailo asked.

"No, I'm up," she lied. "Is everything all right?" Ke'yoko asked nervously.

"Yeah, well, no, not really. I got somethin' to tell you about Ja'rel," Kailo stammered.

"Is he dead?" Ke'yoko asked, fearful. Even though she couldn't stand him, she didn't want to see him dead.

"No."

"Well, shit, couldn't you have waited 'til the mornin' to tell me about this nigga?" Ke'yoko asked, relieved.

"I guess I could have, but I was thinkin' you probably would want to know what happened to him," Kailo said.

"What happened to him?" she inquired, sitting all the way up in the bed.

"Come open the door and I'll tell you."

"Oh, my goodness! How come you just didn't ring the doorbell in the first place?" Ke'yoko asked as she struggled to get out of bed.

"Shit, it's two in the mornin'. I ain't about to be waking people up." Kailo laughed.

"Oh, but you can call and wake me up? That makes no sense." Ke'yoko laughed too. "Bye, boy." Ke'yoko hung up the phone and wobbled down the stairs and opened the door.

"Daaaaang, girl, you big as hell!" Kailo smiled while stepping in the door and rubbing his sister's big, round belly.

"Get off me." Ke'yoko smiled back while playfully smacking her brother's hand away from her stomach.

"Where's Aiko?" Kailo asked, closing the door behind him and following Ke'yoko into the living room.

"Where any five-year-old child should be this time of mornin': in the bed," Ke'yoko said, sitting down on the sofa.

"Shoot, these five-year-olds nowadays be staying up later than their parents do," Kailo replied, sitting down in the chair adjacent to his sister.

"Who you tellin'? Now, wassup wit' Ja'Rel?" Ke'yoko asked, cutting all the small talk.

"Oh, yeah, well, my dude Riley called me; remember him?"

Ke'yoko smiled and shook her head yes.

"He's married," Kailo said, shooting his sister a dirty look.

"It's okay. I can look without touchin'," Ke'yoko said.

Kailo shook his head and smiled. "Anyways, he said Ja'Rel got into a fight in the county, got Tased, and fell back and bumped his head on a steel stool."

"Whaaaat? Is he okay?" Ke'yoko asked, concerned.

"He said he don't know. They rushed him to the Cleveland Clinic. He said we can come up there and see him during his shift tomorrow."

"What time is that?" she inquired.

"He said come before nine a.m."

"Dang, that early? I gotta get Aiko up all early and drop him off at daycare," Ke'yoko said.

"Well, do what you gotta do. I'll meet you at the hospital around eight forty-five a.m.," Kailo said, standing up and yawning.

"A'iiiight. I'll call you when I get there." Ke'yoko struggled to push herself up off the sofa.

"You need some help?" Kailo asked, watching his sister struggle.

"Naw, I got this," she said, finally getting up.

"All right, sis, I'll see you in a few hours. Get you some sleep," Kailo said, walking toward the door.

"Sleep? Nigga, I ain't gon' be able to go back to sleep now. Hell I gotta get up in a few hours. If I go back to sleep now, I'm not gettin' up until around noon," Ke'yoko said, following her brother.

"I feel you. I'm about to hit the gym and work out for about an hour or so." Kailo opened the front door.

"Do a sit-up and a couple of squats for me too," Ke'yoko joked.

"I got'chu." Kailo laughed. "I'll see you in a few, sis. Love you."

"Love you too," Ke'yoko replied as she watched her brother walk down to his car.

Ke'yoko waited until her baby brother made it safely to his car before closing the door and locking it behind her. She headed back upstairs and sat on the edge of the bed, too big to get on her knees, and began doing something she hadn't done in a long time: she began praying. She prayed for Ja'Rel, her mother, and even Ka'yah. Everybody she prayed for played a huge part in hurting her in one way or another, but Ke'yoko knew if she wanted happiness, she would have to learn how to let go of the hurt and anger and move on with her life.

After praying for her family, guidance, and understanding, Ke'yoko felt a sense of relief. She said, "Amen," lay down, and tried to get a couple more hours of rest before having to meet Kailo at the hospital.

Chapter Forty-one

After Kailo left with the news about Ja'Rel, Ke'yoko tried to go back to sleep but couldn't. She lay in the bed wide awake, thinking about different events that occurred in her life and wondering what she'd done so bad to have deserved some of things she'd endured in her life. She was dragging around the house trying to get Aiko and herself ready. After about an hour of fussing, and flipping out, she dropped Aiko off at the daycare and headed up to the hospital. She called Kailo when she pulled up in the crowded hospital parking lot. He told her to stay put and he would come meet her at her car so she wouldn't have to walk by herself. Ke'yoko sat and impatiently waited for her brother. She closed her eyes and said a quick prayer to calm her nerves. She didn't know why she was so nervous. She smiled when she saw Kailo walking toward her car. She opened the door and got out.

"What's up, sis?" he said, wrapping his arms around her body.

"Wassup, big head," she said, wrapping her arms around his waist.

"You okay?" he asked, feeling her body trembling.

"Yeah, I'm good, just a li'l nervous, that's all," she admitted.

"You good. I got'chu," Kailo assured his sister as they turned to walk away.

"Always have." Ke'yoko smiled.

"Damn right, and I ain't gon' stop now," he replied as they walked into the hospital and got on the elevator.

Ke'yoko's body trembled even more as they rode the elevator up. Since Ja'Rel was still locked in the county when he got hurt, they had to keep him on the floor that they kept all the inmates on; technically, he was still a ward of the state.

Kailo and Ke'yoko both stepped off the elevator at the same time. They both began smiling when they saw Riley.

"Hold up, what you smilin' all hard for?" Ke'yoko looked up at her brother and asked suspiciously.

"What?" Kailo asked.

"Damn, him too?"

All Kailo did was smile at his sister.

"Uhhhhh unnt, I thought he was married," she said, disgusted.

"He is, but what that mean?" he said with a wink.

"You a ho," she mumbled as Riley walked over to them, smiling from ear to ear.

Kailo shot his sister a crazy look, hearing what she'd said.

"Wassup, y'all?" Riley asked, giving Ke'yoko a hug and Kailo a firm handshake.

"Hey," Ke'yoko said, feeling disgusted now that she knew his secret.

"What's going on, bruh?" Kailo asked.

Bruh? More like sis. Mental note to self: gots to be more careful.

"The doctor is in there now with him. He's waitin' on y'all so he can tell y'all what's goin' on wit' him. I got a call from the chief and he said the person he got down for next of kin will be up here around ten a.m.," Riley said.

"So what that mean? I'm his wife," Ke'yoko questioned with a slight attitude.

"It mean that since you're not on his emergency contact form, you not allowed to visit him while he's here, wife or not; but since I'm cool wit' ya brother, I'ma look out for you," Riley answered with a smile.

"Good looking," Kailo said, giving him a handshake with a shoulder bump.

"Thanks," Ke'yoko said, still feeling some type of way about not having no rights to visit Ja'Rel even though she was his wife as she walked into his room with Kailo walking in behind her. Ke'yoko looked over at the CO who was standing next to Ja'Rel's bed and then over at Ja'Rel. Seeing him lying there with all those tubes running out of his entire body tore her up on the inside.

"Hello, I'm Dr. Arnell," the doctor introduced himself when Ke'yoko and Kailo walked in.

"Hello, I'm Kailo, and this is the patient's wife, Ke'yoko," Kailo replied. Kailo gave an upward nod to the CO and the CO gave him one in return.

"What's the deal wit' my husband," Ke'yoko said, cutting to the chase. She stood next to the doctor as he lifted both of Ja'Rel's eyelids one at a time and shined a little flashlight into both of his eyes.

"Well, I'm gon' give it to you straight wit' no chaser," the doctor said.

Ke'yoko and Kailo were all ears.

"He took a pretty nasty blow to the back of the head when he fell. He's really lucky to still be alive. Unfortunately, he's paralyzed from the neck down and is unable to speak. One good thing is he's been communicating with his eyes whenever we can get him awake and he has a little strength in his left hand, not much though," the doctor explained.

Ke'yoko shook her head as the doctor continued to talk. Seeing Ja'Rel lying there in the bed, cuffed to the bed like he was some sort of a monster, tore her up even more.

"Wow." Kailo shook his head in disbelief. Even though he didn't like his brother-in-law, seeing him lying there like that had him feeling sorry for him. "How long will he be paralyzed and unable to speak?"

"Well, it's hard tellin' right now. We've done a few CAT scans. His brain is bleeding in a couple different spots, and we're tryin' to get that under control. We got a team of the best doctors working with Mr. Barnes. There's like a ninety percent chance that he'll have seizures for the rest of his life," the doctor replied.

Tears formed in Ke'yoko's eyes and slowly began to fall. Kailo wrapped his arm around his sister's shoulder and pulled her into his body. Ke'yoko was hurt that the man she thought would be her everything was lying in a bed in this condition. She was hurt that the whole story was ending this way, but they'd left her no choice.

"Is there any chance that he can recover?" Ke'yoko asked as she wiped away her tears.

"To tell you the truth, he'll never recover; and if he does, it'll be a miracle. Right now, all we can do is keep observing him and hope for the best. You'll have to get your house set up for him; he'll definitely be needing care around the clock. That's all I have for now," the doctor said.

"Damn, man," Kailo said, shaking his head, feeling sorry for his sister.

"Can I please speak to my husband alone for a few minutes?" Ke'yoko looked at the doctor and then over at the CO and asked. She could not stop crying.

"It's okay wit' me," the doctor replied, jotting down a few notes in Ja'Rel's chart.

The CO was hesitant at first but soon remembered that Riley said he was cool with Ke'yoko and Kailo.

The doctor and the CO headed out of the room. Kailo stayed just in case his sister needed him. Ke'yoko wiped away her tears as she looked down into her husband's lifeless face. It may have just been her mind playing tricks on her, but Ja'Rel looked like he'd aged about ten years since she'd last seen him. She touched his graying hair and then the side of his cheek.

"Ja'Rel," she called out. "Can you hear me, baby? Please, baby, open your eyes if you can hear me."

Ke'yoko watched as Ja'Rel struggled to open his eyes. She was hopeful when she saw his eyelids fluttering.

"Come on, baby, open your eyes," she cheered. "You can do it."

Ja'Rel tried his best to open his eyes. He wanted nothing more than to be able to look at his wife's beautiful face.

"Come on, baby, open your eyes," she repeated.

Ja'Rel finally opened his eyes. Ke'yoko had a huge smile on her face, seeing her husband's eyes open. "That's what I'm talkin' about, baby. I knew you could do it," she said, grabbing his hand.

Ja'Rel wasn't really aware with what was going on or what had happened. All he knew was he was unable to move or speak no matter how hard he tried.

"He's up," Ke'yoko looked back at Kailo and said, excited.

"That's what's up," Kailo replied with a smile.

"Can you hear me, baby? If you can, squeeze my hand," Ke'yoko said to Ja'Rel.

Ja'Rel squeezed Ke'yoko's hand, applying little to no pressure at all, letting her know that he could hear her.

"Good." She smiled. "I just wanna let you know that I know about everything you've done to me. I know about your fiancée, Kassidy, and y'all's two kids. I know that Aiko is really your son. I couldn't believe you thought I was so naïve. I knew about all the drugs you sold; shit, I was sellin' drugs too and even took all your custos from you. Me and Nadia even got Mitch and Jonesy workin' for us now."

Ja'Rel's eyes grew big.

"You know what the killer is? I even know about you druggin' Nadia and rapin' her. Oh, I don't know if you know this or not, but A'Niyah is your child too." Ke'yoko shook her head and chuckled.

The more Ke'yoko spoke about the things Ja'Rel had done to his sister, the madder Kailo got.

"Boy, you somethin' else. I don't know what I done to you to make you do all this shit to me. Crazy thing is, I ain't even mad at you. All I can do is continue to pray for you. I was gon' set you up to fall, just like I did Ka'yah. Yeah, I know I had you thinkin' Ka'yah killed Bo, but naw, it wasn't her; it was me. I'm good, ain't I? God works in mysterious ways because He beat me to you, nigga, 'cause I was comin' for ya head!"

Exposing all of Ja'Rel's bullshit to him felt somewhat like a cleansing.

"Do you have anything to say to your brother-in-law?" she looked back at Kailo and asked.

Kailo walked up to the bed and looked down at Ja'Rel and wanted to spit in his face, but he would never sneak a man while he was down. "Who's the weak-ass muthafucka now?" Kailo asked angrily. "I should turn you over and fuck you in the ass! But I wouldn't put my dick in you even if you begged me to."

Ja'Rel's eyes were as big as saucers.

"All righty then?" Ke'yoko laughed. "I'm sellin' both houses and movin'. You don't have to worry about ever seein' me or the baby. By the way, before I go, I'm givin' Ross the shop. He'll run it way better than you ever have." She smirked.

Neither Ke'yoko nor Ja'Rel knew where he'd got the strength from, but he nearly tried to squeeze the life out of Ke'yoko's hand once she mentioned Ross. Ke'yoko pulled her hand away and shook her head. As she bent down and kissed Ja'Rel on the forehead, Kassidy walked in carrying her newborn in the carrier with Ja'Rel Jr. on her other side.

Kassidy was confused as hell. The only thing that was going through her mind was what was the lady she ran into at the grocery store doing up here kissing her fiancé on the forehead?

Ke'yoko looked down at Ja'Rel one last time before walking toward the door. She walked over to Kassidy, removed her wedding ring, grabbed Kassidy's free hand and placed it in her palm and closed it.

"He's all yours now," Ke'yoko said with a huge smile and walked out the door with Kailo in tow, leaving Kassidy and Ja'Rel both confused.

Epilogue

Ke'yoko stood out on the balcony in her bedroom while taking in the beautiful scenery of the clear, light blue water. It was definitely a sight to see. All she could think about was how blessed she was to be able to raise her child and nephew in such a beautiful and peaceful place. It was definitely paradise. Selling everything she and Ja'Rel owned and moving to Turks and Caicos was something Ke'yoko had been wanting to do ever since she and Ja'Rel had vacationed there. She'd walked away from everything including the streets to finally make her dream a reality.

"Auntie, can me and 'Niyah get in the pool?" Aiko ran out on the balcony and asked, interrupting her train of thought.

"Ain't nobody out there to watch y'all," Ke'yoko said.

"Can you come?" he asked with innocent eyes.

"I'm 'bouta go out there in a few," Nadia interjected, walking out on the balcony with the mail and handing it to Ke'yoko.

"Yessss," Aiko screamed.

"Go get y'all's swimmin' suits on and wait for me by the pool," Nadia said.

"Boys don't wear swimmin' suits," Aiko corrected her.

"Boy," Ke'yoko said, shooting him a dirty look.

"Well, they don't," Aiko said and turned and ran away.

Ke'yoko shook her head and smiled. "That li'l nigga always got somethin' smart to say. I don't know how you gon' handle him and A'Niyah all by yourself when I go to the hospital next week."

"Shit, wit' a lot of hard liquor and some blunts, that's how." Nadia laughed.

Ke'yoko laughed too.

Nadia and Ke'yoko stood silently taking in the sight together as the warm summer's ocean breeze blew across their faces.

"I hope I made the right decision," Ke'yoko finally said while moving a piece of hair out of her face.

"About what?" Nadia inquired.

"About movin' Aiko way over here. I mean, since they lost the evidence in Ka'yah's murder case, she'll be home a lot sooner now," Ke'yoko said.

"Yeah, that was crazy that they offered her a deal without tellin' her they'd lost the evidence and her dumbass copped out to twelve years," Nadia said, laughing. "Aiko will be grown by the time she does get out."

"True."

"This was one of the best decisions you've made in a long time for yourself and your little family. I can handle the business by myself and anything else you need me to take care of in the States. Do you for once, Ke'yoko; it's all about you and yours now. You have nothin' and no one holdin' you back!"

Ke'yoko still had an unsure look on her face.

"You're gonna be givin' these kids an opportunity of a lifetime. How many other kids we know can say they live in such a beautiful place where they'll learn a new culture and a different way of livin'? Shit, half of the kids we know ain't never been off the west side of Cleveland, let alone out of the United States," Nadia said.

"Yeah, I guess you're right," Ke'yoko agreed. "I really appreciate you for comin' out here wit' me to keep Aiko while I have the baby."

"Don't thank me. I already told you that I'll have your back no matter what! You my girl, and I would be a fool to pass up a chance to live in paradise, for free." Nadia laughed. "I got Connie looking after the shop 'til I get back so it's all good. Funny thing, I gave her some responsibility and she is a changed person, not holdin' on to all that jealousy and cattiness."

"That's true, you are in paradise. And if having more responsibility and being in charge is all it took to change her nasty attitude, you shoulda done that sooner," Ke'yoko said, laughing.

"Well, let me get out here wit' these kids," Nadia said and turned to walk away. She took a few steps then turned back around and looked at Ke'yoko.

"What?" Ke'yoko asked.

"I know you'll never admit to it, and I'm not expectin' you to, but deep down inside I know you had somethin' to do wit' that evidence comin' up missin' against Ka'yah, and I wanna say that was real gangsta and I got a lot of respect for you. You a better woman than I'll ever be," Nadia said.

"At the end of the day, you can pick your friends, but not your family," Ke'yoko replied, never fully admitting to anything. Nadia didn't need her to admit it; she knew her hipbone better than she knew herself.

Nadia smiled and continued out of the room.

Ke'yoko began sorting through the mail that Nadia had brought her. A huge smile crept across her face when she saw a letter from Ross. She quickly opened it up and began reading it.

What's up, lady?

I know it's been a while. I hope Turks and Caicos is treatin' you right. There has been so much goin' on since you've been gone. The shop is makin' more money than a little bit. I still can't thank you enough for givin' me the business. You know I gotta repay you some way, even though you say I don't. Harvey, Mitch, and Jonesy told me to tell you hi and to get their rooms ready. Guess what? Me and Sharae got back together. Yeah, I know, but I love her and she's really changed. We're plannin' on gettin' married in the fall and we're expectin' our second child. I'm finally gettin' my son. I want to come out to see you and my godson once you get all the way settled in. I heard about what happened to Ja'Rel. I can't believe Kassidy really packed up and moved back to North Carolina, leavin' Ja'Rel to die all alone. Word on the street is he's livin' in a nursin' home. I hate to say it, but karma misses no one. You might think she skipped over you when you do dirt and just when you least expect it, here she comes knockin' back on your door like Rent-A-Center! Anyways, I just wanted to touch base with you and let you know what's been goin' on. I really miss seein' your pretty face and, between me and you, I still wish you had never been wit' Ja'Rel 'cause I would have loved to get between them thick-ass thighs of yours. I know what you're thinkin', but I ain't married yet so I can still flirt wit' you. I love you, Ke'yoko, and I can't wait to see you. Be safe.

Love always,
Ross

Ke'yoko smiled from ear to ear as she neatly folded the letter and placed it back in the envelope. It was always a pleasure hearing from her old friend Ross. Hearing that he had gotten back with Sharae had Ke'yoko feeling kind of jealous, even though he had made it quite clear to her that they could never mess around on the strength of the relationship he and Ja'Rel used to have.

Ke'yoko placed her hand on her round belly and rubbed it. She couldn't believe that in less than a week she was about to be somebody's mommy. After all the miscarriages she was forced to have, this childbirth thing was really happening and the sad thing was Ja'Rel wouldn't be around to experience it with her. She hated hearing the news about Ja'Rel, but Ross was absolutely right: karma was a bitch, one of the baddest! So in the end he'd gotten what fate felt he deserved.

Ke'yoko was afraid and happy all wrapped into one. If she didn't know anything else, she knew that she would be the best parent she could be, and was going to give her baby and nephew the world.

"Well, baby boy, I guess it's just me, you, Aiko, and Nadia handling business as usual," she said to her unborn child before taking a seat and looking out at the beautiful view, smiling from ear to ear.